The
Hundred-Yen
Singer

The Hundred-Yen Singer

Naomi Suenaga

Translated by Tom Gill

Peter Owen Publishers
London and Chester Springs

PETER OWEN PUBLISHERS
73 Kenway Road, London SW5 ORE

Peter Owen books are distributed in the USA by
Dufour Editions Inc., Chester Springs, PA 19425-0007

ISBN 0 7206 1274 8

Translated from the Japanese
Hyakuen Shingaa Gokuraku Tenshi

© Naomi Suenaga 1997
Originally published in Japan by Kawada Shobo Shinsha, Tokyo
This translation first published by Peter Owen 2006
Translation © Tom Gill 2006

*This book has been selected by the Japanese Literature Publishing Project
(JLPP), which is run by the Japanese Literature and Promotion Center
(J-Lit Center) on behalf of the Agency for Cultural Affairs of Japan.*

A catalogue record for this book is available from the British Library.

Printed and bound in Great Britain by
Windsor Print Production Ltd., Tonbridge

1 The Million-Yen Towels

Seems my ship is always on the verge of sinking.

Am I just too nice, or is it all my parents' fault? Or maybe this sequinned tutu is just too, too tacky and cheap. Whatever the reason, I always seem to be steering with a warped tiller.

'A talented person like you . . .' they say, but they don't give me a job. That's why I can always affect the air of an outsider.

> Love is a miracle,
> Love, love, love
> It's a miracle

On no, not again. Those annoyingly familiar voices echo around the hall. Once that cheap little melody gets into your ear it'll stick there like a piece of gum stuck to the sole of your shoe.

Today my glorious showbiz career has taken me to a health spa in East Omiya, a dormitory town north of Tokyo. The two unlovely voices now filling the concert hall belong to Kenjiro and David, a singing-and-dancing duo who happen to work for the same little talent agency as me. Billed as the 'Duo That Crosses Borders', these two 24-year-olds are supposed to be a Japanese–American combo. Actually, the publicity pack is a pack of lies. The allegedly American David is an illegal Filipino immigrant who's bleached his hair blond. Kenjiro is, admittedly, a genuine Japanese, but the bit about him having graduated from Harvard University is a bit of a laugh, at least to those such as myself who've known him since his days pimping in Uguisudani.

> Fly to me (my love!)
> Fly to my arms (uh-huh!),
> Your perfume (ooooh!)
> Is so lovely (uh-huh).

Uh-huh.

I really hate that song. Every time they do it, it feels like the air is full of poisonous flying insects. The insects seem to come crawling out of my ears, my mouth, across the nape of my neck, and they start dancing all over my body. I really can't stand it.

'Yeeeeaaaaayyyyy!'

'Go for it, Ken-chan.'

Faces flushed from the hot baths from which they've just emerged, a herd of excited housewives stampede on to the stage. It's a broad stage, made of eighty tatami mats, and now it is swarming with pink muu-muus – the Hawaiian-style bathrobes favoured by health spas – as a hundred drunken elderly ladies surround the two idols.

> Is it yes or is it no?
> Is it a little kiss for me?
> Don't want one today (not today!),
> I want you right now!
> (Ah, do the hustle!)
> Uh-huh, you know what I mean.
> Uh-huh, love is a miracle.

I don't need to look at the stage to know what they are doing right now – it's the battle of the backsides. Every time one of them goes 'uh-huh' they wiggle their butts at each other five times. I've seen them practising it loads of times down at the agency office, in front of a video of the deeply revered John Travolta. Their enthusiasm is so moving that it's hard to keep a straight face.

What the hell am I doing in a weird place like this? Time and again I long to be shot of the whole scene; time and again I have to admit that right now this seems to be the only way I can make a living. In this way my thoughts mentally chase their tails around and around the tree.

Just a few months have passed since I started my new life as

Rinka Kazuki of Kink Records, a fictitious label invented by my agency in the hope that people would confuse it with the considerably better-known King Records. Before that I was a 'companion' at a sort of hostess club in the entertainment quarter of Uguisudani. I was doing OK until one day I went and fell in love with one of the customers, and after that I couldn't really concentrate on pampering the rest of the clientele. With a weakness like that you can see I wouldn't have been suited to office work.

Kenjiro, who was pimping at the same establishment, was concerned. The guy I'd fallen for was nicknamed 'the Emperor of West Kawaguchi Nightlife'. He was a notorious playboy in that part of the unfashionable Saitama Prefecture.

'This is the first time it's ever taken me three whole days to bed a woman,' he charmingly remarked as he stooped through the hotel door. But when he emerged from that door a few hours later the casual wisecracking humour was gone.

Uh-oh, here we go again.

I had an idea what it would be like from past experience. This was going to be another monumental hassle in my life – and I had willingly brought it upon myself. How many times had I messed up my life and had to start again from scratch? Couldn't I get the messy business of love sorted out a little more smoothly this time?

After that he swiftly did the rounds of my other customers, beating up each one in turn to warn him away, and it wasn't long before his shirts and mine were swaying in the breeze together on the veranda of a new flat.

Naturally, he wouldn't stand for me taking any more jobs as hostess. 'On the other hand,' said Kenjiro, 'even he would probably let you do a bit of singing. I've had enough of the pimping myself. Come on Rinka, let's hit the entertainment circuit.'

However, the agency that Kenjiro introduced me to took a huge chunk out of our wages, and, although we did indeed hit an entertainment circuit of sorts, most of the stops along the way were far out in the sticks – places like East Omiya. And so, today, as ever, I prepare to take to the stage with a troubled heart.

'So, you would, would you? Well, take *that*.'

The dressing-room rang with the slap of playing-cards on greasy old tatami mats. The matinée was over, and Kenjiro and his fake American partner David were gambling their entire day's pay at poker – as was their wont. Today the MC was taking the pair of them to the cleaners.

'Oh, good grief – lost again. We're broke, David. Even if we chuck in yesterday's pay as well we can't cover this one.'

'What you say?' David looked up at Kenjiro with his meek, weak eyes.

'Call the agency and ask if we can have an advance on next month's pay. I'm just totally broke.'

'All right, Ken-chan.'

'It's Ken-*san* to you, arsehole.'

'Ken-san.'

Poor David was trapped by his illegal status. Knowing that Kenjiro could shop him to the immigration at any time, it made him fawningly obedient to Kenjiro's every word. Eyes brimming with tears, he picked up the mobile.

I had finished changing at last, and now I appeared before them, all decked out in my pink-sequined Chinese dress.

'Rinka? Wow, get a load of that slit skirt.'

'Hee-hee. Kind of sexy, Ken-chan?'

'Stop preening. It's no good trying to turn me on. I've got no money to give you a tip.'

At the word tip, Kenjiro suddenly remembered something. 'Tips? Tips? Of course!' he muttered to himself.

'I can pay up today after all – with this! I'd completely forgotten. Stand back, everybody. Way-hay-hay!'

He got up and briskly yanked down his flies, for all the world as if he were about to piss on the floor. I gave a little ladylike shriek.

It wasn't a pretty sight. Vigorously shaking his pelvis, a motion mastered over many renditions of the 'uh-huh' song, Kenjiro was shaking crumpled thousand-yen notes out of his trousers like a conjurer drawing strings of coloured handkerchiefs from a top hat. They had been put there by lusty old grannies as a tribute to his hip-wiggling skills in the show.

'Those randy old bitches! They were stuffing cash right into my underpants.'

As we observed the unsavoury spectacle, we noticed even a few brown ten-thousand-yen notes mixed in with the blue thousands.

'Go on, count 'em,' said Kenjiro, pointing his jaw at the pile of crumpled notes with a disdain unusual in one who has just been hammered at blackjack.

'The entire contents of your undies, for me? Eh-heh-heh-heh.' The man with the tinny laugh and the silly high-pitched voice was Moody Konami. He was no taller than a schoolboy in shorts and had a baby face to match, although he'd never see fifty again. He was a famous MC, yet with his double-breasted blue suit and black bow-tie, his pomade-encrusted hair parted conservatively at the side, he had the somehow disconcerting presence of a ventriloquist's dummy.

In his youth he'd parlayed his cheeky-chappie look into quite a successful stage career. Naming himself Pretty Konami, he'd found a niche telling comic stories while strumming along on a little guitar and had been a big hit with the older ladies. But on his fortieth birthday he changed his stage name from Pretty to Moody. This proved a disastrous career move. His popularity went down the tubes; the occasional television engagements he'd been getting evaporated, and in no time at all he was reduced to being a camp MC, introducing third-rate touring acts at hot-spring resorts.

There, at least, he remained hugely popular. They loved his baby face etched all over with wrinkles: the incongruity of it made him look like a child impersonating an old man in a school play. Until he minced across the stage, cracking his old jokes in that squeaky voice of his, you just didn't feel that the show had properly begun. He was as essential a part of the hot-spring experience as the wooden buckets that the customers used to throw water over themselves before taking to the baths. He embodied the pleasures of the cheap weekend break for the plebs.

'All right. Shall we make a start then, Rinka?' Today's show was in two parts. Part One was Kenjiro and David with their pop songs and bum-wiggling, then there was a break while the customers played bingo, and then it was time for Part 2: Rinka Kazuki, with 'The Essence of Enka'.

'Full house for you today, Rinka.' Moody's words sent a luscious shiver slithering up my spine, from the small of my back to the top of my neck. It's always been like that for me. The moment you put me in front of an audience every single cell in my body seems to vibrate minutely with some strange new energy: my voice, my expressions, my hand and foot movements, the clothes, agonized over and donned with such painstaking care, the songs I had prepared for this show, everything is going to be observed by a crowd of people I don't know. Each and every one of their lives is about to take a little detour to visit Rinka Kazuki. Ah, the mystery of it, the sheer random chance of it. At times like these I feel at last that, after all, I am a person of some consequence: my hair, my fingers, every flutter of the eyelashes, every breath I take, all, at last, are of some value.

And so, even the stage at a little provincial health spa such as this is an important place for me: a place to refresh my life and my soul. Showbiz people often say that once you've been bathed in the spotlight you can never escape from it. They speak the truth. Once caught in the sparkling waters of that bright white space you can never live on land again. It feels so good to swim in those spotlit waters that life back on terra firma is stifling: you thrash and flail around, gasping for the water like a fish that has accidentally leapt out of the aquarium. I guess I don't have skin on me any more but tight-meshed, silver, showbiz fish-scales. Same with Kenjiro, same with David – covered in smooth, cold scales.

They're right to call these places health spas. The old folks come here to enjoy soaking in the restorative waters of the baths, and we showbiz folk come to refresh our scaly bodies by soaking them in the healing waters of the limelight.

Today's venue is typical. It's a spacious building with an appallingly punning name – the I Love Yu (*yu* meaning hot water in Japanese) – and a whole range of facilities besides the baths and the big tatami room for enjoying the show. It has a video-game arcade and a noodle restaurant, a shopping area with various health products, a boutique, a shop selling cultured-pearl necklaces and a fortune-telling corner – all sorts of seemingly unrelated services, all brought together by some kind of health-spa logic.

The corridor leading to the baths is festooned, as in all these places, with posters advertising stars of the stage that no one has ever seen or heard of:

The man they call the Yujiro Ishihara of the Heisei Era!
The Mystery Man of Tottori
HIROSHI YUMEKAWA!
His hit single
'The Freezing-Cold Blues'
Now on sale!

Heading for the hit parade with a heart on fire . . . it's
SHIMAKO SADO
Taking her show across the nation to meet the fans
with her hot new release
'The Rain Keeps Falling on Your Head'!

Even Kenjiro and his sidekick were up there:

Kenjiro actually looked pretty good in the publicity poster. The tanned skin made him look kind of wild, and he gazed out at the spectator through long, cool, half-hooded eyes. I guess he would pass as a good-looking guy in most people's books, except for the snaggle teeth that would stick out in all directions if, in an absent-minded moment, he allowed himself to laugh – that and the coarse expression of his face in repose. It was the face of a man whose conversational range was limited to money talk and toilet humour.

Then again, I sometimes think that maybe the old trouts who come to the shows at the health spas and hot springs actually like that glimpse of low vulgarity that shines through Kenjiro's suave façade. As the gilt peels off this gaudy statue of manhood, it may look utterly pathetic to you and me, but to the drunken house-wives the process of decay releases a scent of raw pheromone that ignites their animal desires.

Major-league singers have an aura about them. They seem real enough for you to touch them, yet they remain tantaliz-ingly out of reach. But with cheap, minor-league singers, the promoters really have to buff that shiny image like crazy or the punters will get the feeling that if they only stuck their hands out a little bit further they could in fact grab hold quite easily. So it is with Kenjiro and David, and, although I hate to admit it, I guess it's the same with me. You know, there's this thing we often say when we're having a laugh at our own expense, 'Anyway, we're only hundred-yen singers.' And what's wrong with being cheap? Think of the pleasure you get from the sight of those cheap goods all lined up on the shelves of a hundred-yen shop. The sparkle in the eyes of the ordinary folk when they gaze upon those goods is brighter than any you'll see from them in a luxury boutique. Cheap and cheerful; posh and expensive: like yin and yang, there's a place for both in this world of ours – or so say I, speaking as a hundred-yen singer myself.

Sorry she's so cute – she just can't help it!
Introducing the chirruping palm-sized little songbird,
the pride of Kink Records
RINKA KAZUKI
The kid from Kyushu with ballads in her blood!

So here I am, standing behind the stage curtain, trying to calm down my galloping heartbeat, staring fixedly at the bit of velvet hanging right in front of my eyes. And as I stare at it, I notice that someone with a felt-tip pen has drawn a little spot on the inside of the curtain, right at eye-level. No doubt some other struggling artiste put it there in a desperate attempt to keep herself sane.

Because, you know, it's hard to keep staring and staring at that blank piece of cloth, like you're about to shoot an arrow at it; hard for me, hard for Kenjiro, hard for all the magicians and dancing girls and stand-up comedians – all the two-a-penny acts that strut and fret their hour upon this stage. No doubt they all stand here behind this blank piece of velvet with the same feelings chasing each other through their breasts. That eye-level patch must have been stared at so hard over the years by the different performers who stand behind it, day after day, year after year, that I bet it's getting frayed down to the threads. A little more staring and you'd be able to see right through it.

'Ladies and gentlemen, live on stage for your diversion and delight, the top recording artiste from Kink Records, Rinka Kazuki!' Moody Konami's high-pitched voice ushered me on to the stage, generously muffling the second K in Kink Records to make it sound more like King.

'By way of introduction, ladies and gentlemen, Rinka will sing for us "Ballad of the Man of Kawachi". Give her a big hand now.'

Up goes the curtain. The old codgers in the audience go 'Oooh' at the sight of my sexy Chinese dress with the thigh-length slit. The audience starts to pay attention. Through a buzz of background noise the scratchy old tape strikes up with the hackneyed intro to the first song. No place to run, no place to hide, the fake enka singer with the fake smile plastered all over her face is revealed to her audience, arms outstretched in greeting to all.

The likes of us have no fame and no popularity. All we have is our lust for the limelight and our debts. We risk our lives clinging to a ferry that's riddled with holes and liable to sink at any moment. The sea may rage and the waves climb high, but there's no way off the boat. We cannot – we must not – live respectable lives, so there's a desperation about us as we stumble through life.

'Enyakorase no dokkoise! One, two, three, four . . .'

Enka are traditional-style Japanese ballads, so it's kind of customary to shout things like that out before launching into the song itself. All that dokkoise stuff doesn't mean anything; it's just to establish the mood. But why, I hear you ask, am I standing here in a sexy *Chinese* dress, trying to sing an old-fashioned *Japanese* ballad? Is there not something a trifle inappropriate in the combination? Banish such doubts, gentle reader, for there is no room for them in the world of enka. Clothes are clothes; songs are songs. Clothes, songs, moves, you just try and give 'em the best you've got in every department, pack in as much value for money as you can and never mind the finer points of coordination. That is how you survive in this business.

Wobbling precariously in my five-inch heels, I belt out the rhythmic chanting in the instrumental interludes of the Kawachi ballad. I stamp my feet, I shake my head, and a shower of hair-pins and ornaments comes tumbling out of my carefully pinned-up coiffure and scatters all over the floor. Never mind. Keep smiling.

'You're a bit of all right, love.' One of the old codgers has got over-excited and he rises from the audience to come clambering on to the stage. He reckons he's going to dance with me. Moody Konami comes skipping adroitly out from the wings and hauls him away. But while he's busy doing that, another one comes dancing unsteadily up to the stage, and then another. They're peering into my face while I'm trying to sing; they're leering at me with their toothless old mouths hanging open.

'Tsk, tsk.' Clucking sanctimoniously, Moody comes scurrying up to clear them away. I give him a disapproving frown. Hey – this is a danceable number, and it's only natural if people feel their bodies starting to move. Personally I'm glad they're getting into it.

It's going to be easier than usual to get them going today. Good old Kenjiro and David. They've warmed the crowd up nicely with their 'uh-huh' routine. This is going to be a breeze.

It's not always like this. Often when I come on the atmosphere's chilly enough to see your breath. After all, not one of the people in the audience is actually there for the purpose of listening to an obscure singer called Rinka Kazuki. They just happen to have shown up on a day when it's my turn to be the entertainment. Naturally they still nourish faint hopes of enjoying the show, but, unless you hit them really hard with something to grab their attention, the moment their eyes focus on you you'll lose them and the show will carry right on in the same awkward silence. Believe me, there is nothing more miserable than singing in that Siberian cold with the regulation smile all over your face. At such times the awareness of being third rate swells ever stronger, until you're plunged into a bottomless pit of despair.

Even then, however, the situation can be retrieved. You give them a bit of patter – talk about your home town, or the pleasures of the season, how nice the cherry blossoms are this year, or whatever. That's the way to get to their softer side, and when you sing the next number you notice a distinct warming of the atmosphere.

Here at the I Love Yu the atmosphere was plenty warm enough. *Take a pan of water, add chopped vegetables, bring rapidly to simmering point – the vegetables will boil to a mushy consistency.* Here in the auditorium of the health spa we had reached simmering point. The atmosphere was steaming hot and the customers' emotions had come to a mushy consistency. With the slightest gesture of hand or leg, I could make them laugh, cry or get seriously over-excited.

This, of course, is pay-off time, the moment when you really rake in the tips. I have no idea where the custom came from, but they always shove the money at you held between disposable chopsticks. Since the agency ruthlessly rips off our appearance fees, we hundred-yen singers depend on our tips to achieve a basic standard of living. We'd get nowhere if we had to depend on the peanuts passed on to us by the agency. Two shows in a day, and all you get is 18,000 yen – it's ridiculous. The agency's getting somewhere between 30,000 and 50,000 yen and pocketing the difference. And since they only find work for you maybe four or five days in a month – well, there's no way you can live on that.

My salary from the agency last month was just 90,000 yen. But in five shows – two performances each – I made about 150,000 yen in tips. Altogether I made just about enough to scrape by in Tokyo, the world's most expensive city. And I'm doing OK for tips today. I've got thousand-yen notes slipped into the front of my dress and folded around my fingers as they grip the mike. When you do cabarets you sometimes get 10,000-yen notes as well, but you can't expect that kind of treatment at the baths. Still, I am overwhelmed with gratitude at these old folks proffering their crumpled old notes. No way will I use this money on boring everyday living expenses. No, I'll put it towards some smarter stage dresses or spend it on sheet music or buy some CDs by my favourite enka singers to brush up my technique.

'Good luck, girl.'

'Don't forget to come back.'

The curtain slowly descends. The whole audience has been reduced to a hot, thick, creamy vegetable soup. Audience reaction like this is enough to bring tears to your eyes; gigs this good only come along about one time in ten. Milk of human kindness? You'd think a thick lump of the rich, mellow butter of human kindness had plopped down from the ceiling, enveloping the audience, Kenjiro, the MC and everyone around me. They are all lovely people. What more can I say?

'You got well into that,' said Kenjiro, towelling his head, his face red and shiny from the bath. 'Got anything left for the evening show? Forgot to pace yourself, didn't you?' He looked ridiculous, wandering around the changing-room in his flower-patterned muu-muu, a handsome tanned man in an outfit comprised of a top that resembled a billowing maternity dress, paired with baggy trousers designed for old folks that stopped at the knee because his legs were far too long for them. He never seems to mind ambling around in this outrageous gear, and for me it's a struggle not to burst out laughing.

'The lunchboxes have arrived. Shall we eat?'

Lunch for the performers was supplied by a delivery company, and the black lacquer boxes were now sitting invitingly on the grey office desk. Free food, free baths. Life doesn't get much better than this.

'Wow, I'm starving. Come on, let's get stuck in.' I sat down right there in my slit Chinese dress and attacked my pork cutlets. Like most changing-rooms, the one at this health spa was an uneasy compromise between Japanese and Western styles. In forty square metres of floor space it managed to combine elements of a school staff-room, a navvy's digs at some rundown flophouse and the fitting-room at a lingerie store. Part of it was carpeted, with a grey steel desk and a wipe-off monthly planner neatly deployed – indeed, occasionally guys in ties would actually come and do some kind of office work there. But the adjacent area had tatami mats on the floor that were strewn with cushions on which bohemian performers with loud, coarse voices would sit and play cards for money. A small part of the room, modestly concealed behind a flimsy curtain, was reserved for female artistes to get changed and do their makeup. It was equipped with a dresser embellished with a picture of Mickey Mouse and an electric hotpot. The male performers got no such privilege and had to get changed wherever they could.

The cutlets were lost somewhere deep in a thick coating of batter and breadcrumbs, and, when finally located, the meat proved to be about as thick as a salesman's calling card. Amazing, really, that they can make knives sharp enough to cut meat into slices this thin. You have to be grateful for the advances of modern science, I thought to myself, as I sank my teeth into the outer crust of the cutlet.

Just then David, the fake American, came up to me with his tearful eyes and bowed his head before me. 'N-no any b-black?'

I was only momentarily surprised when he shoved the top of his head under my nose. David's always doing that. He frequently bleaches his hair to retain that blond American look, but he lives in fear of the black roots growing up through his scalp and exposing the deception.

'You're fine, David. I checked for you just the other day, didn't I?'

'Really? No any black?' He was truly a pathetic sight, bowing down before me, pointing at his head in a torment of anxiety. He used to ask Kenjiro to check for the dreaded black hairs, but these days his partner was so fed up with the endless requests for reassurance that David got nothing but insults and blows from him when he broached the subject. So now it was me he turned to.

'If there no any black, that all right.'

At this, Kenjiro rose from his cushion in front of the television, which he'd been idly watching while sipping a carton of coffee-flavoured milk, and came striding over to us, glaring furiously at David. Uh-oh. Before I could do anything there was a dull thud and David's knees crumpled. Kenjiro had caught him with a vicious kick to the side of the stomach.

'You stupid bastard, Dave! You and your bloody black hair. Can't you get it through your thick head that people don't want your stinking hair shoved in their face when they're trying to eat their fucking lunch? Stupid fucking bastard.' On and on he went. I took David's arm and tried to help him up, but he shook his head and pushed my hand away, stealing terrified glances at Kenjiro to see if he was still angry.

Kenjiro was lying in front of the telly again, sipping at his coffee-milk. He threw a venomous look our way, snorted contemptuously and carried on watching the box.

'Rinka, why don't you go and have your bath? There's still a fair bit of time before the evening show.' Kenjiro spoke with his back still turned to us but in a relaxed and even tone, totally different from the preceding outburst.

At health spas, the matinée generally starts around two and the evening show at eight. When there are two acts on the bill, like today, each act always gets exactly thirty minutes on stage, but sometimes it's just me, and then I have to keep the punters happy for a whole hour, which means having volunteers on stage to sing duets with me and so on. That can be pretty tough; comparable to running a full marathon, I'd say. Sharing the bill with Kenjiro and David is a lot more relaxing.

'Right, then. I guess I'll have my bath.' I donned my floral muumuu. A free bath between shows is one of the few perks of singing at a health spa, and I like to make the most of it.

'I'm off then. Ken-chan, don't bully David too much, OK? He's having a tough time, you know. Living underground in Japan, pretending to be an American, always worrying that he's going to be found out – you've got to understand.'

'Hah.' The recumbent Kenjiro gave a dry little laugh and rolled wearily over to face me.

'You're too fucking soft, Rinka. The guy's just an idiot. Don't waste your time feeling sorry for him, OK?'

I didn't quite know what to say. I stood there for a couple of moments, eyes downcast, pouting. 'Er, yeah.' And off to the baths I went, with Kenjiro's cynical voice floating down the stairs after me:

'You look great in that bathrobe, you know. Har-har-har . . .'

It was a biggish building. The video-game centres, snack bars, noodle stands and souvenir shops lured the customers in with tinny piped music. Every corner of the place was packed with punters. The audience at the show had been nearly all old folks, but out here there were plenty of little children and couples in their twenties as well – each and every one of them keen to enjoy a cheap and cheerful day out to the max. Admission was a modest 1,850 yen.

The communal baths were the central attraction. The ladies' and gents' each had a dozen or so different kinds: baths laced with medicinal herbs; baths scented with cypress blossom; baths with lumps of radium that supposedly emit health-giving radiation;

all sorts. Saunas and massage-rooms, too, of course. I love this kind of place, and I could gladly stay all day, but I have to watch my step because once I stayed in the hot bath too long, got kind of dizzy and fainted in the changing-room. They had to cancel the evening show, and I was hit with a cash penalty for breach of contract.

'Hey, look who's here.'

'It's that, you know, just now, she was . . .'

'Oh yeah, it's that cute girl who was singing the enka. Hey, how are you doing?'

Funny how people never want to talk to me except when I'm stark naked, crouched on an upturned bucket and trying to wash my face and brush my teeth at the same time.

'Thanks for the show.'

'Yeah, it was really fantastic.'

Through the thick clouds of steam billowing from the baths, I could just make out the broadly grinning faces of a gaggle of matronly ladies appearing and disappearing in the haze. None of them seemed at all embarrassed about being in the nude. Once people are stripped off and sharing a bath, they soon start treating total strangers like family.

'But you don't look twenty-four . . .' I gave a guilty start. 'You look a lot younger than that.' Phew. My 'stage age' is twenty-four, but in fact I'm thirty-four.

'What's your star sign, then?' Damn! Just when I thought I'd got clean away. She meant my Chinese star sign, of course, which depends on the year in which you were born. I had no idea what astrological creature might have governed my fate if I really was twenty-four. The horse? The monkey? Must bluff my way out of it somehow. Time running out . . . Expectant faces starting to look puzzled . . .

'I was born in the year of the cat. Meow!' They all burst out into cackling laughter. There's no such thing as the year of the cat, of course, but they took my desperate little joke in good humour.

'Hey, what was that song you sung? You know, about the third number in the show?'

'Yes, you know. That good one. I wanted to ask about it, too.'

They weren't giving me too much to go on. 'Er, "The White, White Waterfall", was it? Or maybe "Elegy of Michinoku"?'

'Could you sing us a bit, just to remind us? Just the intro, perhaps?'

I softly ran through the top line:

The whistle of the steam train,
Mingling with the howl of this winter blizzard . . .

'That's the one. That's definitely the one.'

'Well, in that case, madam, the name of the song is "Elegy of Michinoku",' I politely informed her.

'Is that so? Well I never. How nice. Do you think they'd have it in the karaoke?'

'Sure they would. It's been in the charts just recently.'

'Hm, I'd love to have a go at it myself later on. Hey, you wouldn't sing us a few more bars of it, would you?'

'Keiko, give the girl a break,' objected one of the other women. 'She's a professional. You can't just ask her to sing for us in the bath. It isn't polite.'

'Oh. Sorry. You're right, you're quite right. I really am sorry. I was forgetting. You're the kind of person who gets *paid* to sing. Us lot have to *pay to be allowed* to sing. Ha-ha-ha-ha-ha!' All the other ladies joined in laughing. They were on great form.

Occasions like this are kind of difficult for me, because they remind me that my whole career is built on lies and trickery. Singer? Me? What for? Who for? Here I am, making out I'm some kind of star, when, in fact, no one has asked me to be a singer; I just used a few handy personal connections to land myself in this position. I'm not a real singer, I'm a fraud. And I'm being paid for it. Some of the people paying me are struggling to get by on a pension. What do I have to give them in exchange for those thousand-yen tips that they can hardly afford? I've only just started this new career as a travelling singer, yet already I've run up quite a tab in that great ledger book in the sky where deeds of kindness and deceit are recorded. What sort of punishment awaits me for all my lies and pretence?

'I, er . . . All right then, I *will* sing for you.' I arose resolutely from the tub, in all my naked glory, showering the surprised ladies with a spray of herbal-scented bath water. I turned to face them as they gasped with surprise. 'I will sing for you the best I can. Please listen while I perform, just for you, "Elegy of Michinoku".'

A sudden hush fell over the bathroom. The old ladies covered in suds suddenly stopped scrubbing, with their sponges in mid air; the housewives sitting dreamily under the massage shower, their shoulders pummelled by jets of warm water, looked up and opened their eyes; the mothers who were just taking their children out to the open-air bath in the back garden stopped in mid stride. All the naked ladies were frozen for a moment as time stood still.

> The whistle of the steam train,
> Mingling with the howl of this winter blizzard . . .

The moment I started singing, that bathroom was my stage. I forgot my nakedness, and the towel wrapped around my head fell slowly to the floor as I sang my heart out amid the wraiths of steam. When I moved into the opening verse of the ballad, I felt myself carried away into the world of the song. All embarrassment was gone. My worthless life, my lack of talent – such mundane things simply evaporated in the steam. For now I was a beautiful woman, deprived by death of the love of her life, standing alone by the Naruse River, in a glorious kimono, singing out her grief to the snowy skies above:

> Ah, even in my dreams I long to be with you.
> Ah, even in my dreams, enfold me in your arms.
> The tears of Michinoku,
> This winter elegy.

The song came to an end. There was a momentary silence in the bathhouse, and then I was engulfed in a storm of riotous applause. Everyone was so delighted that I hardly knew what to do with myself and scratched the back of my head in embarrassment. The beautiful image of the song faded away, and I was once more a dodgy third-rate singer standing naked in a public bathhouse.

At that moment, this really old hag came sidling shyly up to me. 'You sang that very nicely, dear.' And, like a bashful little girl giving a flower to the boy next door, she handed me her pink hand-towel. I knew exactly what the little towel meant, and I felt tears welling up in my eyes. She wanted to give me a tip, but, like everyone else in the bathhouse, she literally had nothing on her. So she gave me her hand-towel – which, at that particular moment, was the only thing she had to give.

'Th-thanks.' My voice was trembling. Ridiculous. Got to get a grip. I pulled myself together and acknowledged her generosity in more fitting manner. 'Thank you very much indeed.'

A murmur went up from the crowd, and a middle-aged lady

unwound the towel on her head and threw it in my direction with considerable force. It slapped into me, and I was still reeling from the sting of the whiplash when a third lady bobbed up from the bath, leering all over her face, and launched another towel at me.

And then they were all at it. Towels were raining down on me from every angle. I couldn't hold them all, my head was covered with towels, my shoulders, too; towels were hanging off every part of my body. They were slapping off me, flopping off me, piling up at my feet in a crumpled towel mountain.

'Glad I did that.' I was talking to myself in an inaudible whisper mingled with an exhausted sigh. I looked up, and there was a picture of Mount Fuji painted on the bathroom wall. In the world of ballad singing I was right at the bottom of that mountain. But right now, just for this one special moment, it felt as if I'd floated right up to the top. Wet towels were splatting into the ceiling and tumbling down on my head and shoulders like some weird laurel of triumph, vigorously massaging my shoulders as they came.

Looking down at the multicoloured flannel mountain at my feet, it occurred to me that I felt *rich*. I somehow scooped up the towels, barely able to hold them all with both arms full, and wobbled out of the bathroom, pushing back the wooden sliding door with some difficulty.

The dressing-room was lined with wicker chairs and a long mirror stretched across one wall at head height. I stood before the mirror for a moment with my arms full of towels. As I observed myself standing there, with all these prizes and rewards covering my body like an ephemeral dusting of light snow, for a minute I really loved myself.

Coming to my senses, I noticed a couple of Korean massage girls in their simple orange work clothes, sitting in the wicker chairs and smoking cigarettes. As soon as they saw me they got up and took all the towels out of my hands, apologizing for putting me to the trouble of collecting them up. Of course, the towels didn't belong to me or to the women who gave them to me; they belonged to the health spa, which lent them to its customers for use in the bath.

'That will be one million yen for the lot,' I said. It was a joke barely worthy of an old man in a greengrocer's, but they looked at each other and laughed just the same. 'No need to bother with tonight's show after all,' I laughed and headed for the stairs leading up to the changing-room.

Looking across the lobby on my way up, I noticed a little group of Filipinas sitting on a sofa and chatting away cheerfully together. They were probably a dance troupe that was staying over before performing tomorrow. The middle-aged Japanese men and women sitting on the opposite sofa were basking peacefully in the youthful aura of the dancers. I'm always struck by the appearance of Filipinos and Filipinas who come to Japan for work. With their dark hair and deep, expressive features, they have a kind of restrained sadness in their eyes that contrasts with the relaxed and jaunty way they carry themselves. I often sense a melancholy about them that makes me wonder whether they can cope with the toughness of their daily lives – but not this time. These girls were noisily talking among themselves, laughing out loud, slapping one anothers' shoulders and thighs and generally having a good time. I was in a good mood myself, what with the million-yen towels, and so I called across the lobby to them.

'Hiya!' The dancers noticed me and waved cheerfully back. At that moment I noticed something that knocked me off balance. There, in the middle of this gaggle of laughing girls, sitting back expansively with his legs crossed like some kind of king, was David.

David – the fake American who was always so worried about his guilty secret being revealed by the glimpse of a single black hair root – was mingling openly with these charming Filipina girls, right in front of the customers, chatting merrily away in Tagalog. Maybe Kenjiro's right after all. Maybe he *is* just an idiot.

Somehow the energy seemed to drain out of me and I tottered the rest of the way to the changing-room on slightly unsteady feet. Little did I know that I was about to have the rest of the stuffing knocked out of me by an even more outrageous development.

'Got a little problem here.' Kenjiro's brow was deeply furrowed. He'd already changed into his gear for the evening show and was standing by the window looking serious. He stared at the mobile telephone clutched in his hand for some moments, then said 'Shit' and chucked it on the floor.

'What's up, Ken-chan?' Giving no thought to the danger of crumpling his stage finery, Kenjiro collapsed to the floor and rolled over on his back, a beaten man. 'Come on, come on, what's up?'

Still he didn't answer. He just lay there, hands folded under his head, staring at the ceiling, lost in thought. He was wearing white trousers and a purple Versace shirt and a white jacket with over-sized shoulder pads scraping against his ears in a way that couldn't have been comfortable.

At length he spoke, a single word escaping from his lips like a bubble released from deep waters. 'Gone.'

'What?'

'They've gone. They've done a runner on us. The whole stinking company.'

'Company? What company? The production company? *Our* production company? Surely not!'

'Sure as sure is sure. I've been trying to call them, but all I can get is a recorded message: "This number is not in use at present."'

'Oh, come on. They've just been a bit too late with paying the phone bill, right?'

'I don't think so. I've got a bad feeling.' Thinking about it, I started to share that bad feeling. This particular month we'd had an unusually large amount of work. These are lean times for the entertainment industry, and I'd been wondering how come they'd been finding so many gigs for inferior acts such as us.

'That bastard of a boss. He's gone for a massive end-of-year closing-down sale, that's what he's done,' said Kenjiro, spitting the words out. 'The same acts for half the price, eh? Of course he got plenty of bookings, the bastard.'

'But what about our pay?'

'We're not gonna *get* any pay.' Kenjiro lay there, eyes closed, pouting like a gargoyle. 'Done a runner,' he quietly repeated.

It's hard to put body and soul into your singing when you've been worrying yourself sick. I knew that, of course, and so I tried to get rid of all thoughts about my troubles and worries by doing deep-breathing exercises before I went on stage. This time, however, the old trick didn't seem to work as well as usual. The scary thing is, the audience immediately senses if your mind isn't on the job in hand. The more they notice that you're off form, the more you panic; the more you panic, the more you overplay the material. There's no relaxation in your voice or in your eyes as they meet those of the audience. Without that relaxation you can't enter fully into the spirit of the song and its lyrics. Mere empty words go drifting up into space and drift pointlessly around the ceiling without ever reaching the audience. In short, the show's no good. Such was the case now. I heard someone failing to stifle a yawn.

Things were pretty bad. At this rate I certainly wouldn't get any tips and I might never be invited back to the place.

And then something happened. I felt a pair of gleaming eyes drilling into me from somewhere in the audience. An old man had risen from his seat and had planted himself firmly in front of the stage. I'd heard rumours about this guy, but I'd never actually met him before. He was ancient, well into his eighties, and he was the most regular customer the place had. He'd sit right at the very back and soak up the sake while he took in the show. His wife had died ages ago, and he lived with his son's family in a state of permanent dissatisfaction. His one joy in life was to hang out at the health spa and watch the free shows while he got drunk. Over the years, these shows had gradually developed from a relaxing pastime to being the main purpose of his continued existence, while the management had come to look on him as a kind of guardian deity of the auditorium.

Old Mr Bravo, that was his nickname. If the show happened to be getting kind of boring, he would rise up and attempt to encourage the hapless performer by calling out 'Bravo!' In fact, his encouragement just drew attention to himself and was the kiss of death to any struggling performer. I could see he was just about to give me the treatment, and did my best to deter him by turning up my ballad-singing to top volume – 'THIS NORTHERN LAND IS OH SO COLD' – but it was too late to save myself.

'Bravo!' The shame of it. Heckled by a crazy old man in front of all these people.

> IN MY HEART I HATE YOU,
> BUT WHEN YOU TAKE ME IN YOUR ARMS
> THE WOMAN IN ME STILL BURNS WITH PASSION.

'Bravo! Braavo!'

> I HAVE GIVEN YOU MY LIFE ... MY LIFE ... MY LIFE ...
> WHAT A FOOL WAS I, WAS I.
> OH, OH, OH, A FOOL INDEED.

'Bravo!' The audience loved him. They were doubled up laughing, clutching their stomachs, egging him on. No one was looking at me any more. All eyes were trained on Old Mr Bravo. He only had the one line, but the more he said it, the more feeling and variety of expression he put into it.

'Bravo! Braaaaaaaaavo!' He was in full flight now. There was no way back for me. I might as well throttle back.

This northern land, this northern land,
The place that quenched the flames of love.

I suddenly became acutely aware that my body was covered with thousands, no millions, of tiny little pores. All those thousands and millions of pores were now opening and closing at the same time, exuding sweat. The bath towel that I wore wrapped around my waist to reduce the pain from the tightly knotted *obi* of my gaudy kimono was now soaking up so much sweat that I could actually feel it getting heavier by the minute.

'Well, it's time to say *sayonara*. You've been a lovely audience. Thank you so much . . .' I finished my mumbled farewells and hobbled miserably off the stage, feeling like I had a hundred-weight sack of rice on my back. Knowing how I'd be feeling, Kenjiro was waiting for me backstage. I sank into his arms as if into a stretcher prepared by an emergency rescue patrol.

'Ha-ha-ha-ha-ha-ha. Don't worry about a little thing like this. You know what they say in the trade: debts, lost love and dud performances are best forgotten. Eh?' Kenjiro hugged me and smiled. Thank goodness he was there.

'I just wanted to get the show right,' I sobbed.

'Silly. There's no point going on about it now.'

'Because I'm a liar. I tell them I'm with a record label, but I've never made a record.'

'Lies don't count unless you tell more than eight, you know that.' Another cheap proverb, but he'd saved me again. He was talking a load of nonsense as usual, but right now it was what I needed. I was feeling better already. 'Besides,' he continued, everyone tells lies. Everyone in the world. Because no one living is true to themselves. Compared with the rest of 'em, you and I are straight as dice.'

Somehow we'd got to holding hands, and he was gently leading me back through the corridor to the changing-room.

'Hello, what have we here?' My white arm was sticking out from my kimono sleeve, and he'd noticed that I had my song list written in felt-tip pen on the inside of my wrist. 'So it was you who painted that giant mural they were going on about on the TV news.'

'Eh? What do you mean?'

'I mean, stupid, that you're a damn fool to write your song titles in those bloody great letters on your own wrist. They can read this in Row Z!'

'Sometimes when I shake hands with people they think it's a tattoo, so they figure I must be a gangster or something and they get scared and pull their hand away.'

'Of course they do, you silly cow.'

'But if I don't write them down, I'll forget them.'

'Can't you remember the names of *eight songs*, Rinka? Talk about shit for brains. It's not like you've got this gigantic repertoire, eh? You and David between you just about take the biscuit. What a pair of morons. Good grief . . .'

'Didn't get any tips this time.'

'Oh, come on. It's only one show. And you got all those towels, didn't you? Those fan-fucking-tastic towels you got.' Of course, the towels. I brightened up. The big number in the bathhouse, the mass presentation of the hand-towels, a tip worth its weight in gold. A million-yen tip. 'Yeah. What about me, eh? I didn't get a million-yen towel. If me and David started swinging our butts together naked in the men's baths they'd be pretty pissed off with us. Turning on the ladies is our only sales point.'

'Well, at least you've got something to sell.' I was about to add 'pheromones' but thought better of it and shut up. I'm no good at comforting Kenjiro.

The Toyota Celsior arrived in Hokima, the run-down district of north-eastern Tokyo that was home to Lucky Promotions Corp.

'Hope things work out for you. Bye for now.' So saying, our driver, none other than Moody Konami himself, turned and drove away, leaving only his Cheshire Cat smile floating in the air behind him. We approached the dilapidated eight-storey building in the middle of a busy shopping street that served as headquarters for our employers along with a number of other dubious enterprises.

As I stood in the lift with Kenjiro and David, my mind went back to my only other visit to Lucky Productions. Then, as now, it had been the three of us. Ken and Dave were already signed to Lucky, and they'd brought me along with them to try to get a contract. The office was a single room in this shabby block, and the president wasn't at his desk at the appointed time. While we stood around chatting and wondering what to do the telephone had rung. It was for me.

'So you're Rinka Kazuki, are you? Thanks a lot for coming along today. Something's cropped up that's taken me away from the office, I'm afraid, but, hey, I've seen your photo and I've heard the tape. You've passed the audition. Now I want you to get out on stage and make us all proud of you.'

It was that easy. A funny thing had happened on the way out, however. The three of us were just talking about stuff while we got our shoes on when we became aware of this huge man towering behind us. He said he was a debt collector and wanted to know where the boss was most urgently. He also wanted to know whether we were in his employ. Things could have turned ugly, but Kenjiro bailed us out.

'Actually we're debt collectors ourselves,' he lied nonchalantly, 'from First Total Finance Corp.' This line seemed to work for the gorilla in the doorway and he let us go.

'Right there I thought there was something funny going on,' I remarked to Kenjiro, as we returned to the office.

'Hark at Sherlock fucking Holmes. Of course there was something funny going on. Funny as a nine-yen coin, Rinka, you silly cow.'

It would appear that Kenjiro had accepted work from this employer while knowing full well that he was an unreliable, fly-by-night sort of person. Or perhaps I should say that Kenjiro knew full well that a guy such as him was not likely ever to be offered a job by a reliable, non-fly-by-night sort of person. He knew he was dodgy himself, and he was comfortable with the situation. Hence Kenjiro was quite unsurprised by the scene that met our eyes as we emerged from the elevator. I, however, had not quite achieved his level of ingrained cynicism and was somewhat taken aback.

'What on earth has happened here?'

The windows were broken; the room was an empty husk. Everything had gone; not a single stick of furniture remained. A chill December wind came cutting through. Right in the middle of the room sat three cardboard boxes. And that was all.

Awfully sorry things have panned out this way – please take the enclosed as a final token of my esteem.

That was the message from the president, scrawled in fat black marker pen on the flap of the top box.

I'll never forget Kenjiro's face as he peered into that cardboard box. Consumed by an agonizing mixture of hope and uncertainty, he pulled back the flaps and stared into it as though stealing a peek at a crystal ball that would foretell his own destiny. His expression took on a most uncharacteristic gravity. And then he froze right there, motionless on his two knees.

'Hnh.' Kenjiro's lip curled, and one cheek froze in a half-formed leer. Then he rolled over on his back, laughing like a hyena, slapping the floor with his hands as the tears rolled down his face. He'd apparently gone mad.

'Rinka! Look at this. Dave! This is unbelievable.' David and I shoved past his writhing body and dived into the cardboard boxes. They proved to be stuffed full of little towels; more like flannels really. Printed on each one was the following legend:

Burning up the pop-charts!
KENJIRO AND DAVID
'Love Is a Miracle'

'I've made it at last,' spluttered Kenjiro hysterically. 'I've done it. I've got my own million-yen towels!' And, indeed, you could argue that these towels were worth a million yen – although only in the sense that they were all we were going to get from an employer who owed the three of us about that much in back pay.

The hysterical Kenjiro was still rolling around on the carpet, scattering the million-yen towels around him, chucking them up at the ceiling. We already had quite a few bookings lined up. In all those health spas and cabarets scattered around the small towns the posters were already up, the programmes already printed, the promoters were relying on us. We weren't going to get paid for those gigs, but we were going to have to do them anyway.

'Hah-hah! Ha-ha-ha! Isn't it great, Dave?' Next to the thrashing and flailing Kenjiro David was kneeling stock-still, like an electric doll that had just been switched off.

Another blast of freezing wind came whistling through the broken window, carrying with it the distant howling of some stupid dog. What sort of New Year was it going to be for us? Already we could hear the hollow ping of the festive drum on some early seasonal advertising floating into the room from somebody's television. A couple of things were certain: we had no spouses or children with whom to share rice-cakes and tangerines, and we could hardly show our faces in front of our own parents at New Year with no money for presents and no job prospects to speak of. New Year was just going to be a drag, with the shops closed and nothing to do. A year older and not a penny richer; the sooner we could get it over with the better.

'I go find him.' David was struggling to his feet, wobbly but vengeful.

'What? What did you just say?'

'I go find boss.'

Kenjiro flushed livid with rage. He looked like one of those vengeful gods that guard the entrances to Buddhist temples with fists full of thunderbolts.

'You bloody idiot.' As usual, these words were accompanied by a hefty kick. David was halfway up, and it caught him right in the stomach. He sank back to the floor, switched off once more.

'For fuck's sake, Dave, what are you thinking of? This thing is *over*. It's all over. Do you really want to go back over this crap again? You arsehole, Dave.'

Still spouting invective, Kenjiro sat down heavily on one of the boxes of towels. The box sank beneath his weight with a faint tearing sound. 'Now listen to me, Dave. Every day is the first day of the rest of your life – that's how to live. You want to look for something new. You don't want to put on the same underpants you took off yesterday, do you? Or the day before yesterday?'

David was lying face down on the filthy carpet, silently weeping. 'Come on, look at me.'

'It no good, Ken-chan. We keep singing, keep singing, we never make big time.'

Even I was angry at his pathetic whining. Actually I wanted to give him a kick myself, but not in front of Kenjiro.

'You idiot, Dave. Don't you have any pride at all in what we're doing now? We're touring artistes, you know.'

'Eh?' Even Kenjiro was surprised at my sudden outburst and turned his attention to me. OK. Time to have my say.

'Dave, which would you rather be: bottom of the class in a good school, or top of the class in a crap school? Which of those two would make you feel better? Well?'

David looked at me with the blank, direct gaze of a breast-feeding child. At the roots of his blond locks, I could make out half a millimetre of black hair.

'Er, bottom of class in crap school?' he essayed.

'That's right, Dave. Er, no, what am I saying? *Top* of the class in a crap school, right?'

'Ah, yes.' Dave's shocking slip of the tongue brought a chill that gripped my whole body. He had just said what I dared not think. *Bottom of the class in a crap school.* Hm. Out of the mouths of fools come wise words. Maybe he had unwittingly put his finger right on our situation. It seemed that the same awful thought had just run through Kenjiro's mind, too. His eyes strayed around the room, wandering from floor to ceiling without settling on any object. Then he abruptly got to his feet and started shadow-boxing.

'Take that! Gotcha! Gotcha! Feint, feint, left, right! I am Mr Drama . . .'

'Yujiro Ishihara! Come on, you're looking good.' I encouraged him. You know, he did slightly resemble Japan's most famous movie hard man – if you didn't look too closely.

'Ow, you got me. You'll pay for that.' Chuckling to himself, Kenjiro started acting out his Yujiro Ishihara fantasy. The chilly grey room started to warm up. 'You gotta have guts. You gotta fight for your rights. Hustle, hustle! Go for it. Give 'em back double what they gave you. Take that!'

It was always like this. Always getting saved from my darker self by Kenjiro and his silly antics. Now he had his leg up for a kung-fu kick and both fists clenched. I threw a towel at his wobbling back. Somewhere at the back of my mind I seemed to hear the ringside bell clanging for the end of Round One.

2 Bright Knight/ Dark Knight

Kenjiro seems to think of me as some kind of Snow White. A fluffy white bunny. A soft little thing that has to be looked after. There are others, however, who curse me as a black-hearted woman: a wicked woman who steals away other people's husbands.

Black to white, white to black – I'm always changing, like some crazy traffic-light.

But the real me is both white and black. Water hot as fire; soft stone.

Daiki Hirose is the kind of guy who can take me just as I am without making an issue of it.

'Go for a drive?' He casually slipped out of the leather jacket he had on over his work clothes and dropped it on to my shoulders. My body was enveloped as if it had just been devoured by some huge creature, and I tottered slightly under the sudden weight.

'We can't just go off right away, Daiki. I haven't washed my face yet. And I want to get changed.'

Guys are always like this. The moment they decide they want to go out, they're ready to roll. It's different for girls.

'You're fine. That tracksuit you've got on doesn't look like pyjamas at all. Just put something over the top and you'll not feel the cold. No problem.'

'I ... Come on, just let me wash my face, OK?'

'No need, no need, you look beautiful just like that.'

Mr Wild, that's my secret nickname for him. Daiki works as a manager on building sites, and he isn't the kind of guy to pay much attention to the finer details. He walked into my life when I was still working as a bar girl in Uguisudani. He was just a casual customer who came in off the street, but, stupidly, I fell in love with him. We've been seeing each other ever since. It seems this rented flat that he calls his office has not yet been discovered by his wife. Ever since I tumbled into the place it's been filled with this sweet atmosphere – sweet as cheap candy.

Neither of us is any good at resisting natural impulses. When he feels sleepy, Daiki will just suddenly topple over, as if someone had just switched him off. It doesn't matter if he's in a bar or standing in the middle of the road, the call to slumber has to be obeyed at once. He's stocky as a baseball player, and can't easily be lifted with a woman's strength. As for me, all the strength drains out of me the moment I feel a pang of hunger: my handbag or the telephone will drop from my limp hands. Cold sweat spreads across me, and I'll even start shivering. One time I got like that just before I went on stage, and lacking anything more suitable I actually scoffed a couple of paper tissues just to calm my stomach. At times like that my brain tells me to hang on a second, but my body just carries on regardless.

And that's how Daiki and I wound up living together. That's why we're going to love each other for ever. It's too late to do anything about it.

That tough body of his is always ready to kick the shit out of any other man who threatens to approach me. Sometimes he gets the wrong idea, but he'll fight anyway. I hate that. But he's like a train with no brakes; he just can't be stopped. I sometimes think that maybe he should have been a boxer or wrestler or something but forgot to get around to it. I reckon there are quite a few forgetful people like that, more than you might expect.

I myself – maybe I forgot to become a famous singer, and I'm living my life in the shadow of that moment of forgetfulness. Or is that all nonsense? Maybe the day when I hit the big time is just around the corner; maybe that gift is just about to fall from the sky. 'Well remembered,' they'll say. The prizes of success will come tumbling down on me like a nice warm shower. Funny.

'Eh, what, you've got one of your . . .' Daiki had spotted my trundle-trolley, sitting there in the hall like a lump of lead. His excitement about the excursion visibly dissolved. My trundle-trolley is a trunk on wheels stuffed with my stage gear: the costumes, the music scores, the greasepaint, the hairpiece, all the things Daiki hates most.

'C'mon, c'mon, let's go for that drive.' I gave him a big hug and put on my most winsome voice. Superficially, at least, he responded, stroking my hair and hugging me back. But I knew things weren't right. Daiki's body is true as a magnet: sometimes it wants to attract another body and sometimes it wants to repel, and the difference between the two modes is perfectly apparent. I'm sure he feels awkward about it himself.

'I'm an understanding guy. I'm not like those old-fashioned men who want to stop their women from expressing themselves. Do what you want to do. I'll back you up, you know that.' Apparently he really has been like that in the past, encouraging the various women in his life to develop their careers. But somehow he just can't with me. Could it be there's something about me, some aura that gets to men, that sends out a message saying 'Tie me down'? To be fair, I wouldn't fancy a man who had no concern at all about his woman going out into the lawless world of travelling players; on the other hand, faced with the prospect of being dominated by a man and not being allowed to do what I want – well, I'd roll over and die. In other words, I want Daiki to suffer, as if he had a stomach ulcer. I can be pretty cruel.

Daiki's just the same. He wants me to struggle. It can't be helped. Both of us are stuck halfway between white and black – and, I have to admit, we seem to be a pretty good match.

'What the hell – I'll go and drink with the boys tonight.' And with that, Mr Wild was out the door. I was left standing by the entrance with one shoe on and one shoe off.

I wonder if it's fun for him, talking to the guys about his girlfriend and stuff. I hate talking to other women. We never talk for long about affairs of the heart, and I naturally run out of things to talk about. They go on and on about their husband's work, or their holiday arrangements, or what they like to eat, or what they feed their children, and I can't wait for the conversation to end. They're stuck in their boring marriages like battery hens in boxes, shut up in the dark and stuffing themselves with food all day.

I heard the sound of the car wheels, rumbling over the road's frozen February surface. Later came dusk, and I trotted off to the station, dragging my trolley-load of misery behind me on its squeaky little wheels.

Maybe I like sad things.

Why do I always rush to get to that wooden stage where no one is waiting for me anyway? Rushing along fit to bust a gut – a capricious woman, a stupid woman. It's ridiculous. The only reward I get for all my singing is the smell of my own hair burning under the spotlights: blazing spotlights in the midsummer heat; heavy kimonos with thick belts; midwinter shows in Sapporo; outdoor stages; singing in the middle of the bone-chilling night; frozen microphones in theatres like fridges; pain in the hands; fingers that feel like they're stuck to the ice-tray; teeth chattering with cold; pain running through my jaw every time I sing. I must be out of my mind.

There are few enough trains on the Musashino Line at the best of times, and when the station PA finally did announce one I cheered up and got ready to board, but it turned out to be just a freight train thundering through: a grey train. I watched a few of these go by, trains that I couldn't board. Why did the tears start to roll down my cheeks? At last I got on a train. It took me from East Kawaguchi to South Urawa, where I changed to the Keihin-Tohoku Line. I was still a long way from Tsurumi, the Yokohama outskirt that was tonight's destination.

Even as I set out on this journey I already wanted to go back home. I always want to set out somewhere, and I always want to go home. I'll tear my body in half if I'm not careful. I'm a spoilt child, that's the trouble – I want it all – but since I can't seem to find any other way to live, all I can do is stamp my feet in frustration.

The tears were coming more freely now. Self-pity? Inner conflict? My tears mean nothing. If I carry on crying, sooner or later they'll stop. I don't want people to see me crying, because they'll just try to attach some meaning to my tears. They taught me a lot of useless crap at school, but they've got no right to tell me the right way to grieve. A woman crying on the train – it's not very respectable, is it? So I just kept standing in the carriage with my head down. But even then someone might have noticed, so I thought I'd just stand by the window and look quietly out at the passing scenery. The leather straps were out of reach anyway. I rubbed my hands together to keep out the cold.

The winter scenery went by in a blur.

There's nothing certain in life, of course, but sometimes it's hard to enjoy the uncertainty. You wish they'd hurry up and get the lottery over with.

There were no autumn blooms colouring the houses crowded along the side of the railway track. Just kale that looked like cabbage.

'I think you dropped this.' An unusually clear voice reached my ears. The woman who had picked up my handkerchief looked to be about thirty. She had seductive white skin that could have belonged to some exotic amphibian – not to any regular office girl, that's for sure. She was decked out in a flapping one-piece that seemed to mingle all the colours of the rainbow – a bit like the view you get on the screen when you adjust your television's colour and contrast – in lamé, too, and with a mink coat over the top of it. A little Louis Vuitton bag dangled from her shoulder. Her fashion sense was terrible.

Beneath this rainbow clothing, I instinctively knew, was a fellow showgirl. She was a stage-fish like me and Kenjiro, covered with the same scales. As I stared at her, she evidently got the same feeling. She looked me in the eye, and said, 'So, which production company are you with?'

How had she guessed? I had no giveaway showgirl gear on me – no fur coat, no Louis Vuitton bag, no sparkling jewellery. My outfit today featured a short-sleeved canary-yellow angora sweater with matching hot pants. I had a white down jacket over the top and knee-high white boots with six-inch heels, and a teddy-bear rucksack on my back. Up top I sported a brown hairpiece, supple as silk, below which my long hair cascaded all the way down to my waist. At my feet was my trundle-trolley with its castors that squeaked wherever I went – an essential item for any travelling artiste. Affixed to the top of it were three stickers, each of them proclaiming 'The Girl Who Brings Out the Blossoms: Kazuki Rinka'. Could it be this that had given her a clue?

'I'm on my way to the Only Yu Health Spa in Kamata,' she said. 'Have you done that gig yet?' Her mobile, amphibious lips were interestingly decorated with pink lipstick on the top one and orange on the bottom. There was something arresting about bad taste on this scale. Her abundant black hair was artificially glossy and done up geisha-girl style, exuding a traditional Japanese atmosphere that went with her loud Western-style clothing not at all. Maybe she was an enka singer, too, and she'd done her hair before she set out to save time getting the geisha look right before the show.

'Heading for that cabaret in Tsurumi, are you? I was there last week.' I looked down at her feet. Sure enough, she had a trundle-trolley, too. Of course, plenty of people take those things with them when they set out on a journey, but not at six o'clock in the evening and not wearing that kind of fashion. Looking around the train carriage, I could see several more showgirl types.

Mostly, when people are coming back from a journey or setting out on one, they have a kind of liberated look in their eyes. They tend not to have a look of total desperation, staring out at the world from faces caked in thick makeup as they go around with their squeaky trundle-trolleys in tow. I felt somewhat cheered. In this carriage alone I could spot no fewer than five trundle-trolley buddies. It wasn't as if I alone were living a particularly weird lifestyle: I was just average.

There are various types of show people who travel around the cabarets and health spas. I read somewhere that there are 1,800 of us enka singers, but there are lots of other singers out there, doing jazz, oldies, folk and so on. And then there are the comedians (solo and double acts mostly), the strippers (or exotic dancers, I should say), the magicians, the guys who work with animals (monkeys, dogs, birds), the impressionists who happen to resemble showbiz stars – so many different creatures, basking in the heat of the spotlight, quietly breathing in the aquarium of the stage.

'Well, good luck then, Rinka.' We had reached Kamata station and off she got.

'Just a minute. What's your name?'

'Don't worry. We'll meet again.'

'No, go on, tell me.' With the piercing clamour of the station's warning bell, the door slid shut between us. The woman's voluptuous, multicoloured lips were moving. Ayako, they seemed to be saying. The breath that came out with the words was white.

'Ayako?'

'That's right. Ayako. You'll see one of my posters at that place you're singing tonight. Don't forget: Ayako!' She blew me a playful kiss and then she was off, her trundle-trolley rattling across the platform behind her.

Left alone in the train, I thoughtfully muttered the name under my breath, 'Ayako.' A voluptuous woman called Ayako who sings enka. Inevitably the image of the great Ayako Fuji came to mind. What was this Ayako's other name, I wondered, and why had she chosen such a silly stage name anyway? As an enka stage name, Ayako carried too much baggage, just as Hibari is too closely associated with Hibari Misora and Harumi with Harumi Miyako.

'Good morning!'

I arrived at the Knockout Cabaret at the stroke of 7 p.m. In the business we always say 'good morning' when we show up for work, no matter what time of day it may be. Munching on the Big Mac I'd picked up at the station, I switched on the electric heater in the freezing-cold dressing-room. It emitted a faint whine, and the filament slowly turned a dull orange, easing my heart to a degree. I opened up the trunk and pulled out the kit I'd be needing for the two performances. I was just ironing the kimono I planned to wear for the second show when I caught sight of the poster of Ayako from the train. There she was, smiling saucily out from the posters of entertainers stuck to the reddish-brown wall of the tiny room.

Not so fast! Naughty boy!
Look out for the National Traffic Safety Campaign theme tune
'Go Slow, Baby'
now on sale from Bolydor Records, with the sensational B-side
'Look Straight Ahead'
recommended by the All-Japan Truckers' Association!
The hot new release that's burning up the Boricon Bop Chart,
from the beauty who prays for every driver's safety
Ayako Buji!

I was never going to forget this name. *Buji* means safe and sound in Japanese, and this terrible pun was taking an awful liberty with the name of the magnificent Ayako Fuji. Similar liberties had been taken with the trade names of Polydor Records and the Oricon Pop Chart. I laughed until I dropped the iron on my foot. I had to make friends with this girl. At last I'd found a girl I could have a good laugh over. Until now people had made a fool of me and people had loved me. That was all very well, but now and again it would be nice if I could be the one making a fool of somebody else. Ayako Buji indeed. 'Not so fast! Naughty boy!' indeed.

On the poster Ayako Buji was smiling elegantly in a navy-blue kimono with a policewoman's cap perched on her head at a jaunty angle. I stood in front of this glorious image, shoulders shaking, body writhing, stabbing at the poster with my finger while I laughed till I was struggling to breathe.

'What an idiot.'

I was so busy laughing at Ayako Buji that I didn't notice the time. When I remembered to look at the clock it was already eight. I'd have to hurry up and have my pre-show meeting with the band.

I was in the pink, spangly Chinese dress that I often wore at health spas. This was my first time at this cabaret, and I would have to take careful note of what I was wearing to avoid future trouble. I recorded what I wore at each establishment in a diary I maintained just for that purpose. Every cabaret has an A&R man who checks up on every singer that comes his way. The check covers everything – singing ability, appearance, etiquette and clothing – and you know they're quietly marking your scorecard somewhere over in the corner of the room. A singer who wears the same clothes two or three times or sings the same numbers every time she appears seems kind of shabby and, naturally, doesn't get too many bookings.

Consequently, we singers are forever trying to work out how to scrape together the money to buy clothing and scores. Even so, most of us are in the red. Getting the music arranged is a pricey business for a start. You can't just play the band a CD of some hit ballad and expect them to play it straight off. No, you have to get somebody to arrange the song in parts for the kind of small band you get on the circuit, and that costs around 30,000 to 50,000 yen for a full-part score. Mind you, these days times are hard for the arrangers, too – most of them are retired bandsmen – and since they need customers to put food on the table, some of them have dropped their prices to around 10,000 or 20,000 yen.

Most singers can't earn a living from appearance fees and sales of original songs. Most rely on some other form of income – a day job, perhaps, or a patron. To get work they will sleep with cabaret managers, and some will actually sell their bodies to make the money to buy clothes.

In my own case, first of all I have no original songs. I have none, yet I still tell the big lie, going around the country as if I were a real singer. For stage-clothing I mostly make do with other girls' cast-offs, cunningly fixing them up to conceal the fact that they aren't new. Kimonos are the most expensive item, of course, but I know a second-hand dealer who lets me have them on the cheap, and I actually end up spending more money on the belts. A smart new *obi* can do wonders for a second-hand kimono. Singing lessons are another major expense, and here I rely on a teacher in Asakusa who happens to have high expectations of me for some reason. I am the only pupil he teaches for free. It's much the same story with the scores – there's this crusty old arranger who happens to share my tastes in music, and he wrote up thirty scores for me all for nothing. 'I'll not take a penny from you,' he said.

All things considered, I guess you could say I'm quite a canny young woman. Perhaps I have more talent for begging than for singing. But a professional recording début for free? That's one thing I haven't managed to figure out yet. Still working on it.

You know that Hiroshi Yumekawa who sings 'The Freezing-Cold Blues' and appears on all those hair-implant commercials? His recording career was launched with gangster money. The man himself is a yakuza, senior consultant to the H Gang. Speaking of that kind of thing, old Shimako Sado – 'The Rain Keeps Falling On Your Head' – found a pretty ridiculous way to finance her first national release. She knew this élite business-man, the president of a real top-flight company, whom she'd known since her days working as a bar hostess. She buttered him up nicely and then told him she'd love to have the honour of per-sonally organizing a party to celebrate the company's thirtieth anniversary. In the end it was the president's own money that paid for it all, but Shimako did such a great job on him that he wound up handing her a budget of 10 million yen – and feeling good about it to boot. Shimako managed to set up the event for 7 million, by battling over the cost of renting the banquet hall and scrimping on the food and invitations, and spent the remaining 3 million yen on producing a CD of the company's 'Thirtieth Anniversary Theme Song' and a poster to promote it. On the day of the party she did a special one-woman stage show as her own personal gift to the president of the company. And, of course, the president was delighted. What an idiot.

I seem to spend my life surrounded by idiots. This business is a lawless zone, it's pure anarchy – that's what I think, anyway. Nobody *wants* these singers to sing. They just damn well do it anyway, to please themselves. But hang on a second. Even the really big stars weren't singing because people wanted them to when they made their débuts. Some producer gave them their break because he figured folks might possibly want them to sing for them in future. In the beginning they're all just singing for the hell of it. Later on, paths diverge: some reach the point where people actually want to know what they're going to come up with next; others seem to carry on singing just for the hell of it right to the bitter end.

*

'We'll start with the first two verses and choruses of "Love Wanders the World". Tempo as stated on the score, please. Then we'll run the next two songs together...' I explain the playlist to the boys in the band. Like all the bandsmen I've known, they listen to whatever I say with totally expressionless faces. They avoid eye contact and flip over the pages of the score with limp, listless hands. I am quite inured to their studied apathy.

Just occasionally I can bring a spark of life to their dead-fish eyes, like when I give them their cans of coffee. They immediately return to their normal zombie-like condition, but just for a moment, as the can of coffee arrives in their hands, their eyes light up with something that is almost human. These guys make about 150,000 yen a month. That is the price of securing their allegiance to a particular cabaret, but it's nowhere near enough to sustain life in Tokyo, where rents are sky high and it costs a small fortune to support a wife and family. One time there was this bass player who didn't drink the can of coffee I gave him. He just put it under his chair. Later on I caught sight of him standing next to a canned-coffee vending machine trying to sell it to passers-by. However, most bandsmen resort to more orthodox survival tactics: they work for two or three different places. Once the cabaret closes, around midnight, they head off to some late-opening host club and play their instruments until dawn to entertain the wealthy ladies who patronize those places. They do that more or less every night, and to make things worse they are often guys who dreamt of being jazz or blues musicians, yet they have to play the despised enka night after night. All in all, it's a stressful occupation.

'When I was young I dreamt of being the new Clapton. But now I'm just old and clapped out.' They make pathetic jokes like that and laugh among themselves, and it's not healthy, jovial laughter, more like the slow wheezing of a broken-down bellows. They are obsessive economizers. They hardly eat, so they don't have enough fuel to display emotions. Their facial expressions are limited to the area below the nose. Above that, nothing moves. The pre-show meeting with these guys is enough to suck half the vitality out of any singer. I wish they'd do something about it.

'Well, you've got to have the occasional laugh or you'd never be able to stick it.' It was the drummer who spoke. He was the most senior musician of the lot. I'd heard the line before, from the labourers who worked for my darling Mr Wild. Sometimes I'd bring them some snacks at the building site, and they'd always be going on like that. It made sense: the lifelessness of these musicians stemmed from a lifetime spent playing a guitar every day the same way a labourer digs holes. This thought made them seem a little more likable.

'Ladies and gentlemen, please put your hands together for the hot new artiste from Kink Records, Rinka Kazuki and her Golden Show!' With the MC's words, the twelve good men and true of Teruji Yoshinami and his New Gorgeous Towers cranked into action. It started with a pathetic pattering sound on the drums, and then the brass came in. The intro music before the singer came on was the same every night, and it was exactly the kind of cheap, exaggerated fanfare you'd expect from a third-rate cabaret.

The bandsmen had an average age of about fifty. Each and every one of them was dressed in a sky-blue tuxedo with matching bow-tie, and their feet were clad in white enamel shoes. They had long hair that quite failed to match their worn-out faces, and altogether their look was a cheesy leftover from the 1960s.

Bash, clang, wallop on the drums; skirl, squeak, squeak on the clarinet; dendekka, dendekka on the guitar. Again I'm reminded of my visits to building sites. As the musicians sit there emitting these industrial sounds, an expression of gravity gradually suffuses their faces. The noise, which has been oddly muffled like some distant tribal incantation, swells to new heights as the seething brass joins in. And then it fades away again, leaving just a restrained drum roll drifting across the room. A certain tension spreads through the audience, rather like when they're about to announce the winner of the Grand Prix at the All Japan Recording Industry Awards Night. OK, so it's a fairly meaningless, customary kind of hush that falls upon the room, but, still, some of the customers are impressed by the slightly indecent intensity of it all, and one or two of them swallow their gum. And then a little bud of music starts to grow out of the drum roll and it blossoms into a riotous jazz session, before coming to an equally abrupt halt: zazazaaa (zing zing); boom b-boomboom boom (baaooogh); chakachaka, chakchak, chakety-chack, zinggggg.

Oh, for goodness' sake, I'm thinking to myself as I stand there waiting in the wings. What sort of monster could reasonably take the stage after an intro like this? I feel tired already. But there's no turning back now.

'Good evening, everybody. My name is Rinka Kazuki. That's Kazuki written with the characters "Summer Moon" . . .' They can't hear me, the mike being turned down too low. Happens all the time, but I still feel somewhat discouraged.

Japan's been in recession ever since the bubble economy went pop at the start of the 1990s. It's like an ice age for the entertainment industry. A lot of cabarets have closed, and those that are still around are desperate to save money. The first place they look for savings is the entertainment budget. They can't afford big-name acts such as Yoshimi Tendo or Takashi Hosokawa any more – which, in a way, is a good thing, since it means more gigs for us unknowns, but from the establishment's point of view they'd rather not be putting on these low-grade gigs at all However, since they advertise themselves as cabarets, they have to put on some kind of show to draw a line between themselves and the various hostess clubs and bars that are their competitors. As a bare minimum, that means providing a floor that is big enough to dance on and some kind of live music.

But there's no respect for the musicians: we're seen as a nuisance. The bandsmen are cooped up in a tiny dressing-room, where they dine on convenience-store snacks and watch the cockroaches and mice compete for the leftovers. As for the singer's dressing-room, it could easily be mistaken for a miniature rubbish dump: battered old sofa with the springs coming out, tiny little television with a crack across the screen – and, to cap it all, when you finally do get to sing, the mike's turned down almost to zero. You see, recently customers have started complaining that the singing's too noisy. What with the craze for karaoke sweeping the country, a lot of ordinary people have got it into their heads that songs are for them to *sing*, not for them to *listen to*.

But I won't be beaten that easily. This is my livelihood we're talking about. I need those tips. I summon up the inner strength of one who has risen from the ranks of hostesses to take centre stage. I scan them all from here – the punters, the hostesses, the waiters in their black dinner suits, the lighting guy and the sound guy. Having worked on the floor of a cabaret myself, I know exactly what they are all thinking and how they are likely to behave. Just watch me.

'Well, here comes the cherry-blossom season again . . .' Just saying 'cherry blossom' was enough to stop the waiters in their tracks; the hostesses, while continuing to chat to their customers, threw a quick glance in my direction. 'Yes, it's that time of year again. Soon they'll be in full bloom. I love those cherry blossoms, you know. I see the ones in here have bloomed a little earlier than the rest.'

Like the entertainment industry in general, cabarets take great care to adjust their interior decoration to reflect the changing seasons. In February practically every single one of them proclaims a Festival of Cherry Blossoms and festoons the premises with pink plastic blossoms. They also make the hostesses wear pink dresses and generally spring-like fashions. Some of them even give free drinks to people with *sakura* – the character for cherry blossoms – in their name.

'As you can see, I'm dressed all in pink for tonight's show', and I tilt my head to show them the plastic cherry blossoms adorning my hair-do. Some of the waiters put their trays to one side and give me a round of applause. 'Oh, I say – applause. Actually, ladies and gentlemen, those people are cherry blossoms, too.' (A little joke. An accomplice planted in the audience is also called *sakura*, because like real cherry blossoms they attract the general public.) I got a little laugh out of the waiters, and the mike suddenly got turned up like a loudspeaker. OK, the house had noticed me, and the hostesses were starting to pay attention, too. Now for the audience.

'When the blossoms are out, there's nothing nicer than a picnic under a cherry tree, right? And if you like a drink, well, sake and *sakura* just go together perfectly – or so I'm told. Sadly, ladies and gentlemen, this little lass from Kyushu can't handle the hard stuff; booze just doesn't agree with me. Looking down from the stage at all you good people enjoying your drinks, well, I envy you.'

'All right!' Support from some guy in the audience. The customers' faces are starting to blossom. Guys half getting up from the sofa to look at me. We're in good shape.

'If only I could be sitting there with each and every one of you, sharing a drink while we get to know each other. But since I'm a girl who can't drink a drop, please allow me to do the next best thing and share a couple of drinking songs with you: "Dreams in My Sake Cup", followed by "My Sake and My Memories".'

'Woo-woo-woooo!' Drunken customers cheering and whistling, jostling and craning their necks to get a better view of me. Customers competing to shout humorous words of encouragement. I had evidently won them over. In fact, it was rather pleasing to note that the customers' excitement had reached the point where the hostesses started to look at me with faces full of an intense and predictable jealousy.

Ah, this sake, come and dull this sadness of mine . . .

Customers are getting up from their seats, blowing kisses and waving their hands; hostesses are clinging on to their customers, frowning furiously as they struggle to keep their attention. The atmosphere in here is hot and thick as boiling stew. No need to worry about the microphone any more: it's been turned up to ten, with an excessive dollop of reverb thrown in for good measure. The lighting guy is pulling out all the stops, too; he's even got the old mirror-ball spinning for me. A crowd-pleasing show is good news for the management. To keep them on my side, I take care to put plenty of steamy love ballads into the playlist. A fisherman's sea shanty at this point would be a sure way to get the mike turned down again.

'This is for you, darling. Keep up the good work, OK?' A key moment: the first tip of the night – and it's a big one, 10,000 yen, no less. Actually that's not necessarily a good thing. If the first tip of the night is a big one like that, it makes the other customers feel shy about handing over the 1,000-yen notes that are the singer's bread and butter, and at the end of the night you're likely actually to end up with less tip-money to count. So I swiftly tuck the 10,000-yen note out of sight. I particularly want to keep it away from the prying eyes of the bandsmen. Stage etiquette dictates that you should give about a quarter of your tip-money to the boys in the band. Most people find some way of reducing the outlay, but it's a lot harder to wangle once they've spotted the portrait of Yukichi Fukuzawa peeking out from a fold in your kimono. The Meiji-era educationist has had his face on the 10,000-yen note for as long as I can remember.

'That singer Whatshername got three 10,000-yen notes the other night, and do you know what she left for us? A measly 3,000!' An incident like that stays permanently engraved upon a bandsman's heart. It's the stuff of legend. Unless you make suitable amends, it can ruin your reputation in the business. The resentment never fades. It's a deep, festering wound, and they probably carry it with them to the grave.

On the label of the bottle, I write the date we parted,
My tears softly fall as I bite back my grief.

I'm singing like a lovelorn sex kitten, but inwardly my mind is calculating faster than any super-computer. With this long-sleeved kimono I'm wearing, how high do I have to raise my arms to conceal from the audience the 10,000-yen note tucked into my sleeve? And if I stick out the elbow of my microphone hand a little further than usual can I create a blind spot that will stop the boys in the band from spotting the portrait of Fukuzawa? At the same time I'm scanning the faces in the audience for any tell-tale sign of an intention to hand over money. Got to wait for the right moment to descend from the stage and move among the punters. Here we go. As I approach their territory, still singing, I spot one of them rummaging in his briefcase. He's looking for his wallet. He's found it. He's clamping a banknote between his disposable chop-sticks. Mike elbow up; activate blind spot!

Drunk again, drunk with the sake of my memories

I descend upon the audience with my arms outstretched, like a giant fruit bat, my huge kimono concealing tip activity from the band. I have to get in among the punters fast. My extravagant gestures have nothing to do with the emotional climaxes of the song; they are timed to hide any further 10,000-yen notes from the musicians. When I get 1,000-yen notes I quickly tuck them into the top of my belt, proudly displaying them to the audience.

Zuchachaaaaa, dochachachaaaaaa . . . tantantara!

'Thank you very much, and good night.'
Phew. All over.

After two shows in the big kimono, my takings for the day came to 37,000 yen, which was not too bad really. I was just counting the crumpled banknotes on my way back to the dressing-room when someone addressed me.

'Think you're pretty damn smart with your flashy kimono and its stupid sequins, right?' A solitary woman was spitting these words at me. But her face was smiling. She was wearing a purple lamé dress, so simply designed that it looked as if she'd just wrapped her swarthy body in a purple bath towel. She wore no jewellery, carried no accessories. She had transparent high heels a bit like Cinderella's glass slippers. You could see her feet inside, bare from ankle to toe.

'You go around the country, carrying your own bags and squawking those silly enka, do you?' There was a sneer in her voice. 'Ha-ha-ha, what an idiot!' She kept her arms folded, further expressing her contempt by standing at an oblique angle as she poured scorn on me. Everything about her expressed the deepest contempt. I was irritated, but also a little intrigued by this raw display of textbook nastiness. Some kind of joke? For now I'd wait to see what came next. But she just carried on being nasty.

'Not a bad night for the tips, eh?' She ran a brownish finger across the row of banknotes clenched between my fingers. 'Enka, huh. Talk about easy money. Stand up in front of them in one of those posh kimonos and they'll chuck money at you, even if the singing's crap.'

'Come 'ere and say that again.' When I get angry I tend to lose my ladylike manners and I forget to suppress my rural Kyushu accent. This is dangerous; it happens about twice a year. I start talking Kyushu dialect and completely lose my temper. I'm like some wild animal, totally out of control. It's like that Kafka story, 'Metamorphosis'. Last time it happened was about six months ago. I got into a fight with Mr Wild and we just about wrecked the apartment. He was clearly going easy on me because I was a woman, but that just made me even madder.

'Ain't you got no bloody manners? And who the hell do you think you are anyway?' In the corner of my screaming heart there was one tiny part that wanted to make sure Kenjiro wasn't watching this unseemly performance. Not that there was any reason he should be here tonight, but still, I didn't want him to see me like this. I wanted to carry on being a fluffy white bunny for him.

Now the woman was telling me her name. 'Kaho Jojima.'

'What about it? I'll sort you out, you bitch.' My eyes grew ever wider as I moved in on her. I drew myself up to my full height, which was just about high enough to make a grab at her throat. I thought I had her, but somehow I missed. I had a couple more tries, but each time my hands snapped shut on empty air. She had these huge tits that stretched her spandex dress so tight there was nothing to grip on.

'I do jazz,' she said. 'That's why I can't make a decent living at places like this. And it doesn't matter how much I work on my voice – I'll never get the kind of tips you get.' Suddenly I understood. Come to think of it, I had heard a snatch of this girl singing 'Stardust' when I came in. She'd been the warm-up act. I hadn't paid much attention; she'd seemed a cold, unfriendly kind of woman. Perhaps I could give her a spot of advice.

'It's your own fault if you don't get any tips. Did you remember to greet the audience properly?'

'I know about that, stupid. If I bowed and scraped and arse-licked the way you do I'd have no trouble. But you can't sing *jazz* after humiliating yourself like that.'

'Well, you're the one who decided to sing jazz. If you're so sick with jealousy, why don't you just shut up and quit?'

'I don't need you to tell me that. I *am* going to quit. Today. That's it. I quit.' Then she burst into tears. Her makeup started running, streaking her face and making her look like a miserable raccoon. She was going to quit. Quit singing. Today. How was she going to eat? I felt my anger gradually giving way to pity.

'Really? Well here's a little parting gift then, from me.' I pulled out one of the crumpled banknotes from my wad and quickly held it out to her. But, hell – it was a ten-thousand! Damn it, I should have looked more carefully. I couldn't very well take it back and replace it with a one-thousand-yen note now, so I somehow concealed my utter dismay and pressed it into her hand with feigned equanimity and an attempt at a sympathetic smile.

She also gave a little grin as her hand closed on the note. 'Thank you.' And then, with her big dark eyes fixed upon me, she slowly lifted it up and pressed it to her nose.

Snort.

She loudly blew her nose into my 10,000-yen note, crumpled it into a little ball and quietly pushed it into my pocket.

'And the best of luck to you, too. Bye.'

Click-clack, click-clack, the sound of Cinderella's glass slippers faded into the distance. I was so shocked at this inexplicable turn of events that I stood there for a few moments, slack-jawed and speechless. The bong of a grandfather clock echoed down the cabaret's dusty old backstage corridor, announcing eleven o'clock.

I didn't have time to moon around like this. If I didn't get changed quickly I was going to miss the last train. I got into a fluster. I was just about to untie the string on my kimono belt when I suddenly remembered the boys in the band. I hadn't given them their share of the tips.

Bzzzzzzzz . . . The hair-drier in the dressing-room was a battered old thing, and I wouldn't use it for drying my hair for fear of the sparks. But on this occasion it came in handy.

'Good as new.' The note had a slightly starchy consistency after I'd finished drying up the jazz girl's tears and snot, but it was a 10,000-yen note for all that. Harsh treatment had not diminished its value. I scrunched it up into a ball. It was the colour of dead leaves and looked like some weird fruit from a South American tree. Giggling to myself, I rolled it around on the palm of my hand.

'The bastard.'

Today's bass player had been the pits. Apparently he was one of these musicians who'd come into the business for the love of jazz, and he couldn't stand the simple rhythms of enka. He'd totally messed up my performance of 'Come With Me to Dear Old Noto' by trying to stick some smartass jazzy melody into it.

Absorbed in thoughts of revenge, I'd allowed the clock to get to half-past eleven. I'd have to fly to make the last train; it would leave at 11:45.

'Shit.' I didn't have time to get out of the kimono. Not for the first time I'd have to dash for the station in all my stage finery, dragging my trolley behind me.

I zoomed down the cabaret's corridor, with my kimono skirts all over the place and my faithful trolley squeaking and rattling over the bare concrete floor. The band's dressing-room was at the end of the corridor. I shoved open the door. All twelve of them were assembled in the little four-and-a-half mat room in their shirtsleeves, watching some kind of variety show on the television.

'Sorry to burst in on you like this.' I treated them to a coquettish flutter of my mascara'd eyelashes. The old drummer who was leader of the band seemed to like this and gave me a little smile. I shyly approached him and held out the crumpled paper.

'Here you go – funeral dumpling for you.' He stared at it for a for a few moments, but I fancy he discerned at once that this odd little lumpy thing was, in fact, constructed from a 10,000-yen note. He burst out into a strangled fit of laughter that could have meant surprise or could have meant delight. The bassman got in before him and snatched the thing out of my hand. The whole room went berserk.

'Ta-ra for now.' I gave them a cheeky wink and waved bye-bye. Suddenly filled with good humour, all twelve bandsmen waved back at me in unison. Hey, maybe it wasn't such a bad end to the evening. Why had I bothered to get so worked up about stuff that didn't really matter? An eye for an eye, a joke for a joke.

Emerging from the cabaret I ran pell-mell for Tsurumi Station with my hair blowing about in the wind. There was night dew in the air, and the moisture on the asphalt made the trundling sound of my trolley's wheels sound nearly an octave lower than usual. The trundle-trolley always faithfully reflects the prevailing weather conditions.

And that dear old trolley is faithful to me, too. Wherever I go, even if I go somewhere ridiculous, it always trundles faithfully along behind me.

I hurried through the entertainment district, with the smell of the smoke from the grilled-chicken stands, the smell of sauce and perfume, all these different smells getting mixed up in my hair. The flashing neon lights reflected in the dewy asphalt. Here and there, gold-coloured things scattered around the road to the station. Gold coins dropped by someone?

I always look upon my surroundings in a blurred, dreamy sort of way, but like a high-performance camera I zoom straight in to focus on any coin that might lie in my path.

'Just a gob of spit . . .' The sparkling coins were nothing more than little pools of phlegm – as usual. I'm always having to steer my little trolley through these gleaming coins that people leave behind on the pavement.

Mustn't be distracted. Got to keep my wheels clean and get myself safely home. Full steam ahead.

East Kawaguchi Station. No good phoning Daiki – there's no way he's going to come and pick me up in the car. I'll walk home to him.

'Hi there, I'm home.' A woman of my age, coming home in the middle of the night, kimono-clad, drenched in sweat and pulling my trunk behind me: Daiki used to laugh about it when we first started living together, but after two years he doesn't seem to see the funny side any more.

'Ah, hi there.' He briefly glanced up from the late-night tele-vision programme he was watching and gave me a little smile. But there was something in the air that wasn't right. I felt a prickling sensation spreading over my skin. Better give it no attention; probably just my imagination. I felt irritated with myself for always overreacting to little things that don't matter.

'Well, I'm off to bed,' he said, sounding kind of angry. His words were like a spark of static in the supercharged atmosphere. Having confirmed my identity with that one little glance, he wouldn't once look me in the eye. Then, without another word, he disappeared into the bedroom. That hurt.

'How much longer are you going to carry on doing this?' If I closed my eyes, I could clearly bring to mind Daiki's words the last time we had a fight about my singing work. 'You're going to give it up sooner or later, right? What's the point of carrying on with it?'

What was the point? There was no point. But there was something I believed in that made me do it. What was that something? 'Success.' That would be the simple answer – and one that people would understand. But we fishy folk of the spotlight know that this bumpy back alley we travel is not the road to success. Maybe the thing I believe in is to be found somewhere in that same zone between black and white where Daiki and I got together.

He'd left the television on. Looking around for the remote control to switch it off, I bumped my knee against the coffee-table. A teacup fell off and smashed on the ground.

Crash.

Daiki's a Sagittarius, born in December. I gave him that cup for his fortieth birthday, just a couple of months ago. It was a blue teacup by Richard Ginori.

'Wow, this is fantastic. It's much too good to use.' He loved that cup. Most of the time he kept the cup and its matching saucer on display on the bookshelf. Very occasionally he would reverently take it down and carefully drink some tea from it. Tonight he'd been sitting there, all on his own, drinking coffee. Out of this cup. An intensely painful wave of regret came welling up from somewhere deep within my breast. There was nothing for it but to quietly close my eyes. Even so, hot tears forced their way through my closed eyelids and splashed softly on the floor.

I hung up my kimono on its special lacquered stand. It looked like some kind of scary monster. I was again surprised at how huge it looked with the two arms spread out like that. A creature from another planet, out to invade the earth. How much longer was I going to do battle with this beast?

I got in the bath. I recalled a poster I'd seen stuck on a telegraph pole in front of the station:

Temporary Help Wanted at Sushi Restaurant
One thousand yen per hour

A thousand yen an hour – as jobs go, this one would pay much better than what I was doing now: no overheads, and Daiki wouldn't get annoyed with me like tonight. But could I really do a job like that? Working at a sushi restaurant – just as a disposable part-timer, with no prospect of becoming a master sushi chef. No doubt if I got into a job like that I'd soon start feeling the smart of some painful emotion I couldn't control. Underneath my spotlessly laundered white apron, my shiny scales would start to throb and pulse. I'd be in trouble if anyone found out. But one day someone *would* scent me out – probably another guy with scales, who'd carry me off with him.

Or if that didn't happen, those aching scales would get me into some other kind of trouble in the course of my routine everyday life. The pure, white starched apron, the friendly smiles of the sushi chefs, the occasional visits of the young sushi master's wife, all very wholesome – and all the free sushi I could eat. Every day the promised wages would be paid to me, no matter how much or how little I worked; tick-tock, regular as clockwork. 'Ah, that was delicious. Thank you very much. Well done.'

But then my scaly skin would seek out a target. It could be any-one – a customer or one of the chefs? – the more fun the better. It would be the young sushi master. I'd end up getting emotionally involved with the young sushi master, and my days would stop going tick-tock. I'd be happy, the young sushi master would be happy – but what about the others? The balance sheet wouldn't add up any more. Would the shop end up being devoured by me and left in ruins? Or would the young master and I succeed in making the enterprise sparkle like a star in the night sky? The dice could roll in any direction. Anyway, that feeling of having rolled the dice would remain in the palm of my hand. That's a very special feeling.

I carefully washed myself all over with soap. Since I wear the kimono, which leaves the back of the neck exposed, I sometimes used to get Daiki to shave the hair on my nape. He used to do quite a few other things for me, too. He'd cut my hair for me, and brush it, and help me with my makeup . . .

I entered the bedroom. In the darkness I could faintly make out a Daiki-shaped mound under the futon. A big guy. Today he was sleeping with his back turned to me. He always did that when he was upset about something. His sleeping breath filled the room with warmth. The hostility had gone out of the atmosphere. I slid into bed beside him. It felt narrow, although it was a full-sized double. The sound of heavy, regular breathing drifted through the darkness.

I remembered the voice of that woman I met at the cabaret, that weird woman with the jazz and the weeping. Surely I'd heard that voice before somewhere. What was her name? Kaho Jojima. I had this powerful feeling that I was somehow in her debt. I can't ignore intuitions like that; they usually have something to with reality.

The sound of the telephone's ring cut through the night. Who could it be at this hour? But the answering machine kicked in right away. I could hear the low voice of the recorded message out in the other room. Should I get up and answer the call? While I was still wondering what to do, another visitor came to me through the darkness. It was Daiki's hand, insinuating itself under my silk pyjamas, seeking out my breast. I moved away. But the hand came sneaking back in.

He came rising up from the amniotic world of sleep, and now the tone of his breathing was changed – from the regular exhalation of a sleeping man to the rough panting of a wild animal, roaring in my ear. This was no longer the ill-tempered man who'd been watching television but a different man altogether. A man whose brain was half asleep. His hand was seeking me out. I felt an overwhelming sympathy for this man. The roar of his barbaric breathing, the muted echo of his waking anger, penetration without communication, that was all there was between us today. The tense beat of his heart beneath my hand, rising in tempo to match the squeaking of the bedsprings. And he took me with him. It's easy enough for me to feed the flames of my own desire. I had only to move my body slightly back and forth to find my own boiling point.

This body I was stroking in the darkness was almost obscenely healthy and muscular. It reminded me of Kintaro, the powerful little boy of Japanese legend who used to wrestle with bears and tear down trees with his bare hands. Every time I felt out the shape of the sleeping body, I felt close to fainting with sheer desire. I could feel the stirrings of sympathy on his part, too.

This'll be all right. From now on. Us.

3 Mercedes-Benz Events

'That Hiroshi Itsuki', said Kenjiro, champing on his gum, 'the way he sings, it always seems like he's holding his shit in and enjoying it.'

Mr Itsuki was singing his heart out on the television screen above the café counter.

'Don't you think, Rinka?'

'Don't be disgusting.' Kenjiro is such a pathetic guy that I always feel relaxed in his company. 'Honestly, Kenjiro, why do you always have to talk like that when we're eating? I wish you wouldn't.'

He gave a loud, course laugh. Money and shit: as I may have mentioned, these are the only two themes in this man's conversational repertoire. I was disgusted as usual but returned to my curried rice anyway.

'I'm done.'

'Tasty?'

'Yep – except for the conversation.'

He guffawed once more. Kenjiro viciously stubbed his cigarette out in the ashtray, stood up and swilled down his water.

'Hey, mama. The bill.'

'Coming right up, Ken-chan.'

We emerged from the café on to the familiar streets of Uguisudani. This is Kenjiro's home turf.

'I rang you up last night.'

'Eh?' I found myself blushing. That telephone call last night – the one that came just as Daiki's hand was reaching out for my breast – it must have been Kenjiro. Why is that men instinctively seem to know when a woman they fancy is making love? It's almost uncanny. I reckon Kenjiro has a certain feeling for me, and he's always ringing up just when Daiki and I are about to do it. Or, if it's not him, it's some ex-boyfriend interrupting us at that very private moment. Do they have some kind of radar? Or is Daiki the one with the psychic powers? Maybe some animal instinct makes him sense that another man is thinking about me, and he takes me to bed before they call. Either way, this thing has happened too often to be mere coincidence.

'So, do you have some urgent business today?'

'Nah, not really. Sorry about that, suddenly calling you out all this way.' He said he felt vaguely worried about me. He hadn't found any work since the production company we'd been rely-ing on went belly-up, leaving us with nothing but the boxes of 'million-yen towels', and he was guessing that I must be in the same boat.

'Oh really, Ken-chan. I thought you might have some tasty job to tell me about.'

'If I had I wouldn't be in the mess I'm in now. But, hey, what about you? Singing in all those cabarets. Nice work. Ah, you women get all the good jobs. It's all right for some.' I was slightly irritated by that remark, but there was some truth in it. Cabarets are places designed for men to pick up women, and if a male singer such as Kenjiro comes along and starts wiggling his hips the way he does – well, he'd be lucky to get out of the place alive. Still, I had to argue back at him somehow.

'It's not like just any woman can wander in and get work. Have you noticed there's a recession on? The guys who hand out the tips are short of cash, too. You won't find too many girls who can make as much as me out of tips. It takes effort, you know. The clothes and all that.'

Yet another coarse guffaw. Overwhelmed with laughter, Kenjiro suddenly squatted down in the middle of the road. A car came up from behind him and the driver braked with every sign of irritation. He would surely have hit the horn, only Kenjiro was wearing his black lamé shirt and his black trousers and had slung his silver fox-fur coat over his shoulders without bothering to put his arms in the sleeves – I guess the driver was somewhat over-whelmed by the gangster image.

'What's the matter with you, Ken? Come on, get off the road. It's dangerous.'

'Heh-heh! It was just so sweet, the way you got all upset.'

'You making a fool of me?' He was twenty-four, I was thirty-four, but he didn't know my real age. My stage age was ten years younger – the idiot thought I was the same age as him. I am pleased when I get away with this kind of deception, but sometimes there's an unsettling side to it as well. I don't want people to think that I have the emotional maturity of a 24-year-old. Of course, I'd also be upset if people thought I was older than I really am; and, naturally, I'd be even more upset if someone guessed my age just right.

'Ken-chan, I've got an idea.' A naughty thought had floated into my mind: let's have a bit of fun at Kenjiro's expense. 'Sorry I've been keeping you waiting so long.' I grabbed his arm and pulled him into a side alley. It was the narrowest of spaces between two office buildings, and the two of us just about squeezed into it.

'Nobody's watching us, Ken-chan.' I tittered and stuck my lips out at him. 'C'mon, give us a kiss.'

'Er, what?' He gave a squeal of surprise.

'C'mon, get on with it.' He looked so serious. What a sight; what a joke. I was about to burst out laughing, but somehow I held it in – laughter now would break the spell and we'd revert to being just good friends. No – this would be my supreme performance. On with the show.

I put my hands around Kenjiro's shoulders and drew myself to him. Should I wrap my legs around him? No, perhaps that would be going too far. But, then again, let's do it anyway.

'You d-d-damn fool, Rinka. What are you playing at?'

'C'mon, pucker up.' I pouted at him again, and he rewarded me with a formal little peck.

'Eh-heh-heh.' He's giggling, the idiot. He's up for it and no mistake. What a pillock. What a sorry excuse for a man. OK, I'll show him.

'Try again.'

'Eh?'

'Try again. Try harder.'

'W-w-what's up with you?'

'Give me a *real* kiss. C'mon, burn me up, cowboy.' Talk about shit for brains – he was looking all serious again. So, what next? I swallowed my spit. Was he going to make his move? And if he did?

What then? I was a little disconcerted. What if he really did get serious? What if he really wanted me?

'You fucking idiot, I'll give you more than you're bargaining for.' With an angry snort he shoved me away from him, pulled out his cigarettes and lit one of them with an unsteady hand. 'I'm not going to take you in a place like this.' His melancholy downcast eyes; the timing with which he exhaled his cigarette smoke . . . At that moment he looked like the coolest man alive. But then he carefully looked me over and gave a little grin.

'Let's head over there.' I looked in the direction indicated by his finger. A street of cheap hotels, with prostitutes wandering about in front of them.

'You – you bastard!' But he was already heading off in the direction indicated and didn't appear to hear my muttered objection.

'Taxi!' He stopped a cab for what would have been a three-minute walk. Talk about stupid.

So there I was, holed up in a room at a shabby love hotel. Kenjiro was rushing about in a great fluster, looking for something to open his bottle of beer with.

'Found it. Here it is. Heh-heh.' He wasn't capable of holding two glasses in one hand, but he tried to do it anyway and dropped the pair of them. He bent over to pick them up and accidentally poured half the beer on to the floor. 'Tut, what's the matter with me?'

How on earth did this happen? An adult sort of person would say 'because I was lonely' or 'because there was something missing from my life'. They'd find some cool rationalization and put a lid on their real feelings. A less mature person would say, 'This kind of thing always starts off with things you can't explain.' But, as for me, at heart I simply seem to like making trouble for myself. Where would my thoughts lead me? The one thing that did occur to me was that the likes of Kenjiro and I simply had too much time on our hands.

'Rinka.'

I was still sitting on the side of the bed wondering absently about things as Kenjiro sat down beside me.

'Ahem.' He cleared his throat.

Oh my God. He really is a pathetic guy. Shit.

'Here's what I think about love.'

For crying out loud. What's coming next? Come on, do me a favour.

'Love is like a train, running along the track. And the last station is marriage.'

What was he talking about? Putting his arm around my shoulders, body all aquiver, how could he be so tense at a time like this? And what was all this talk about the future when we hadn't even done anything yet?

'I want to keep on running – with you – though I don't know how much I can do for you.'

What? Why all the homespun philosophy? He was a simpler guy than I'd realized. He sounded super-serious.

'I want to be useful to you. I want to be by your side. I know it sounds really corny, but – I want to protect you.'

He really was naïve, innocent. Until this day I never realized he was that kind of guy. Oh no, I think I'm going to cry.

'So that's about the size of it. Please, let's carry on being friends.'

Please, let's carry on being friends? Such pretty sentiments are seldom expressed in rooms in shabby love hotels. He was flushed with embarrassment at his own eloquence, and it made me want to look after the poor little thing. Yes, I thought. Let's be friends for ever. Let's be buddies. It would be easy to take the next step and become lovers, but in your case it's better to stay this way, just as we are. Almost as if my thought had communicated itself to Kenjiro he stretched out a hand to shake on our friendship. I gladly extended my own hand and gave him a warm, firm handshake.

'Right, let's get on with it.'

'Eek!' Suddenly Kenjiro was stripped down to his underwear and had me pinned down on the bed. I struggled to resist, my arms flailing around as if I were a stranded fish flapping around on dry land.

'Stop it! Stop it!'

'Shut up and keep still!

'Get off me. Get *off!*'

'I told you there's no final station for the love train. We're gonna fly down the tracks, baby. We're gonna keep on flying. We're gonna go screaming past the stations. There ain't no brakes.'

'Um, ummm.' He had his hand over my mouth to stop me screaming.

'And you're going with me – all the way. Straight ahead, all the way down. You want it, right?'

'No, I don't!'

'I'll *make* you want it. I'll give it to you three times today. Doesn't matter if I use up my strength – I haven't got a job to go to tomorrow, or the day after tomorrow, or the next day after that, I may never work again in my whole fucking life.'

'Eeeeeek . . .' Just as I was letting out this almighty scream, another sound came to my ears, a repeated heavy thumping against the bedroom door. Someone was trying to kick it down. It got Kenjiro off me. He went rushing to the door, and now I could hear him talking to somebody. Who could it be?

'I tell you I'm not going to open the door.' He was shouting at someone. 'It's all right, Rinka, I'll keep you out of this. Do me a favour and pop into the bathroom for a minute, will you? This won't take long.'

'What? Why? What's going on?'

'Shut up and do as you're told.' Cowed by the savage look he gave me, I took refuge in the bathroom. There was a small water-proof clock in there. It said 3 p.m. What the hell was I doing in a place like this at three o'clock in the afternoon? I still had my day-time clothes on.

The bathroom had a transparent plastic door. Peeking through it, I could see Kenjiro, apparently engaged in a fierce argument with the television.

'If you don't like it, we're through.'

'That suits me just fine.' On the television screen was the face of a hysterically sobbing woman; next to her was a naked man. The two of them were in a room that looked identical to the one we were in. It was the room next door. I immediately felt the colour drain from my face. I'd heard of these love hotels with closed-circuit television systems where the customers got to see each other on the job, but I'd never dreamt that Kenjiro could sink so low.

'I've been framed.'

Overwhelmed with self-pity, I emerged unsteadily from the bathroom.

'You idiot. I told you to stay put.'

'Did someone say, "I've been framed"?'

The woman on the television screen was quivering all over. She put her hands to her head and writhed in misery and rage.

'So you *have* been doing it. I knew it.'

'I haven't done anything – yet.'

Kenjiro and the woman on the screen carried on their shouting match. I started crying. And then I thumped Kenjiro as hard as I could.

'You stupid fucking pervert!'

'Ow, that hurt. You've got it all wrong, both of you.'

The woman on the screen gave a sudden scream. 'Rinka.'

'What? You?' The woman on the screen was Kaho Jojima. The jazz singer I had met last night.

Kenjiro shouted back at her, 'I thought I told you not to bring customers in here. I told you to do it in that other hotel.'

'I had a hunch about today. I've had my suspicions about you two for quite a while.'

What did she mean – you two? I spoke to her in a ragged voice. 'Your name's Kaho, right? You and me only met last night, at that show.'

'Rinka, I knew you before that.' At that moment, a couple of the pieces of the puzzle in my head finally came together. I recognized Kaho's voice.

'Please don't call her. It's that girl again, I know.' I'd heard that plaintive, half-choked voice before, faintly, in the background while Kenjiro was on the telephone to me. Whenever he rang up to see how I was getting on, I'd hear this woman's whining voice nearby, trying to get him off the line.

'You said you only loved me. You said you wouldn't sleep with anyone else. You promised.' Kaho carried on denouncing Kenjiro. She had wrapped her naked body in a sheet. The style was oddly similar to the dress she'd been wearing when we first met. 'You promised.'

Behind Kaho I could make out the figure of a balding middle-aged man hurriedly pulling on his trousers. Eventually he tiptoed quietly off screen, and I heard the sound of a door closing in the corridor.

'Kaho!' Kenjiro shouted at her. Pathetically enough, she sounded pleased just to be addressed by him.

'What, darling?'

'That customer – did he pay?'

'What?' She looked around her. Kenjiro flew into a rage.

'Shit. That bald fucking bastard.' He booted the door open and rushed out to the corridor. I was left staring vacantly at Kaho's face in the screen. She looked back at me for a while, then sadly stood up and walked off camera. The screen was left empty, save for a crumpled double bed. Love. People falling in love with each other, people falling in love with people who didn't love them back, it seemed that the whole messy story of love was written in these scattered sheets, lying there like the windswept ruins of some ancient monument. A deep sense of emptiness came over me. Alone in the room, I switched off the television and lay face down on the bed.

'GRAAAAAAAAAAGGHHHHH!'

Some woman had jumped on me and hit me in the back with a forearm smash. Now she was going for the strangle. It was Kaho. I should have locked the door before abandoning myself to my melancholy thoughts. Too late now, however: an all-girl death match was under way.

'You bitch, Rinka, you seduced him. I saw you.'

'No, no. You've got it all wrong . . . ugh.'

'It's too late to worm your way out of this one.' I'd never realized how alarming it could be to have a naked woman riding you like a horse and screaming at you. I felt a moment of acute gladness that I hadn't been born a man. Kaho was raining slaps down on me with her big floppy tits swinging in all directions. I soaked up the punishment, but I kept my eye on her. I'd fight back with words.

'You've got to take better care of your man if you don't want him taken off you.' The moment I spoke, the rusty taste of blood told me I'd bitten my lip. At times like this it's so important to talk through gritted teeth.

Kaho carried on thrashing me until she finally ran out of power and collapsed on top of me in a flood of tears. I was too far gone to push her off.

'Hey! Get up quick. We're in the shit.' Kenjiro was back in the room. 'It's the law. We've got to get out of here.'

'What?'

The hotel management must have called the police – hardly surprising, given the racket we'd been making. Thinking coolly and rationally, however, was there really any need for me to escape? OK, I was doing a fairly shady sort of job. Pretending to be a singer with a famous label when I'd never recorded a song in my life, lying about my age – but these things were merely a bit dodgy, not actually criminal. On the other hand, if I got arrested the cops might find about Kenjiro's past and present activities in the pimping department, and if the investigation spread further they might even discover that Kenjiro's 'American' partner David was an illegal immigrant from the Philippines.

'Come, on come on. We've got to get going, for God's sake.'

Spurred into action by Kenjiro's entreaties, I opened the window. Luckily we were only on the second floor. Maybe we could jump out. It would be a bit hard on Kaho, however, as she was stark naked and the February air outside was bitterly cold. I suddenly remembered Kenjiro's silver-fox-fur coat and dashed to the closet.

'Here, put this on.' I threw the coat at Kaho and she promptly burst into tears again. She sat there howling as loud as she could, like an oversized baby. A woman weeping openly, in front of another woman who isn't even her friend, not even bothering to hide her tear-stained face, there's something about a situation like that that a man would never understand.

We stood there gripping the balcony rail. Kenjiro had struggled into his trousers, but he was naked from the waist up.

'I'm going to count one, two, three, and then we're going to jump. OK, my lovelies?'

My lovelies? Kenjiro was totally insensitive to the feelings of women. I started to feel some sympathy for Kaho, although she'd just been beating me up.

'I'm scared, I'm scared.' Kaho was quivering with fear as she looked down from the balcony. 'I'm no good with heights.'

'Shut up. We'll all jump together. You'll be fine. Now then – "a-one and a-two and a-three . . ."' Kaho stepped softly off the balcony into space '. . . is what I'm going to say, and then we'll all jump, OK? Kaho!'

'You bloody fool, Ken-chan. You mustn't talk that way. Now you've made Kaho jump off on her own.'

'Oh shit!' This hopeless man, it really was too much.

'Hey, Rinka, look. She's got her head stuck in the azaleas. Look at her big arse sticking out from the fur coat. Oh man, this is too much. Look at her, just bloody look at her!' He was laughing his silly head off.

'Kenjiro . . .' This man has neither blood nor tears in him. He'll drive a woman to tears, he has nothing in his head but money-making schemes and lavatory humour, and when he sings all he can manage is the 'uh-huh' song. The useless bastard. Let's just jump off this stupid balcony and go home.

'Right,' he said. 'Let's go. Ready?'

'Er, um, just a sec. Hold my hand, OK?' Who'd have thought it could take so much courage to jump from a balcony on the second floor? I stood there gripping the handrail, knees knocking together. Suddenly it looked a lot further down. A jump like that wouldn't kill you, but if you messed it up you could easily break a few bones or dislocate something. Shit, how did I get into this mess? In broad daylight, too. What is this, some kind of cheap romantic novel?

I closed my eyes to get ready to jump. Somehow Kenjiro got the wrong idea and kissed me on the lips. Oddly, however, it was quite a restrained little kiss, like a kiss between friends.

'We'll talk later.'

And with those words of his, we stepped off the balcony.

Kenjiro's brown-dyed hair sparkles in the afternoon sunlight, and for a fleeting moment he seems to float there like an angel. His naked chest curves in beautifully, and you'd think the wings of Pegasus could grow out from his delicate shoulder-blades at any moment. How pretty. I wonder if I look that pretty, too. If I could just go straight up to heaven from here, I'm sure it would be a lovely feeling. Reclining on a cloud, casually looking down at the world.

Ah . . .

The tickling wind comes to touch my ears, my forehead, every part of me that pulses. The wind blows on everyone the same – a comforting thought. You could call it pleasant, this feeling; it wouldn't even be totally wrong to call it relaxing. And right now I'm sparkling, I'm shining. I wish someone could see me now, anyone. Look at this angel, look at me.

The fall only took a moment, but it played itself out for me in super-slow motion. I'd have liked to float on the breeze a little longer, only the ground got in the way. Amazingly enough, I bounced when I hit the lawn, and rolled across the hotel garden.

Bonk. With a dull thud, I lost consciousness. Someone was screaming out my name, and I felt several stinging slaps on the face.

You'll have to slap me harder than that.

Eventually the pain wandered off somewhere and I was embraced by some warm animal. I felt warm and comfortable, as if I were soaking in a hot bath or curled up in a sunny spot in the garden. But it also felt as if the warmth was spilling out from something pulsing through me that had burst. Blood. It was blood. I never knew it was such hot stuff.

So is this the end of me? What a ridiculous way to bring the curtain down. Is this a whole life? Is this all there is to it? I don't want to die. I want to carry on living, even if I have to crawl on the ground.

Kenjiro, Daiki, David, wake me up, even if you have to hurt me. I want to eat. I want to sleep. I want to love. I want to sing. I want to do stupid things. I want to suffer.

I'm conscious. I can see something. An old-fashioned Japanese inn. A pond. There are so many lilies floating on this pond. It's a wide, wide pond – huge. Beneath the lotus leaves the golden backs of ornamental carp drift slowly back and forth. I have seen this place before. I was three years old. We had some relatives who were running a big country inn. I sometimes went there with my mother. A white parasol, the strangely soothing noise of the midsummer cicadas. The inn was big enough to have outhouses, with elegant ebony tables standing out in front of them. The pond surrounded all the buildings like a castle moat, and it appealed to my childish curiosity.

'Hey, look at that.' The lazily swimming carp had whiskers as long as a child's fingers. Along with my little cousins, I gazed upon them in awe. The waters of the pond came all the way up to the side of the inn, and we could glimpse the carp through the floorboards of the walkway that ran around the outside.

'Aren't they pretty.'

'They're all shiny.'

There were wet rocks, gleaming in the August sunlight; the trees and flowers were reflected in the waters of the pond like a photographic negative. And where there was a little shade you could see all the way down to the bottom of the pond. Great round boulders, coated in delicate lichen and studded with the sleek jet-black carapaces of diving beetles. The luscious golds and reds of the fish drew the fascinated eye toward them.

'I wonder if the water's cold.'

'It looks so cool.'

The delighted children looked at each other. But one face was missing: mine.

'What's happened?'

'Somebody help.'

When had I fallen in? I didn't really know myself. The frenzied sawing of the cicadas suddenly faded far away, the terrified screams of my little cousins were muffled and distant. The water wasn't cold at all. There was a tepid warmth to it, and as it seeped into my ears and nose and mouth, I could feel nausea on its way. Every time I opened my mouth to scream, strands of weird pondweed and bitter-tasting insects came floating into it. I opened my eyes to a world of green. Fish flitted past, fast as darts. My two feet touched bottom. The stones were covered with slippery weeds; unable to get a footing, I slipped and slid from stone to stone.

I'm choking. I can't bear it any more. Am I going to die? I don't want to die. A wave of unbearable pain wells up from somewhere between my eyes and nose.

I thrashed around with my arms and legs as hard as I could. My body slowly floated upwards. My face broke the surface. This was how I learnt to swim, long before all my friends did. I'm told that when the grown-ups finally came running to the rescue, they saw me swimming boldly across the pond, and they stood there for a moment in shock before they could take any action. Behind me I could hear voices calling me to come back and get out of the pond, but I kept swimming ahead. Eventually my great-uncle plunged noisily into the pond in pursuit. I swam away from him. It was a very big pond. As I swam across it, I could hear somebody laughing at me from one of the rooms. It was a guest at the inn, who was right in the middle of discussing an arranged marriage – the formal clothes, the serious atmosphere, the incongruity of the three-year old child swimming in the carp pond.

And then I heard another laughing voice. I looked up to see who it was, and there was this man, looking out from a little room in the far corner of the grounds, beating his hands on the window and laughing with his mouth wide open. He looked big enough to go and work for a company, but he had this strange hairstyle with his hair cut straight just above his eyebrows like a little schoolboy. He had a towel hung across his chest like a bib. The hand that wasn't beating at the window gripped a spoon. Apparently this man wasn't allowed to step outside his room. I had the feeling that my uncle didn't want me to see him. At last my uncle caught up with me, put his hands over my eyes and dragged me to safety.

Other occasions when I'd fallen came floating back to me. There was the time I went on a picnic with my parents. The three of us were sitting on top of a cliff, looking down at the broad expanse of light-purple vetch spread out below us. Absorbed in the beauty of the scene, I toppled slowly off the cliff and into the vetch. The dramatic sort of thing my friends were reading about in their schoolbooks actually happened to me.

I've come close to death more than once. But I've never died.

I'm lucky. With luck this good I've got to think that I'm in God's good books.

'Lucky we all got out in one piece.'

When I came to, I was in Kenjiro's apartment. The woman called Kaho was there, too; David as well. Apparently I'd rolled over and hit my head on a fence post after landing in the hotel garden and gone out like a light. Kenjiro had carried me away from the scene and bundled me into a taxi.

'Why don't you stay here tonight and get some rest?' Kaho's suggestion reminded me that I was supposed to be living with Daiki. I sat up in bed. Apart from a few minor aches and pains, I seemed to be in fairly good shape.

'What's the time? I've got to get home.'

'Well, at least have a cup of tea before you go.' At Kaho's suggestion I kept the blanket wrapped around me. The room was so sparsely furnished it had no atmosphere at all, with just a few bits and pieces of nondescript mail-order furniture and some plastic storage boxes. There was a clock. It said 7 p.m. I calmed down a bit. I was expecting Mr Wild this evening. I'd have to go home at some point. These days he rarely went to his other home. In the early days he used to spend only a couple of nights a week at our love nest, but these days it was his main base, and he would only 'visit' his wife about once a month. It was a total mystery to me why she didn't seem to make an issue of this. I can only guess that, knowing his reputation as the Emperor of West Kawaguchi Nightlife, she had given up trying to enforce the marriage vows.

'You're worried about that boyfriend of yours, right?' With a bored expression on his face, Kenjiro got up to go to the kitchen.

Kaho chimed in. 'Who'd have thought the Emperor of West Kawaguchi Nightlife could have got so tame,' she chuckled.

'How do you know about him?' I flared up and was about to make a grab at Kaho's throat, despite the failure of my previous attempt. Kenjiro tried to calm me down.

'He's an acquaintance of hers. Kaho used to work in West Kawaguchi. She used her own name. Most of the girls use stage names, right? But this girl believes in hiding nothing. That's her style – letting it all hang out, any time, any place.'

'Shut up, Ken. You never know when to stop,' Kaho scolded Kenjiro while looking away from him. At that moment I had an inkling of why this woman couldn't get a man to love her. It was a relief – she obviously couldn't have had a thing going on with Mr Wild. When I have a bone to pick with a guy I always look him straight in the eye. That's the one time you should never take your eye off him. Men hate nothing more than a woman who grumbles at them while letting their eyes wander around the room or even complains about them at the same time as doing something else. The body language says you don't really expect anything to come of the criticism; it means you're getting old and you don't really care any more. Men are very alert to that ageing of the spirit, and none more so than Mr Wild.

'Shall I tell you what her nickname used to be in those days, Rinka?'

'I don't care, Kenjiro. Say what you like.' At my reply, Kaho gave me a sulky look, pulled out a cigarette from a packet of Capris and plonked the box down on the coffee-table. The Capri looked ridiculously small and delicate between her sensually out-turned full red lips, more like a toothpick.

'They used to call her "the Imperial Banquet of West Kawaguchi Nightlife". Funny, huh?'

'Oh, whatever.'

'By the way,' – I tried another tack to put my suspicions to rest – 'which clubs were you working at? And do you know which of the girls Daiki liked to have sitting with him there?'

'She wasn't working at a club, Rinka. Try massage parlour.'

Kenjiro's teasing voice infuriated me. 'What?' This was too much. The very thought of my Mr Wild playing around with this jazz bitch's melon boobs! 'Did he ask for you?' I grabbed Kaho by the shoulders and shook her violently. But when I saw a word start to form on her lips – still holding the cigarette – I hurriedly withdrew the question. 'Oh, forget it.'

Just suppose Daiki hadn't picked Kaho out from the catalogue of women for sale at the massage parlour, it would only mean he'd helped himself to some other cheap prostitute. Besides, if Kaho still remembered Daiki's face when he hadn't even been with her, it would indicate that he must have been crazy enough about this other girl to be a very regular customer. Had Daiki been juggling the jazz melon boobs, or unknown boobs? Either way, I really didn't want to know the answer, ever.

'Rinka . . .' Kenjiro was gazing at my tear-stained, quivering face with a show of concern. 'Are you really that keen on the guy? I never realized.'

Kaho was less disposed towards sympathy. 'Look at her, whining like a little puppy dog that got caught in the rain. What a fucking fake.'

'Now you lay off her.' Kenjiro quietly but firmly shut Kaho up, seizing her wrists before she could start hitting me again. Then, with a very serious expression on his face, he turned to me. 'Um, there's something I want to ask you about that guy. Is he, like, good in bed? You know? Go on, give us a clue.'

'Just fuck off.'

Breaking Kenjiro's hold on her wrists, Kaho continued, 'I wasn't at work when I met Daiki. He's a hot-tempered guy, always getting into fights on the street. But one time, when he didn't even know me, he saved me from a pervert who was messing me around.'

'I see . . .' Released from misery, I flushed with pride and smiled all the way to my double molar. 'He's a great fighter is Daiki. The little darling's never been beaten.'

My enthusiasm was infectious. Kaho's eyes sparkled. 'That I can well believe. He's like a bear or a gorilla. It only took one punch. The other guy didn't know what hit him.' She glanced at Kenjiro. Just for a moment a hint of fear and envy flickered across his face, before fading like a fleeting mirage. 'I was so overwhelmed by what he'd done for me that I felt like giving him a free ticket to the massage parlour – or maybe a pack of a hundred – but I didn't.'

'Why not?'

'Because I reckoned he'd pick some other girl to do his massage.'

I laughed out loud, like a chicken about to be strangled. She might be kind of dumb in other ways, but Kaho really had the right instincts about men. Right on the money. I even found myself starting to like her a bit.

'Here is apple for you.' David emerged from the kitchen, bearing a plate of apple slices. Kenjiro picked one of them up with a grin.

'Honestly, David, talk about a guy with time on his hands. What the hell is this? You didn't have to turn them into works of fucking art.' David had carefully left part of the peel on each slice, cutting it into two points that looked like the ears of a sweet little rabbit. It's something girls like to do. Kenjiro shoved one of the slices into David's mouth and aimed a flying kick at him.

'But they more cute like this,' the force-fed David struggled to explain himself indistinctly through a mouthful of apple.

My mobile phone still hadn't rung, which probably meant that

Mr Wild had gone off somewhere for a drink with the lads. The clock on the wall said half-past seven, and I was feeling too weary and lazy to get my stuff together and go home right now. Perhaps I'd stay until nine. Kaho was just ringing up to order pizza. My clothes were dirty and my hair was in a filthy mess, so I asked to use the shower.

Entering the bathroom, I got a shock that nearly made me faint clean away. As I slipped out of my dress I discovered that I was wearing somebody else's knickers. I only use conservative white or pink underwear, but these were frilly black pants, so high on the hip it was positively indecent. Someone had taken mine off and replaced them with these. Who?

Buffeted by the unexpected force of the shower, I took a step back while various alarming scenarios chased each other across my mind. Could Kenjiro have taken advantage of me while I was unconscious? No, he didn't have that kind of spitefulness in him, although he had plenty of other kinds, and a wimp like David wouldn't have the balls for trickery on that scale. No, it had to be Kaho.

I shook the water out of my hair like a lion tossing its mane, chucked on a bathrobe and wrapped a towel around my head, turban-style. Then I opened the bathroom door and flew out to confront Kaho. I intercepted her on the way back from the front door with the pizza.

'Hey! Just a bloody minute. You come over here.' I pulled Kaho into the bathroom and showed her what I had on under the bathrobe. 'What the hell are these?'

She took one glance at the frilly little thing and started explaining in a very sincerely apologetic tone. 'Oh, I really am sorry. This is the only kind I have.'

'What?'

She gently explained that I had experienced a moment of incontinence during my fall from the hotel balcony. I flushed profusely. What an idiot. That warm, comfortable feeling I'd had, like soaking in a hot bath or being curled up in some sunny spot, it hadn't been blood leaking out of me at all. I'd simply pissed my panties. Luckily, Kaho added with a laugh, Kenjiro had been too preoccupied with getting away from the police to notice this embarrassing mishap of mine.

I can't do anything to defy this woman any more. I can't put on airs in front of her either. Damn it, she's got me over a barrel. I hung my head in shame.

'Actually, they're probably just about dry by now – your knickers.' Still clutching the box with the pizza in it, she pointed her chin towards the washing machine in the corner of the bathroom. Just above it was a small tumble-drier. Behind the Perspex panel I could make out various items of clothing I'd been wearing earlier today, all mixed up together. I opened the door and pulled out a pair of perfectly washed white panties with a little ribbon on them – definitely the underwear I'd put on this morning. They were still hot from the drier, so I waved them to and fro a few times, as if I were waving a white flag in Kaho's direction.

'But, you know . . .' (I could hear Kenjiro's voice from the living-room. He sounded cheerful. In the back room, which adjoined the bathroom, I could see the stage-clothes he wore when performing 'Love Is a Miracle'. There were lots of outfits, all neatly hung up in the plastic covers in which they'd come back from the cleaners. There were some of Kaho's dresses, too. In fact, there was so much gear hanging up there that you could barely make out the colour of the wall. The designs were all totally outrageous – the kind to make any burglar regret taking the trouble to break in. You couldn't expect anyone who spent much of their time wrapped in this kind of stuff to have a normal outlook on life.)

' . . . the truth is, it's great that you're going to quit singing. When you said you wanted to go back to West Kawaguchi, that was music to my ears.'

'Come off it, Ken. You know perfectly well you forced me to say I'd quit. You make up these stories to suit yourself.' Kaho was complaining to Kenjiro with her eyes turned away from him as usual, and she was making the tea at the same time. David had apparently gone home.

'Still and all,' said Kenjiro, 'it's a shame we're getting a Mercedes when we don't have a show to go to in it.'

A *Mercedes*? What was all this about? I stayed there in the corridor, listening in to the couple's everyday conversation with a mounting sense of shock.

'I can still get some shows.'

'Now just a minute. You're not gonna be doing any shows. It's Kenjiro and David, and that's all.'

'OK, OK, I've got it. I'll be taking some time off from singing.'

'Time off? *Time off*? Who are you trying to kid? In bed last night you said you were going to quit singing for ever. You don't want to be messing around with a microphone, you silly bitch. You can't make enough to eat, the production companies are all bent, and the whole fucking business is a nest of conmen and rip-off artists. Look, there's no point getting into that kind of world unless you can hit the big time. Go on, let's see you do it. Let's see you turn yourself into a jazz superstar. Let's see you get some smart foreign big shot into bed and help yourself to a wad of his cash. And let's see you fucking well bring some of it home to me.'

'Oh, Ken, all your talk's so silly I can't even be bothered to get angry. I suppose I do –'

'Do what?'

Kaho leant forward towards Kenjiro and looked him straight in the eye. 'I suppose I do love you quite a lot.'

Oh, big mistake. I stood there in the corridor, clicking my tongue. She'd got it the wrong way around. If you look a man in the eye when you tell him you fancy him, it puts a big psychological burden on him. *That's* the time to look somewhere else. Silly Kaho – she hadn't got a clue. It occurred to me that in my heart I was unconsciously cheering her on from the sidelines. True to form, Kenjiro responded to Kaho's moving declaration by getting up to switch on the television.

Kaho carried on talking, with a nervous flutter in her voice. 'Still, Ken-chan, at least we've got the Mercedes to look forward to. I know it's what you've always wanted.'

'You're right there. Only second-hand, but what the hell? A Mercedes is still a Mercedes.'

Honestly, if you spent any time in showbiz, you'd think the Mercedes-Benz was the only car in the whole wide world. Every luxury foreign brand gets hauled into the abyss and turned into worthless junk by guys such as Kenjiro.

'I think I can get the loan sorted over at West Kawaguchi,' said Kaho.

'You reckon it'll be OK?'

'I'll do the best I can. So don't forget about my little reward.'

'OK, OK. Man, I'm tired.'

Little reward?

''Coz I do want a little reward, Ken. I want you to stop making me promise to do stuff when we're in that bed together. Like, telling me to stop singing and all that.'

'Shut up, Kaho, you stupid cow. I'm not taking orders from you.' Kenjiro lay down on the tatami mat to look for the television remote. He found it under the coffee-table and changed the channel. On the screen a familiar male singer was singing his heart out with a mixture of pain and pleasure on his straining face. Kenjiro gazed fixedly at him for several moments, his eyes growing rounder and rounder, like a little child who's just been given a new toy. At length he spoke. 'You know, Kaho, that Hiroshi Itsuki –'

Kaho must have heard the line before. 'I know, I know,' she grumbled, her eyes turned away from him. 'Give it a rest, will you? We've got this pizza to eat.'

4 The Voice King

I'm heading for Asakusa on the Tobu Line. The view from the train window is full of the fresh new green of May. Only if I close my eyes can I see a lingering image of the long-gone cherry blossoms.

The sight of cherry blossoms is supposed to be a fleeting pleasure that comes but once a year, but since I got into the travelling-show business I've been able to extend that pleasure, enjoying the blossoms in different parts of the country over a couple of months. You see, the cherry-blossom season comes to southern Japan first and then proceeds northwards. Long after the blossoms have come and gone down south in my native Kyushu, their arrival is still awaited up in Hokkaido. And since people all over Japan like to have singing and dancing at cherry-blossom time, we entertainers tend to travel with the cherry-blossom front, skipping back and forth along the line as it snakes across the country. This year I started in Okayama in south-west Honshu. When the blossoms had fallen from the trees in Okayama, I moved on to Hakone, and then north to Fukushima, always following those blossoms.

At night-time the blossom-laden trees swell forth like the ample posterior of some enormous woman. Beneath the dense blooming expanse, all the drunken merrymakers, young and old, men and women, enjoy themselves listening to me sing. This is the time of year when we strolling players can make some decent money for once, but this year all my appearance money has been paid up front in the form of 'million-yen towels'. This means that my only chance of survival is to haul in the tips like crazy. I set out with enough money to pay the train fare from Tokyo to Okayama but not for the return journey – like one of those World War II kamikaze pilots who were sent off on their missions without enough fuel to come back. These have been truly desperate days for me . . . But the feeling when I manage to pull in the big tips is something else. I literally feel like jumping for joy.

'What's the point of carrying on with that sort of stuff?' I can almost hear Daiki's gloomy voice behind me. What, indeed, is the point, I wonder?

A train window in May; fresh, blooming green bursting out everywhere in full force, flowing past the window like water. Turn, turn, turn: the seasons keep on turning and there's not a thing I can do about it. Who doesn't feel a little buzz of happiness when winter gives way to spring? I know I do.

And there are many stations in this world of ours. If a train sets out, it eventually has to arrive somewhere. That's how things are. So as long as you get on board, you know you can get somewhere. A good thing that is, too. That little feeling of something accomplished is always ready and waiting for you somewhere, as if someone had put it there to stop people from going mad. And I tend to think that in a seasonal country like Japan that feeling is even stronger, because you know that each season will finally lead to another.

Thank goodness for that, eh?

Oh dear. Speculation like this will never fill the emptiness in my heart that comes from all these days spent singing the same sad songs.

The train will pass through Takenotsuka and then through Umejima, and eventually it will quite definitely arrive at its terminus, Asakusa. We'll be there in about twenty minutes, and then that little feeling of accomplishment will warm me inside. It's a gradual feeling, more gradual than the growth of these fingernails or the lengthening of my hair or the emergence of new cherry-blossoms. It's something I could easily have gone through my whole life without noticing, but now I notice it.

Thank goodness for that.

The whistle as the train pulled into Asakusa was a fanfare loud enough to hurt your ears. The giant iron caterpillar gradually slowed its shuffle until at last it came to a shuddering halt.

Pssssssshew. The train let out a long, relieved fart. Then it expelled the people on to the platform like so many little rolling lumps of crap and lay there empty like a dying caterpillar with its many orifices still lolling stupidly open. The very sight of it made me almost faint with nausea, so I scampered off down the platform as quick as my little legs would carry me.

It was a fifteen-minute walk to the home of composer Teruo Hikari. On the way it's always fun to do a spot of window-shopping at the peanut vendors and shops selling ornamental hairpins, so I knew I'd have to be careful not to arrive late.

'Ah, you're here. Good grief, what have you done to your hair?' Teruo had a good laugh at the state of my hair, left spectacularly blonde by leaving the bleach in too long. I laughed, too, out of embarrassment.

'Yeah, it's a mess, isn't it? I was bleaching it while I watched TV, and I'm afraid I fell asleep halfway through. When I woke up it was like this.'

'Well, you're a funny one and no mistake. It suits you just fine, but what are you going to do about it at show time?'

'Something tells me it won't go too well with the kimono, so I'm planning to use black hairspray just for the shows.'

Teruo Hikari laughed again. He was a classy composer who'd written material for some famous enka singers, but he'd never become very well-known himself. He was in the habit of blaming his relative lack of advancement on his aristocratic pedigree. He came from a good family, with generations of doctors and professors before him and enough money to ensure a comfortable lifestyle. He seemed to think that this had dulled in him the desire for success.

'You've got guts, Rinka-chan. Just talking to you is good for me. You give me that feeling of determination. So, no need to pay for the lessons.'

Teruo will be sixty-five this year. He dyes his white hair black, and he always wears jeans and a cheerful tracksuit top in primary colours featuring some cute little motif, a teddy bear or something. These brave attempts to retain a youthful appearance are typical of composers in the enka world. He looks dreadful, truth to tell, but still I harbour a secret admiration for his stubborn refusal to accept the creeping onset of old age.

'Oh, by the way, I've got Yumekawa coming a little later.'

'Yumekawa? What, you mean Hiroshi Yumekawa?' Well I never. So Hiroshi Yumekawa, who had made his recording début with 'The Freezing-Cold Blues', was a fellow pupil of Teruo Hikari. Teruo told me that he had eight travelling enka singers under his wing, but Hiroshi and I were the only two who didn't have to pay.

Soon the cool tones of the piano were echoing through every corner of the house. Once the lesson started, Teruo's wife came in with a charming smile and a tea set on a silver tray.

'Ah, just put it over there,' said Teruo and she did as instructed and withdrew, still smiling.

'OK, now, open wide and give me a C.'

I always struggle somewhat at this moment. It's like the moment when the dentist asks you to open your mouth, and I hate going to the dentist. I feel a resistance, as if my throat, my jaw and my tongue were being detached from my body and lent to someone else.

'Aaaaaaaaaa.'

'Wrong. Listen carefully to the piano. You're about a fifth of a tone flat.'

Was I really flat? One time I did actually dare to challenge Teruo's judgement. He was most upset, said that he might be getting on in years but he still had perfect pitch, and in the end he actually recorded my voice and played it back to me to prove his point – and, sure enough, I was flat.

'When you sing enka, you really have to *taste* the words, so you've got to enunciate clearly. And since you have to express extremes of sadness and pleasure you have to be able to turn up the emotional voltage and still keep firm and clear. At times like that you don't have the leisure to fuss about looking for the right note. You have to put your whole body and soul into the performance.'

That is something very difficult to achieve. But the sheer enormity of the challenge fascinates me. Songs, I'm convinced, have wings. That's why they want to fly into the sky like wild birds. You may capture one on the palm of your hand, but just as you give a sigh of relief it's liable to fly straight off again. But don't worry, even if it escapes today, you can always recapture it tomorrow if you put all your strength into the chase. Although it may escape you again the day after tomorrow. That's why I always try to keep a real close eye on my songs. It also explains why I always take the time to put on a decent kimono for a show, however heavy it is to drag around, however bothersome to get into and out of, however hot I may feel under the lights. Taking all that trouble over preparations is worth it because it puts you into a serious frame of mind that you take with you on to the stage. That way even a clumsy person like me can look after her songs properly.

'I was wondering what song to use for today's lesson,' said Teruo, his fingers resting delicately on the keyboard, and I saw him smile at me through a little mirror he kept standing next to the piano so that he could check the facial expressions of his students while still playing the accompaniment. 'In the end I decided we'd go with "The Crimson Thread of Life" because I think it's the one best suited to your voice.' 'The Crimson Thread of Life' is a happy song, often sung at wedding ceremonies and other festive occasions. And yet its melody has a certain wistful quality to it, and enka singers tend to perform it as if they're about to die of loneliness. I always feel that people overdo the miserable bit, so when Teruo picked out that song I decided to give it a more celebratory interpretation. I started by putting on my biggest full-facial smile. Teruo looked somewhat taken aback when he caught the smile in his mirror, but he refrained from comment and started to play the tune.

> We were fated to be together, before we were even born.
> I have that feeling . . . a crimson thread tied you to me,
> So let us be together until we die, you and I.
> I will call you husband, and you me wife.
> The crimson thread binds the two of us for life.

I got through one chorus before the piano came to an abrupt halt.

'Ahem.' I could see Teruo's shoulders shaking. He was soundlessly giggling. 'I admire your spirit of adventure, Rinka, but isn't this going a little too far?'

'Sorry. I really don't know what to make of these lyrics.'

At that moment a roar of laughter came rolling out of the shadows and a man emerged from a corner of the room behind me. It was Hiroshi Yumekawa.

'Sorry about that. I just had to laugh,' he said. 'I arrived early today, so I thought I'd listen in to your lesson for a bit. What a hoot. Thought I was going to die laughing.'

'Go on, Hiroshi, tell her.'

'Tell her what? That there's more to self-expression than dollops of exaggerated vibrato, you mean?'

'I have high hopes of this young lady, Hiroshi. Isn't there some way of making her understand this song?'

'Hm.' Yumekawa knitted his forehead in concentration and lapsed into silence. He was a better-looking guy than I'd have guessed from the publicity posters. His hair was combed right back and stiffly pomaded, and he had prominent dark eyebrows. He was wearing a green tracksuit, and for some reason he was sporting a fat gold necklace and matching bracelet.

'I don't know what sort of man you're seeing at the moment,' he said at length, only to be interrupted by a snigger from Teruo, who knew all about my private life.

'Don't be fooled by that blank expression, Hiroshi. She's having quite a tough time in that department.'

'One of us victims of love, eh? Well, she should be able to sing it properly then.' Yumekawa explained that he used to be married to a woman who was prone to illness. They had children, but eventually she died. Later he remarried, and his feeling on the occasion of the second wedding ceremony had been precisely those of the song 'The Crimson Thread of Life'. Then he told me to sing it as if it were mine and my present boyfriend's special song.

Me and Daiki.

Either treat it as a song of celebration for a past wedding or as a love song of the present, he suggested. That way I would grab the hearts of the kind of people who gather to listen to enka.

'There's more than one kind of celebration in the world,' he said. 'Most people think celebrating is what you do when a zero becomes a plus. But you can also celebrate a minus becoming a zero.'

When somebody loves you, you should feel happy – or, rather, grateful. I've certainly had that feeling. Most people in the world never have the experience of being loved by someone whom they really fancy, but I have. Maybe that's good enough.

> Lu la, lu la la
> Love has gone away.
> And I am left, left freezing,
> Freezing, freezing,
> With these blues,
> With these freezing-cold blues.

Now it was Yumekawa's turn for a lesson. He sang with incredible power. I could see the glass vibrating in the windows and the veins standing out on his temples. His mouth was opened so wide you'd think his jaw would fall off at any moment, and he was so absorbed in the song that you half expected to see his own spirit come floating out of that open mouth. The song was absolutely drenched in emotion. Fantastic. Very good, Hiroshi.

Just then, in an excess of pathos, he drifted slightly out of tune. The piano stopped immediately, and Teruo whipped him across the back of the legs with a bamboo switch.

'Ouch!'

I knew it was pretty painful, having felt it myself. Teruo kept the switch standing next to the piano, and when our lessons were really heating up he'd use it on me – rather like a Zen priest smacking an acolyte – to concentrate the mind. In fact, he'd used it on so many pupils that the lower half of it was splayed out in all directions like some animal's tail.

'Ow!'

'Ugh!'

'Eek!'

Time and again the switch came down on Yumekawa's shin or on his bottom. Would it be very cruel to question the value of what these two grown-up men were doing, all covered in sweat? But I was painfully aware that, like them, I had entered of my own volition into a labyrinth with no exit. Was there still a chance I could turn back? Listening to Yumekawa's blues, interspersed with yelps of pain, I instinctively put my hand to my neck. I also tucked my hand into the opposite sleeve and felt the thin arm concealed within. Amid the warmth of my own body I could clearly feel those slippery silver-blue scales again – just as I suspected. No, there's no turning back for me. I love the water. I want to dive once more into the aquarium of the stage. Laughable really. Both those guys, and me, too, all victims of the desire for self-expression.

I want to be an expressionist. Such a commonplace desire; there is probably more of that desire floating around Tokyo than air. People gifted with brains and beauty are more numerous than pebbles in Tokyo. But the knack of satisfying that desire is not something you can buy in a supermarket, so people are forced to choose between the pain of abandoning the dream or the pain of following the dream and falling into one of the many potholes along the way. In which case you might as well fall down the hole.

When I started out doing the shows my friends all said the same thing: don't do it; no good will come of it. Once I went into singing anyway, they hurriedly rang up a few people they knew in the business and advised me to avoid getting mixed up with so-and-so, that I'd be better off with so-and-so, etc. And if I talked about how I enjoyed doing the shows they'd say, 'You may be having fun now, but just you wait – there's trouble ahead.'

Regrets? I've had too few to mention. I chuckled. It reminded me of the day I fell in the pond. I swallowed an awful lot of water. I was struggling. When my feet touched the bottom, they slipped on the slimy weed. But what's wrong with getting slimy? And what's wrong with swallowing gallons of water? I might slip and slide, I might ship lots of water, but I wouldn't die. Or even if by some remote chance my body *were* to die, that would still be better than if my spirit died. The electric current of desire to sing was running through me, and the breaker switch was broken.

The realization came to me in a flash, like a sudden accident. When the thought hit me, the words that popped out of my mouth were 'Ah, the pain.' Why on earth had I resolved on such a difficult course of action? I started talking to myself in Kyushu dialect. 'Damn.'

You know who understands this kind of feeling? Kenjiro.

'You're dead right,' he says. 'That's it, that's it.' One time, he said, 'I'm in my room, all on my own, OK? And I'm super busy. But then this thought comes to me, Ooh, wouldn't it be lovely to wank myself off right now. No, I mustn't. But it's too late. I've just got to have that wank, even if means neglecting all sorts of important stuff. Because if I don't, I know I'm not going to make any kind of progress today with all those important tasks. Maybe it's a bit of an exaggeration, but my whole life seems like a kind of rush-hour traffic jam. So I go ahead and have my fun. And, of course, it does feel great. And that's all there is to it, really.'

Pleasure is a matter of life or death.

'Er, Rinka . . .' Yumekawa had finished his lesson, and now he came sidling up to me as I was putting my shoes on in the hall-way. I could hear his bracelet and wristwatch clinking together. 'I hear you're really raking in the cash on the circuit, although you haven't got any original songs.' I was annoyed. What business was it of his?

'That's fantastic, that's really something.' He gave me a patronizing pat on the shoulder. I unceremoniously shoved his hand away.

'Look, if you've got something to say, just get on with it.'

'Don't scowl at me like that. I've got an interesting proposition for you. I'm going to bring out a second CD. Look at this.' He pulled a leaflet out of his back pocket and unfolded it under my nose. The leaflet said that Hiroshi Yumekawa was going to be releasing a new CD in March of next year; that it was going to be a duet, entitled 'Rumba For Two', and that there was to be an open competition to find the female voice to pair with that of Mr Yumekawa on the recording.

'It's a great number, "Rumba For Two",' he said. 'I think it would be perfect for you.'

'You're suggesting I should enter this competition?' What a silly idea, I was thinking. If I had the time to waste on taking extra lessons to enter some stupid contest that I wouldn't win anyway – well, I'd sooner use the time on doing a few extra shows and making some cash. I didn't need this.

'Listen, Rinka, I'll let you into a secret. This kind of audition is fixed right from the word go. The production company already has the winner decided, and they just run the audition so that they can turn down hundreds of other kids to make the winner look good and generate a bit more publicity for the début. Just to get a bit of a buzz going, you know?'

'I know that. I wasn't born yesterday. But at the same time the record company and the promoters keep their eyes peeled for any hot talent that shows up in the field, and if they spot someone good they give her the runner-up prize with a view to doing something with her later. So it's not necessarily a complete and utter waste of time to go in for the audition. That's what you're trying to tell me, right?'

'No, silly, that is *not* what I'm trying to tell you. What I'm saying is that I want to make this record with you. The pre-ordained winner of this audition is . . .' He stuck his forefinger straight out and put it to the side of my temple; I gave a little shudder, as if someone had just put a gun to my head. 'You, Rinka Kazuki.'

'What?' Hang on a minute. Did a guy like Hiroshi Yumekawa really have the power to decide something like that all by himself?

'Sure I have. What I tell them goes. So how about it? If you don't fancy it, I'll give up and look elsewhere. But won't you come and see the president of the recording company with me?' Yumekawa was all a-quiver, and every time he quivered I could hear a metallic clinking. At first I thought it was the bracelet again, but on second thoughts maybe he had a bunch of keys rattling in his pocket.

'Hello, you two. Still here?' Yumekawa's shoulders gave a start as Teruo emerged from the back of the house, and he made a flustered farewell.

'Just on our way. Many thanks for the lesson, Mr Hikari.' He led me by the hand into the car park. 'I'll give you a lift to the station. Come on, in you get.'

Chewing busily on his gum, he reached into his pocket and hauled out a bunch of keys. So I'd been right about the clinking sound. But, good grief, look at the size of it. There must have been fifteen keys in the bunch. What on earth could he be doing with so many keys? Fishy. He produced a key from the bunch like a card shark extracting the queen of spades and used it to open the door of his white Mercedes.

'Sorry it's kind of untidy – but come on in.' The door swung open, but I decided I wouldn't be getting in. The only question was how to decline the invitation. Sorry, I never get in cars with strangers. My mother makes an awful fuss about it. No, that wouldn't work. He'd just say, 'Well, your mum ain't watching now.' How about this one, then? I only get into my boyfriend's car. 'What a boring woman,' he'd say. I didn't fancy being thought of that way either. OK, I'll try this one:

'I'm awfully sorry, Mr Yumekawa.'

'Why, what's up?' Yumekawa gave me a perplexed sidelong glance.

'Well, I'm very superstitious, you see, and I'm afraid I've got a thing about white cars. I never ride in them.'

'Oh, really? I see.' Yumekawa's face suddenly brightened. 'Into feng shui, eh? Same as me.' He gave a little laugh. 'OK, I'll give you my calling card for now. Give me a ring if you're interested in that thing we were talking about just now, OK? Well, bye for now.'

After he handed me the card, Yumekawa suddenly put on a really serious face and pointed his finger at me through the car window. 'You *will* give me a ring.' And with a grin that showed his teeth, he was off.

Phew, what a relief. That had been a dangerous moment. There's something not right about men who carry that many keys around. Mind you, a guy with just one or two keys cuts a pathetic kind of figure. It's like you can read the whole pattern of their boring lives right there. I like a guy to have about five keys on his ring. If Yumekawa had had five keys, I guess I might have got in his car.

As I followed the crowd across the road at the pedestrian crossing I studied the backs of these people intent on the shopping for dinner. I'd be lying if I said I had no interest in Yumekawa's proposition. It must be a very nice feeling to have your CD on sale across the nation, even if it's only a duet. There'd be the photoshoot for the cover, a process that people in the music business always talked about as if it were the most tedious chore imaginable. I'd love to talk about shooting the cover photograph in that same bored tone of voice: which clothes to wear, what hairstyle to choose; consultations with Yumekawa; this won't do, that won't do; the rivalry would be that much more intense with the nation waiting to see the result. It could be fun – and I could imagine the people talking about the song after it came out:

'That girl in the photo with Hiroshi Yumekawa, she's kind of cute, eh?'

'Lovely voice, too.'

'Actually I think she sings better than Yumekawa.'

'Of course she does. *Much* better.'

I was nearly salivating at the thought of it. It would be just too fantastic. By and by I got back to Asakusa station. It was before the rush-hour, but the place was still buzzing with crowds of people. People struggling along clutching heavy-looking bags of shopping in both hands, housewives tugging their children along behind them, elderly couples, all these people – and all the people packed into this train, and the girl serving at the platform kiosk, and the station official telling people to stand clear of the closing doors – imagine them all listening to my song. It would be incredible. I nearly fainted with pleasure just thinking about it. My obsession with fame was overwhelming.

The train left Asakusa and headed for Koshigaya New Town, where I would be changing trains. I had skilfully grabbed a seat in the crowded carriage, and now I opened up the magazine I had bought at the kiosk. I looked up at the passengers standing in front of me, hanging on to the leather straps. The men's Adam's apples were hanging there in front of me like a row of real apples in an orchard. They were all the same colour; they were all fresh and smooth.

My thoughts drifted back to a time in my childhood when my habit of looking too closely at other people's throats nearly cost me my life. I was four. My grandfather took me to see a show starring the great enka singer Miyako Harumi. She was to perform at some special event to celebrate the anniversary of the founding of the Yahata steelworks or something. She had recently attained superstar status, thanks to a colossal hit she had with a song called 'The Man I Fell in Love With'. I was too young to understand what the lyrics were all about; I just sat next to my grand-father and listened to her voice. I was amazed. What was going on? Her voice seemed to be *rolling* somehow. Later on, I learnt that there was a name for this vocal technique favoured by singers of enka and folk songs: *kobushi mawashi*, a variation on the vibrato used by opera singers. At the time, however, I was just struck dumb by the wonder of it. I went right up to the stage and stood there staring at her throat and mouth. And the great Miyako Harumi actually noticed me looking up at her and gave me a little smile while she was singing.

It was a revelation. People who became famous by singing were a breed apart – they were born with some sort of little ball in their throat that made their voices roll. Somehow I got that notion into my head. As it happened, my father and grandfather were both very fine singers, and if I touched their throats, sure enough, I could feel the little ball. It was just sticking out a little bit, like an old-fashioned lemonade bottle with a little glass marble for a stopper. When the owner of that little ball started singing, he or she could make it go around and around at will and send down a shower of beautiful music on those who listened, shining with all the colours of the rainbow, as if someone had squeezed out all the tubes of paint in the box at the same time.

Alas, however, I myself was not one of the favoured 'ball people'. My voice did not roll. How I wished I had one of those special balls in *my* throat. The nearest thing I had was a rubber superball. They were in vogue among children at the time. Mine was a couple of centimetres across and had all the colours of the rainbow on it. Determined to become a singer at any cost, I swallowed my superball. The ball was small enough to put in a child's mouth but not small enough to get down the throat. It lodged halfway down. In the middle of our living-room was a square hole a couple of feet deep, where we put our legs to keep them warm under the heated table in the winter months. But this was summer and the hole was uncovered. Suddenly unable to breathe, I fell into the hole and lay there, thrashing around at the bottom. My mother came flying, her face white with fear. Somehow she sensed that I had something stuck in my throat. She fetched some soy sauce from the kitchen and poured it straight down me. Looking back, I have to say it was a drastic remedy, but it saved my life. The soy sauce induced vomiting, and after an awful struggle I finally managed to cough up the 'voice ball'.

I had my rainbow-coloured superball taken away from me. I

also dislocated an arm in the violence of my struggles and was taken to a creepy old mansion with 'Bonesetter' written over the entrance and pictures of skeletons all over the place, where I was taken into a treatment room where the walls were covered with Noh masks collected by the goat-faced doctor who gave a loud war cry as he popped my arm back into its socket – an altogether shocking experience. To this day I can't listen to Miyako Harumi without recalling that bone-setting clinic and feeling myself shrink with fear.

I instinctively put my hand to my throat. Have I developed a voice ball since then? After all, I can just about do the trick with the rolling voice these days, even if it does sound like 'dollops of exaggerated vibrato' at times. Hm, perhaps there's just a little ball there, like a pearl, a little pearl, sleeping in an oyster at the bottom of the sea. Every time another wave passes over, the layers of the pearl get that tiny bit thicker – that mother-of-pearl, that rainbow radiance, pure white, but with so many different ways of shining. That's my voice ball. Wouldn't it be nice if it really did grow that way?

5 The Little Dance of the Bones

When Hawaiian shirts appear on the streets, they are every bit as welcome as the cherry blossom to travelling-show folk. They herald summer, season of outdoor festivals, fireworks, the seaside and the beer garden, season of many engagements for the popular entertainer. Even Kenjiro, who had been joking cynically that in his case show business was just like no business, managed to get a few bookings. Going to work in the Mercedes Kaho bought for him had really gone to his head. He had lost what last remnants of shame he may once have had and wiggled his bum more outrageously than ever when doing the 'uh-huh' song with David. All in all, he was on great form.

I was doing all right, too. I found myself a new agency, and last night they actually treated me to quite a riotous welcome party at one of the clubs. I wore an iridescent silk kimono that was lavishly praised by all, and I was so pleased by all the fuss being made over me that I ended up on a drunken crawl through the transvestite bars until three o'clock in the morning.

The taxi dropped me off just before four. Without even bothering to get out of my kimono, I headed straight for the kitchen and put an apron on over the top of it. I had set the timer on the electric rice cooker to have the rice ready and steaming at around this time, and my first task was to make some nice fresh rice balls for Mr Wild, who had a trip scheduled to the far side of the Boso Peninsula for a spot of sea fishing.

Lately I'd had very few opportunities to behave like a good wife to Daiki – never mind that I wasn't strictly his wife anyway – but this fishing trip was a big chance for a woman who hardly knows her way about the kitchen to act the good wife by putting together a first-rate lunchbox. Elaborate cuisine just gets in the way of outdoor leisure activities, and making a set of simple rice balls is actually the best kind of service a dedicated housewife can do for her man. As it's also the simplest kind of cookery in the world, that suits me just fine. I would do him proud.

I was just in the middle of squeezing the rice into little balls, concentrating furiously on the job in hand, when Daiki got out of bed. I kept my back turned to him, letting him see the apron-strings, while smirking quietly to myself. My forehead was covered with sweat, but I wasn't going to let him know I'd been out on the razzle all night. I squeezed the rice balls as casually as I could and hummed a little tune to myself.

'Why, thank you, Rinka. Fancy you being up and working so early in the morning.' He gave me a little hug from behind, the tooth-brush still in his mouth. He didn't seem to realize that I'd been up all night. I was relieved. My little deception had apparently succeeded.

Inside each rice ball I put a generous helping of *mentaiko*. This spicy cod's roe is the most famous gourmet treat from my home town of Fukuoka, and this was the best kind, from Fukuya, the company that first came up with the recipe. They'd had a special sale of goodies from Fukuoka in a department store the other day, and I was too nostalgic to resist. I wrapped the rice balls in sheets of dried seaweed and the job was done. I added some tasty pickled radish and wrapped the whole in bamboo leaves. I put the rice balls in a paper bag, along with some canned whale meat and canned potato salad, and tossed in a bunch of bananas for dessert. A flask of green tea completed the set.

Getting everything neatly bagged up brought a strangely satis-fying sense of accomplishment. I examined the bag from various different angles, gloating with glee.

'Have a lovely day, darling.'

Daiki put his boots on in the hallway in great good spirits. His tanned body looked great in his stylish angling gear. 'Let's see. It's just before five. If I set out now, I should make the seven o'clock meet at the quayside quite comfortably. By the way, you're free for supper tonight, aren't you? We're all going to the usual sushi shop tonight. The master there is going to prepare today's catch for the table.'

'Meaning that you're rock-solid certain you're going to catch something today?'

'Of course. We've never yet come back with a goose egg.'

'A goose egg?'

'A zero, an empty net. We never get a goose egg, because I always leave the silly goose at home.'

'The silly goose? Oh, I see. Me.'

'Exactly. Everyone knows it's bad luck to have a woman on board. Now look after the flat while I'm gone, OK?' Daiki slung the empty coolbag over his shoulder. I accompanied him down to the street.

I love it around 5 a.m. Even when you're so lifeless and languid that you're about ready to collapse into bed, the world in its morning glory is so beautiful that it makes you want to stay up just a little longer. You go out on to the familiar street, and suddenly it isn't familiar at all. Once the clock passes 6 a.m. the street starts to glow with gold, and amid the silence you sense the pulse of the new day about to start. But my favourite time of day is just before that, when the dawn is still pale and white, with a refreshing hint of lilac. The thin air seems to absorb all the time that has passed before this new day, and all the hurly-burly of the days gone by, and returns everything to still silence. It's that moment when my own ending mingles with the day's beginning. I take a deep breath and become absolutely empty myself.

'See you then, silly goose.' The engine came crisply to life and I watched Daiki's Pajero until it disappeared from sight at the bottom of the road. I was just turning away to go back to the apartment when I was stopped in my tracks by a familiar voice.

'Oi, Rinka, what are you doing up at this time of the morning?'

A green Mercedes had pulled up alongside the block of flats. It was Kenjiro. What on earth was he doing here at a time like this? He stuck his face out of the window and spoke to me. 'Nice body-work, don't you think? Took it to the carwash again yesterday. Maybe I'll have it washed again today.' He sniggered lasciviously. 'Fancy a ride, Rinka?'

'I haven't slept, and I'm out of fuel myself. Another time, OK? But anyway, what are *you* doing up and about so early this morning?'

'Me? I'm just off to Sendai for a three-day stint doing shows in a beer garden there. Man, I'm so, so sleepy. I've got Dave in the back. Oi, Dave. Dave. Wakey-wakey!' David was sound asleep on the back seat, curled up in a blanket with a look of pure innocence on his face.

'There's no need to wake the poor thing,' I said. 'Look how deeply he's sleeping.'

'Huh! Sleeping like a baby while I have to do all the driving. I could fall asleep at the wheel myself any time. Why don't you get in, Rinka? Talk to me to keep me awake.'

'Eh? What the hell makes you think I'm going to drop everything and go to Sendai with you?'

'Because that's how things are working out today. I was just driving past and, purely by chance, there you were.'

'No way, Ken-chan. I'm practically asleep on my feet.'

'No problem. You can sleep in the car. There'll be grilled ox tongue for you when we get to Sendai. C'mon, let's go.' Kenjiro opened the door, grabbed my arm and tried to pull me in. We were just larking about there, arguing whether or not I was going to go with him and squealing with laughter, when it happened. Kenjiro's face went white as a sheet. A huge man had his collar in a vice-like grip. The giant growled softly at him.

'And what's your business with this woman, jerk?'

'Daiki!' What was he doing here? I looked around, and there was the Pajero that I had just seen off, back home and parked right behind Kenjiro's Mercedes.

'I somehow got this feeling that I ought to turn back. Lucky I did – eh, punk? Think you can pick women up in the street with a Mercedes and some flashy threads, huh?'

'Leave it out, man. D'you wanna ride, too? I'll give you one.'

'What the fuck?' Daiki's fist tightened. Kenjiro kept his eye on him and started to tremble. But he didn't yield at all. This was it. It was all up for Kenjiro. I made a desperate effort to keep blood off the street.

'Stop it. Please, stop it, both of you.'

'You're lucky you've still got that fancy Mercedes in one piece, my friend. I was thinking of driving straight on and giving you one up the backside.'

'I'm glad you didn't. I'm not into anal.'

'You know, I really shouldn't be wasting my time talking to a pathetic shrimp like you . . .' Daiki started cracking his knuckles. Kenjiro seemed to have decided that war was inevitable. He looked up at Daiki as insolently as possible and gave a derisive laugh.

'Well, if you're so fucking busy, mister, why don't you just fuck off and do your fishing, eh?'

'I'll stop you fishing for women first.' Daiki swiftly raised his fist and squared up to use it.

I can stop this fight. The intuition came to me suddenly. The build-up to the fight was too long to be real. With all this sparring it was more like a haiku contest than a fist-fight over a woman with men's honour at stake. If I made the right move I could prevent real violence.

The next moment my throat reverberated with a tremendous scream, so high pitched it was almost ultrasonic. All that enka singing had done wonders for my vocal chords. It was a scream to bring the telegraph poles crashing down, to bring the birds plummeting senseless from the sky, to leave Mr Wild and the Uh-huh Man unconscious on the street, to smash every window and pop every eardrum in town.

It didn't actually do all those things, of course, but it was effective just the same. The two men covered their ears in panic, and lights appeared at windows all down the street. People who had been sleeping peacefully moments earlier appeared bleary-eyed and pale on their balconies, wondering what on earth was going on. Looking down at the street, they could see a woman clad in full kimono, involved in some kind of altercation with two men, one leaning out of a green Mercedes-Benz, decked out like some kind of junior gangster, the other a giant of a man, dressed for a fishing trip. Good grief. They soon retreated indoors, probably hoping it would prove to be a bad dream.

And then the three of us were left alone in the silent street again. Two big tears rolled down each of my cheeks, my nose started running and, my voice gone, I just stood there hiccup-ping noisily. The sight of me in this state quelled Daiki's fighting spirit. He unhanded Kenjiro's collar, roughly shoving him away, and, to my surprise, slid his hand under *my* collar instead. Kenjiro gulped and held his breath. Just below the material of my kimono I could feel that great hand moving about in a very naughty sort of way.

Daiki burst out in a loud, triumphant guffaw. Kenjiro looked irritably about him, and gradually the fighting flames faded from his eyes. Giving a final hiss of disgust from between grated teeth, he turned on the engine of the Mercedes. Daiki carried on laugh-ing and laughing, as though he found something unbearably amusing in the situation. Suddenly the back door of the Mercedes flew open and a man came shooting out of it with surprising momentum, straight at Daiki. Caught off guard, he cried out, staggered backwards and fell on his backside.

'What?' The man looked around him nervously, a suitcase dangling from his hand. It was David.

'Already, are we there?'

'Idiot. Shit-for-brains. We're not in Sendai yet, you fucking moron. Get back in the fucking car.' Stung by Kenjiro's scolding, David hurriedly climbed back into the car.

After the Mercedes had departed Daiki gave me my orders. I was to accompany him to the seaside, kimono and all. I tried to protest, but he just scooped me up, legs flailing, and chucked me unceremoniously into the back seat of the Pajero.

The engine started. He was a man used to getting his way. Maybe he was worried that Kenjiro might come back again after he'd gone. Outside, the air had started to warm up, and through the car window I could see the sky turning cobalt blue, pregnant with the new day. Soon we'd be back to the usual baking city streets. What would the day bring? I wondered, as I drifted slowly out of consciousness.

I was terribly tired and hungry and somewhat hot. Although this was a summer kimono, made of silken gauze designed to let some air through, any kimono is liable to get sticky around the waist area. I wanted to change into something more relaxing. I wanted a shower. I was hungry and sleepy. Want to get undressed. Worried about getting wrinkles in the kimono. Want to wash my face, wash my hair. Want to sleep.

I slept.

It's always like that with me. I can fall asleep anywhere, and I don't open my eyes until it's time to wake up. Today I had nothing whatsoever on my schedule, and so I would not wake up for over seven hours.

Brrm, brrm – the vibrations of the Pajero as it drove along were comforting to my tired body. Inside my sleeping flesh, my bones were doing a little dance.

I awoke to find myself lying on a futon in an unfamiliar four-and-a-half mat room. The place had a lived-in feel to it. There was washing hung up to dry all over the room, including items of baby clothing.

'Ah, you're awake.' A woman I didn't know, holding a baby in her arms, was peering at my face. 'Daiki said to look after you,' she explained.

Daiki. Her familiar use of his personal name convinced me for a moment that she was his wife. Stunned, I sat bolt upright in the futon. In fact, it turned out she was his older sister. She was running a bar on the ground floor of the house. She was a mama-san. And indeed, she was wearing a bright-red trouser-suit that was out of place in a homely room such as this. She had a pear-shaped head with her hair bundled up at the top. Although we had never met before, she combed back my stray hair with her long white fingers, talking to me as she did so.

'Daiki told me to give you something to eat when you woke up, something easy on the stomach. I've got it all ready, so I'll just go and get it. Oh, and I hung up your kimono to stop it getting crumpled. And Daiki also told me to give you a rubdown with a damp towel and a light dusting with baby powder to keep the heat rash off.'

Ahem. Excuse me, madam, but I am not a baby.

Before I knew it she had me dressed in a very mama-san-style floral négligé, and my skin was free of that nasty sweaty feeling and silky smooth once more. I'm sure Daiki was joking when he said all that about the baby powder and stuff, but she took it all seriously and went right ahead. She was a very straightforward person. When I checked up on my kimono, I found she had hung it up very correctly on the appropriate stand. With its two arms spread stiffly outwards it looked like a giant kite. There was an overbearing authority about it that seemed to condemn its owner for indulgence in casual daytime napping. Despite the efforts of Daiki's sister it was already thoroughly crumpled and had several stains on the collar. Oh dear. I had only just got it, on credit from the Isetan Department Store, and now I'd have to put it out for cleaning. Just cleaning these things costs five thousand yen. Expenses like this soon ate up the money I earned from singing – in fact I couldn't make enough to keep myself. I was OK for the time being, because Daiki paid the rent and the utilities, besides footing the food bill, but without him I wouldn't be able to get by.

> Sponge off your parents till you've sucked them through.
> If they've got no money then a boyfriend will do.
> In this old word two things we don't need
> Are men who crush our dreams and girls who sing for greed.

They ain't no use to you nor me,
So kick them and beat them, one, two, three.

Inwardly humming this little fragment of masochistic home-made enka, I slurped up the bowl of egg porridge the mama-san had made for me.

'I expect you'll be bored on your own up there,' said the pear-head mama, her voice floating back from halfway down the stairs. Actually I would have found it very relaxing to take it easy on my own, but I did as she suggested and followed her down into the shop.

A handsome man, just like my father . . .

It was three o'clock in the afternoon, yet there were customers in the bar. I realized that at this time of day it must function as a karaoke café. Acutely embarrassed in my floral négligé, I stopped in my tracks and tried to struggle back up the stairs.

'Oh I say, what a perfectly charming young lady.'

'Don't be shy, love, come over and join us, please.'

Although it was still broad daylight outside, a dozen or more housewives had occupied the bar, dressed to the nines in glitzy fashions more suited to the night. Some kind of ladies' karaoke circle. Full of misgivings, I picked up the hem of my négligé, which was trailing on the stairs behind me, and reluctantly carried on down and approached the ladies. One of them addressed me.

'So, I hear you're the singer that's scum . . .'

'Sc-scum?'

'Yes. The singer that's come to entertain us today. The mama told us all about you, dear.'

Oh yes, ha-ha. Of course. Never mind that it was my day off and I'd only just got out of bed, they expected me to sing for them. And in a négligé, too. It is the curse of our profession. If a watch repairer shows up at a bar, no one asks them to fix their watch. If a greengrocer strolls into a café, no one tells him they fancy a salad so can he hand over a lettuce and a couple of tomatoes. But if you happen to be a painter or a singer, people expect you to perform for free at the drop of a hat and will be most upset if you try to object.

'We professional singers have to be ready to sing in any situation – and we have to do it properly, too, otherwise people will start talking.' I recall my friend and fellow singer Shimako Sado telling me that once. However, there are some people who take the opposite view. They don't take kindly to the likes of me singing in private, informal situations as if it were a real concert. Bar mama-sans are such people. Many of them are good singers themselves. They're amateurs, of course, but they're still proud of their voices. When the likes of Shimako and myself start singing in their establishments, they often feel resentful because they're not centre stage any more, so they dilute the drinks, overcharge you on the bill and generally make their displeasure felt. Of course, we singers have our pride, too, and in a perverse sort of way we'd be quite upset if our singing *didn't* provoke jealousy among the mama-sans. We want stuff to happen when we sing. Just a little commotion. The moment it dawns on us that people see our singing as no different from that of any other punter at the karaoke we feel as if we've just been sentenced to death. Well, anyway, the fact is I was totally exhausted and in no mood to join in with some amateur sing-along. But what could I do?

'OK. I'll go with song number ten, "Your Wild Hair".'

I'm worn out. I'm covered in sweat again. The sweat is making the négligé stick to my body in places. Actually, there's only one kind of place where I can relax fully and enjoy singing in private, and that's a transvestite bar. There I can mess around with the songs, change the words – 'I reach out and touch your wild face' rather than 'your wild hair', for instance – and the hostesses will laugh with me but never at me, because they never forget to accord me the respect due to a pro. Once it gets to about five in the morning you may overhear one or two slightly disconcerting sounds – the buzz of an electric razor coming from the toilets, as one of the girls deals with her five-o'clock shadow, or an irritable catfight of the kind gay people tend to get into when overtired – but apart from these minor distractions it's really a very relaxing environment.

'Right, let's ask Mrs Nakajima to sing next.'

'I say, Mrs Nakajima, you're no mean singer yourself.' Repressing the urge to weep at their dreadful performances, I dutifully compliment each of the ladies in turn. Perhaps I overdo it just a tad, for it isn't long before one of them gets a little over-excited and says, 'I wonder whether I should put out a CD as well...'

'I think you should. But I don't know if it's quite the done thing for women of our age to make their recording débuts...'

When the talk turns to CDs, a girl like me, owner of an entirely fictional recording career, really should bite her tongue. Yet, somehow, I feel anger and pathos and general disgust building up inside me. Where does it all come from, I wonder? Eventually, I hesitantly start to address them.

'Er, excuse me, everybody.' They notice the gravity of my expression, and their hands pause in the act of flicking over the pages of the karaoke songbook. 'I'm very sorry to say something that you may well find rather strange.'

'What could it be?' asks one of the ladies brightly. I am so embarrassed about the utterly pathetic thing I am about to say that my voice is already shaking and close to tears before I even start talking. But I pluck up my courage and say it anyway.

'Please give me some money.' As expected, the ladies look at each other in some perplexity. 'I know I'm not at all famous or anything, but I do actually get paid for singing. A hundred yen will be plenty. I couldn't accept more than that anyway. Please.' I finish my request in a half-strangled voice. The company, in such good spirits until just now, is plunged into a silence both sudden and profound. I fear I may have spoilt the party. I should have kept my big mouth shut. But if I hadn't said anything my heart would have died a little death. So I went ahead and said it. Please forgive me. Humour me. I had to say it, for the sake of my own future.

'Oh, I *see*.' The ladies soon recover their composure. 'Actually we *were* being a bit naughty, weren't we?'

'Of course we were. You've got to draw a line between those who get paid for singing and those who have to pay to be allowed to sing.'

The ladies all burst out laughing. That's a relief. I hear the clink of coins as they shuffle spare change in the palms of their hands: my honorarium. Of course, this is the first time in my life I've actually come right out and reminded people about the custom of tipping. By enduring the intense humiliation of having to do something so totally unthinkable, I have somehow postponed for a while the day when my entire heart fades away and dies. But it is a victory won at great cost; part of my heart is dead already.

'Here you are, love. Is this the right way to do it?' One of the ladies skilfully pinches a hundred-yen coin between the two unseparated halves of a pair of disposable chopsticks. It's kind of nice; just like a real tip for an enka singer. Held by this little forked sliver of forest life, the silver coin gleams dully. This is a fitting reward for me, no? I'm always getting more than I deserve.

Noisily hiding the coins away in my pocket, I thank the ladies. I have 1,600 yen. I should be able to buy a pair of stage socks with that. As I may have mentioned, I don't like to use tip-money for daily living expenses; I like to use it to buy myself something special.

As for the pear-head mama, she was bustling around behind a counter in the corner of the shop, taking telephone calls, making coffee and so on. She showed no sign of having noticed the little drama we had just played out.

Eventually there was a call from Daiki, giving word that he was back from the trip and that I was to make my way to the usual sushi shop.

'You wouldn't want to put on that kimono again,' said the pear-drop mama. 'The lining was simply drenched in sweat, you know. Why not have a shower? I'll lend you something simple to slip into.'

And so once again I found myself having a shower in the bathroom of a perfect stranger. Beyond the frosted glass of the shower-unit door I could make out the mama's pear-shaped head.

'How do you find the waters?'

I gave a little snort of laughter. How do you find the waters? That's a funny sort of question when someone's just having a shower. Anyone would think I was soaking in a luxury herbal hot spring or something. She was a funny sort of person, come to that.

Dripping all over, I opened the shower door. The mama was gone, and there was a one-piece dress, white with blue polka dots, lying neatly folded in a rattan basket. There was also a brand-new pair of knickers in a supermarket carrier bag. No bra, though – ah, I should have guessed, the dress had a pair of cups sewn into the front. She really did think of everything. It was one of those halter-neck dresses, with a little ribbon to tie behind the neck, leaving the whole of the back exposed. With the flared skirt below, it had something of the 1970s to it. I put my hair up to match.

'Well, I'll be off then.' I slipped on my sandals and left the house. I put the hundred-yen tips in a plastic bag along with the disposable chopsticks that had held them, and walked along with the bag dangling from my hand – not that I had any particular purpose in mind for it. It was only about a fifteen-minute walk from here to Daiki's regular sushi restaurant, Hiro-zushi. As I went clacking along the street, I realized that I was thirsty. I bought a can of juice at a vending machine. Bought with money I'd earned by singing, it tasted especially sweet but also kind of bitter.

I came across some waste ground by the side of the road and stopped. It was roped off with a sign clearly stating 'No Entry'. I slipped under the rope and into the plot. The evening air was hot and sticky, and it wasn't long before the summer mosquitoes were feasting on my flesh. I squatted down amid the flourishing silver grass that covered the ground and stuck the chopsticks that had held the hundred-yen tips into the soil. I clapped my hands together two or three times and said a brief prayer. These chopsticks formed a grave marker. A little bit of my heart had died and was buried there.

I arrived at the sushi restaurant soon after, vigorously rubbing at the mosquito bites behind my knees.

'What's with that outfit, Rinka? You'll catch your death.' The moment he saw me Daiki grumbled about the borrowed dress, took off his work jacket and dropped it over my shoulders. The lovely dress disappeared, and I looked like a peasant.

Naked from the waist up, Daiki nibbled at his sushi.

'We had a great catch today,' he remarked.

'Rinka, you'll never know how much we owe to Mr Hirose.' The young workmen, all of them with their hair dyed brown, greeted me one by one, each making it clear how deeply he respected Daiki. I got all flustered. Why is it that young manual workers are always so sexy? One of them had long hair tied at the back and an earring. Another had apparently used a pair of scissors to slash the neck and sleeves of his T-shirt. They were so beautiful that it really didn't matter what they did with their clothes and hair. Anything looked great on them. I mean, they looked like teenage pop stars.

Yum-yum.

No fewer than eight beautiful young men, of all different types, lined up in front of me like a row of juicy grapes. It seemed a bit of a shame not to have a little taste of at least one of them. But these boys had surprisingly strict morals. One time I did have a go at hitting on one of them, in a humorous sort of way, you understand, pretending to be drunk. I got nowhere.

'Sorry, miss, no can do. Mr Hirose saved me from messing up my life with glue-sniffing. There are some things that just aren't on, know what I mean?'

I suppose I did know what he meant.

'Hey there, master. The young lady's arrived, so can you do us the special now?'

'Coming right up.'

As ordered by Daiki, the master of the sushi restaurant sliced up some freshly caught mackerel and placed each slice on its delicate bed of rice. It was far more delicious than I could possibly have imagined.

'Wow! This is fantastic. Did you really catch this yourself today? Amazing.'

'Oh, you know, about par for the course.'

Although still a little chagrined that the building-site Adonises were off limits to me, I had to admit that Daiki had something that could beat the whole lot of them put together. It was the fact that I knew I could rely on him. To someone like me, always sailing perilously through the choppy seas of life in a shabby little boat, he was a kind of anchor. A lover, yes, but a father to me as well. I couldn't cheat on this man. In a way, though, I had, in fact, been cheating on him from the very day we met, because I was in love with singing – head over heels in love. To Daiki, my singing career was the old enemy, the one enemy he couldn't fight off. I suppose anyone would see a lifelong dream such as mine as a permanent rival in love.

'The rock-fish is a bit of all right, too, eh?'

'The grilled bream's out of this world.'

The crowd of beautiful boys arrayed along the counter swapped plates of fish around with such unbridled enthusiasm that it looked like some kind of crazy ball game. Gradually, the meat of the fish they'd caught became part of their own flesh and blood. Men were shoving chunks of ice into my glass with their bare hands so fast I didn't have time to object. Then other men would pour shots of *shochu* into the glass, and we'd have another round of toasts. I really couldn't drink this much. I was just wondering what to do with it all when Daiki seized the glass of burning liquor from my grasp and tossed the whole glassful down his great thick neck. I could only gaze on in wonderment.

'Oh, hello, dear. Come on in. On your own this evening?' The master gave a hearty greeting as another customer came through the door. Somewhat unusually for a place like this, the new arrival was an unaccompanied woman; to my intense surprise it turned out to be Kaho Jojima. She was wearing a skin-tight, moss-green suede tank-top with nothing underneath it and ragged cut-off jeans that didn't really look as if they'd been cut at all – more as if some outrageously powerful man had ripped off the legs from the thigh down. On her feet were trainers worn slip-shod and sockless. It was the kind of summer look that only a dark-skinned woman can get away with, and I did actually feel a slight twinge of jealousy.

Kaho spotted Daiki before she noticed me, and started frolicking around him as though she might fly to his arms at any moment. Daiki didn't know where to look.

'It's Kaho, isn't it?' he said with a shy laugh. 'No more trouble with perverts after that time, I hope? Everything OK?' Yes, Daiki was the kind of guy who would protect a prostitute from a pervert in the street. That was the kind of thing I really liked about him.

'Hello, Rinka,' said Kaho. 'I'm on my own tonight, because Ken's gone off to Sendai. I'm glad I bumped into you. Nice to see the emperor after all this time, too.'

The sushi shop attracted a mixed clientele. It was popular with show people and construction workers alike, but the two groups didn't overlap that much, and Daiki didn't know about Kaho being Kenjiro's girlfriend, which was all for the best really, considering this morning's encounter. Nor do I suppose that Kaho would ever guess that the man whose mighty power had once come to her rescue had been on the verge of using that same power against her own lover earlier this very day.

'Ugh, more stupid building work tomorrow.'

'Today was just an inspection day at the site, so the work was easy. Tomorrow we're starting on a new project, way up in Miyagi.'

These labourers travelled around the country, going from one building site to the next, staying in cheap inns – their lifestyle was just like ours. They showed their white teeth and laughed together.

'Tough, ain't it?'

'Oh, it's tough all right: 3D doesn't describe it; more like 4D.'

'Ha-ha-ha. Make that 5D – no, 6D.'

Listening to the drunken lads complaining about their jobs, Kaho and I exchanged looks and laughed. We shrugged our shoulders. You see, all that talk about '3D' work – meaning work that is Dirty, Demanding and Dangerous – is a regular part of show people's conversation, too, including the little joke about 4D, 5D and so on. You have a chat with Kenjiro one of these days, or Moody Konami, or Hiroshi Yumekawa, or Shimako Sado, and you'll probably hear them cracking the very same joke.

'Dirty, demanding, dangerous . . .'
'Demeaning.'
'Delayed payment.'
'Doss house. Dump.'
'Deprivation – of love, that is.'
'Devil take the hindmost.'
'Deeply in debt.'
. . . and so on.

The fish on the table were rapidly transformed into happy-looking skeletons, and by the time each skeleton had been picked well and truly clean Daiki and his crew of young workers were well and truly drunk. They'd had so much cheap liquor they could barely stand. Kaho and I ended the evening the best of friends, and as we, too, needed some assistance to stay on our feet, we put our shoulders together as we walked out of the shop.

'Got a problem, pal?' Daiki's voice sounded like the low growl of a wild dog. It was street-fighting time. I was too plastered to recall the next day exactly who the sacrificial victim was on this occasion. Some unlucky passer-by, maybe; some other stressed-out guy, just like Daiki, who had something eating away at him day after day. It had nothing to do with women. All I had to do was find somewhere to sit down and doze off, lulled by the pleasant sound of bones being smashed somewhere far away. Occasionally my eye would open and catch a glimpse of the men, with flowers of fine fresh blood blooming on tightly pursed lips or blossoming from the temple. Nothing to do with women. A cool night wind caressed the back of my neck. The men were bustling around with firm, determined faces, the way they do at festival time, when they carry the portable Shinto shrine through the streets. Their voices were bold and vigorous. There was a very Japanese atmosphere about the whole occasion. The master of the sushi shop was merrily joining in, too. Something told me the shop would be closed for the day tomorrow. Not one of those men knew fear. The beautiful youths were just incredible. There seemed to be about six men fighting on the other side. However, Kaho and I felt certain that our side would be victorious, so we slipped peacefully off to sleep. So long as the men danced so nimbly around us, not even a gnat could get near us as we lay there on our bed of silver grass. Cool, so cool.

It felt really nice. I hadn't had a night like this in a long time. Even the moon was round as a hundred-yen coin.

Snore.

6 Kimono Garage

Spun silver, spun gold: the gorgeous colours of the turning leaves form beautiful patterns all around me, anticipating the onset of autumn. It's late August, and the heat of summer lingers on, but it is part of the enka singer's art to emulate the leaves in anticipating the turn of the season. Now she must put aside the light stage-clothing of summer and don the heavy-brocaded kimono that people associate with the coming season – and it is her pride to wear it lightly, as if she and her kimono might drift away on the autumn breeze at any moment.

I smiled quietly to myself as I set to work to get the mighty kimono wrapped around me, alone in a garage that didn't even have a mirror. Tonight I would be singing popular songs in an old-fashioned tavern, the kind of work I most detest. It's a common enough story. The owner of a pub, bar or sushi shop happens to know someone in the entertainment business, happens to like a good sing-song himself and asks his pal in the production company to send someone along to perform at some kind of celebratory bash – twenty years in the business or something. The shop is usually quite large, and the customers are all company directors and the like who've known the owner for a decade or more. Naturally you can expect to rake in at least 40,000 yen per show in tips at this kind of event.

And yet, I don't really appreciate the tips I get at these shows. It's not like at the health spas, where people are moved to reach for their wallets because they feel well disposed towards me. No, these tips are obligatory – they even come wrapped in a special decorative envelope because the donor knows it's the done thing to tip the singer at these events. I feel totally disgusted with myself when I take that money home. Another thing about these gigs in taverns is that they're great opportunities to sell tapes of your original songs – only in my case, there are no original songs to sell in the first place, so that doesn't mean a lot to me.

But the worst thing about this kind of show is the miserable fact that the establishments don't have dressing-rooms. One time I was asked to get changed in a tiny little toilet. Even I had to complain about that one. I mean, how are you supposed to get a full-sized kimono on in a room that's too small to open a trunk in? Seeing my point, the client thoughtfully suggested a dusty old broom cup-board as an alternative. When even that failed to meet with my approval, he proposed that I get changed in a car he had parked outside on the street. Lost for words, I just gazed despairingly up at the sky, at which moment he had a bright idea. How about this dog pen he had in the back garden? It was more spacious – why, there must have been all of sixty square feet of floor space in there – and it was high enough for me to stand up without bumping my head on the top of the cage. If we put a sheet or something over the whole thing, it would make quite a decent changing-room, no? How about that? Putting on a formal long-sleeved kimono in a dog pen. I somehow swallowed my rage and gave a ladylike smile. Well, I say. What a unique dressing-room. I climbed into the cage, heaving my trunk in with me. There was no resident in there, but there were plentiful signs that the pen was in use – the smell of left-over dog food, for example, competing with that rank odour so characteristic of man's best friend. Not what you'd call the ideal environment. Anyway, I opened up the trunk, got out the large plastic sheet I'd bought at the hundred-yen shop and spread it over the floor. I took my shoes off and stood on the sheet. This would have to do. At least it was a couple of notches up from the toilet and the broom cupboard. So thinking, I unfolded my collapsible coat hangar and used it to hang the kimono from the top of the cage. At that moment the door of the cage was shut with an abrupt clang, and a member of the tavern staff started covering the whole cage with a sheet. The fellow addressed me:

'Excuse me, Linda . . .' I bluntly pointed out that my name was Rinka. 'Ah, Rinka. Um, about how many minutes will it take you to get changed?'

'How many minutes? Well, this is a formal long-sleeved kimono, you know. Even if I hurry I'll need at least fifteen to twenty minutes. And then I've got to do my make-up, of course.' 'Well, anyway, could you be as quick as possible, please? I'm awfully sorry to hurry you like this, but, you see, Jasper will be coming back from his walk in a little while.'

I don't think I have ever been quite so insulted in all my born days. I'm never going to forget that name: Jasper. Why should I, Rinka Kazuki, have to hurry my preparations for the sake of some stupid mutt?

I kicked open the door with a clatter and emerged from the pen snorting with fury. Once I was fairly sure there was no one around, I started getting changed right there in the open air. It was midsummer, and my body warmth soon attracted a swarm of mosquitoes, the long-legged kind with the black-and-white stripes. They were making quite a banquet out of me, but somehow the itching didn't bother me. Actually I felt pretty good. It was dusk, and although the daylight was fading to grey there was still something to be seen as I stripped off in the backyard there. It's not every day you see a naked women getting changed outdoors, and there were quite a lot of houses with views of the yard. Old men started to appear at the windows, gawping at me in slack-jawed amazement as if they'd just seen an alien touch down. Hi, guys. Look, it's not my fault. Blame the establishment.

That was then. This time I'm in a garage. Well, I guess you could say it's an improvement. At least it's got some room in it. I finished putting on the kimono, put my daytime clothes and handbag into the trunk and carefully locked it. In my line of business you've got to have a good, stout, lockable trunk. It's like a safe.

When the show was over I adjourned to a sushi shop in East Kanagawa. I'd rung up Kenjiro, David and Kaho on the mobile, and the four of us were going to have a few drinks. I was going to treat everybody, since I was in a hurry to get rid of the tip-money I'd received without really deserving it.

'I guess you can't very well refuse a job like that – can you? – even if you do really hate it,' said Kaho, smiling wryly as she poured some beer for me.

'Of course you can't,' said Kenjiro, waving his chopsticks around for emphasis. 'That kind of show may be kind of shabby, but it's important to the production company. They've got to look after their old clients. Don't forget, there are over a thousand travelling singers who can't get enough work to feed themselves because the work's just not there. Sometimes the production company will go to one of those crummy bars and *ask* them to put on one of their singers – as a special favour, you know. Let's not forget, guys like us need all the work we can get. You should be grateful for any that comes your way, Rinka.'

'Yeah, but the trouble is, that's the *only* kind of work I'm getting these days.' I gave a little pout, which merely served to enrage Kenjiro still more.

'You silly cow. Who the hell do you think you are? These places may be nothing special, but you do get star billing, right? If you're tired of it, why don't you get a job at a club, eh? Same place every night, singing duets with salarymen? How d'you like that?' As he warmed to his theme, Kenjiro waved his chopsticks ever more vigorously and flicked droplets of soy sauce on to his shirt. Kaho struggled to wipe off the stains with a napkin, while Kenjiro returned to the attack.

'Rinka. You're not seriously thinking of aiming for the big time, are you? At your age?' I was flustered. The incident with Hiroshi Yumekawa the other day passed through my mind. He'd asked me to record a duet with him, and I still hadn't given the man an answer. How could a girl like that have thoughts of stardom on her mind?

Flatly denying my own inner desires, I replied, 'Of course not, Ken-chan. Come on, you must be kidding. Dear me, the things you say.' I even managed a somewhat forced laugh. After all, what am I? Just a low-grade travelling singer who's never recorded a song in her life. Kenjiro and David do have a CD out that you can buy in the shops, but it's self-produced with money that Kaho raised for them. In the end they're just low-grade travelling singers, too. Still, we are supposed to have some kind of pride in our profession, are we not?

'Listen to this, Rinka. The other day a famous singer, who shall remain nameless, came into this very sushi bar. Apparently she saw our poster up on the wall, and do you know what she said? "There's something so disgraceful about these singers who produce their own records. The way they put themselves about like that, even though nobody wants to listen to them. I'd like to give them a piece of my mind. I'd like to say, 'Hello, darling, don't you know that what you're doing is generally considered to be embar-

rassing?' Ah, but life is too short to waste time on their sort."
Doesn't it piss you off when some old bag who thinks she's special
because she used to be something way back when goes on about
the likes of us like that?'

As a former show singer Kaho wasn't going to be left out of this
conversation. 'Well, you know what I say about our kind? At least
we're free. That's something, isn't it? OK, we're just singers – we
don't have any power or fame – but, still, you can't beat that feeling when they like your work and bring out the tips, because you
know they give you the tips just because they like your singing –
not because you're famous or it's the done thing or whatever. Ah,
my singing – it was great, it really was fantastic.'

Spurred on by their passion, I, too, started to warm to the theme.
'Dead right, Kaho. These famous singers – the way they go on as
soon as they start selling a few units, you'd think they wouldn't be
seen dead in a health spa or a snack bar. But what's wrong with
singing in place like that? If you can please the punters, it doesn't
matter where you do your singing.'

'That right. That real right.' David cheerfully added his support. 'By the way, Rinka . . .' he continued, and suddenly got up
and stood right in front of me. I was a little unnerved. For a
moment I thought he was going to ask me about the deal with
Hiroshi Yumekawa, but my fears proved unfounded. '. . . no any
black?' He shoved his platinum-blond locks in my face, and I
feigned shock and amazement. Kenjiro moved in with the usual
flying kick.

'You stupid bastard.'

'Ow! Sorry. But I got nightmare about black hair, because I no
bleaching it these days.'

Kenjiro bashed David over the head with an aluminium ashtray
he found lying on the counter. David carried on making feeble
excuses as the cigarette ash spilt down his head.

Perhaps feeling some pity for him, Kaho pulled David away
from Kenjiro and gave him a protective hug. 'Cut it out, Ken.
David's doing the best he can, you know. Don't forget, he could
have been doing nice steady work at that Chinese restaurant if
you hadn't bullied him into becoming a singer.'

'Oh, whatever . . .' Sensing the mood of the meeting turning
against him, Kenjiro returned to his previous theme. 'Guys like us
sing because we've got nothing better to do. It didn't have to be
singing. Anything would have done, yeah? So long as it was smart
and flashy, and brought in the money without us having to do too

much real work.' I was stuck for a reply. Somehow I had the feeling that he'd got a little too close to the truth for comfort. 'Like, supposing some bloke came up to you and said how would you like to do a spot of acting, for really good money, say. What would you do? Say the guy flatters you, tells you you've got fantastic acting ability and all that. Whatever people might say in a situation like that, just about everybody would go for it in the end, 'coz it would seem like more fun, right?'

'Er, I wonder,' said Kaho.

'Um, maybe,' said I.

'What I'm saying is, cut the crap about how *singing* means so much to you. If you've got so much time on your hands for pompous whining, don't you think you might as well use the time a little better by figuring out how to bring in bigger tips?'

'Hm, maybe.'

'I guess you're right.'

Encouraged, Kenjiro stuck out his chest – not that there was much of it – and loudly proclaimed:

'In fifty years' time we won't be around any more. You only live once. So if you've got enough spare time for thinking about stuff, you might as well use that time to *do* stuff – stuff that pleases your body, stuff that pleases your soul.'

Kaho stared vacantly into space and said, 'Oh my God. Philosophy.'

Kenjiro sniggered and put one foot up on his bar stool. Then he slapped his hand down on the counter and said, 'Friends, we are people who live by the soul.' Great line.

Kaho's eyes were moist and she clung passionately to Kenjiro. 'You really are fantastic, Ken.'

We didn't really know what we were going on about, but somehow it felt right at the time. It was a good night out.

The following morning, while I was still half asleep, the sound of a calendar page being torn off came to my ears. September already.

'Oh, sorry. Did I wake you up?' Daiki came over in his work clothes and gave me an affectionate peck on the cheek.

'Er, what time is it?'

'It's six o'clock.' Six: he always gets up at around this time. He gets up so early that I'm hardly ever able to get up with him. I feel kind of bad about it, so I always wash the rice and set the timer on the electric cooker the night before, so at least he can have freshly cooked rice with his breakfast.

'September, eh?' Mr Wild gazes intently at the numbers on the calendar. I blearily look at them, too, from the bed. We may be looking at the same numbers, but our concerns are doubtless very different. For me, it's just a question of how many bookings I've got and how many more may come in during the course of the month. That's all. According to Mr Hirata, the boss of the agency I'm working for these days, the company functions as a sort of employment agency of last resort. Besides myself, there are about 120 artistes on the books, and every one of them is short of money. Seems they're all people who, for various reasons, just can't get along in regular society – some are drug addicts, some have criminal records, some are girlfriends of gangsters – but they also love music, or they're good at talking, or they're good at telling lies that make people feel good. Finding a place in society for these people – by sending them out across the nation to hot-spring resorts and cabarets, to festivals and events, there to perform as singers, comedians, MCs, magicians or strippers – such is the mission of Mr Hirata's talent agency.

We are all very grateful to him. However, with such a large family to look after, there is a limit to how much work the agency can find for each of us – in my case, about five bookings a month. Also, the money for each engagement is bad. Compared with the production company that Kenjiro and I used to be in, this one pays about 5,000 yen less per show, so a measly 13,000 yen. The way things are right now I really can't live by singing alone. Maybe I should start learning magic tricks and MC stage patter, or I'm never going to get rich.

What sort of concerns does Daiki have on his mind, I wonder, as he gazes at the numbers on the calendar? The number of days he has building work scheduled, payment dates agreed with clients, various instructions to issue? Perhaps, too, he's wondering how long it will be before his wife finds out about his double life. Maybe he's thinking, I should go home for a spell by and by. How much longer will the missus believe that I'm living in a dormitory at some rural construction site? Maybe she already thinks it's been too long.

'Fancy getting up and going to the building site with me?' Mr Wild is clearly in a good mood – probably because I haven't been getting much work lately. Oh, I know all about his thoughts on the subject; he showed me exactly how he felt about it last night, perhaps a little more frankly than he intended. He kissed and caressed me so delicately that he might have been putting the finishing touches to an oil painting – and then, well, it was hammer and tongs time. Ah, the pleasures of love. Once we were snuggled up comfortably afterwards, he broached the subject: 'I like your singing, don't get me wrong. I really think you've got talent. But from the point of view of the general public, who listen to you at hot springs and so on – well, they think you're just another tuppenny-ha'penny singer from nowhere, right? That kind of bothers me.' I'm used to that line.

Here's another one he quite often comes up with. 'The young guys at work keep asking me about you, Rinka. "That girlfriend of yours, she's a singer, right? When's she going to make her recording début? She wants to get on the big New Year variety show some day, right?" I really don't know how to answer them, truth to tell.'

Although I never try to hit back at Daiki, I could, if I wanted to, make a slightly similar complaint about him. 'I like you, Daiki, don't get me wrong. I think you're a real nice guy. But from the point of view of the general public – well, they think I'm just being trifled with, or even tricked. That kind of bothers me. My girlfriends keep asking me about you, Daiki. "You're living with a married man, yeah? When's he going to get divorced, then, so he can make an honest woman out of you? If he really loves you, he'll be wanting to marry you, no?" I really don't know how to answer them, truth to tell.' However, that isn't really how I feel about us – far from it. So I've never actually tried that line on Daiki.

Just then, the doorbell rang. Who the hell could it be at this hour of the morning? Daiki blanched.

'It's the wife.'

'What?' Our cover had apparently been blown. Mr Wild was plunged into confusion. Despite the fact that my belongings were scattered all over the room, he rather futilely grabbed my pink slippers and hid them behind the closet. I just cowered in the corner holding my breath, eyes wide and staring. I didn't want to lose everything. I wanted to keep things just as they were. Love: it's the finest stage a man and woman can share. And it only shines when you're away from the world of humdrum, everyday existence. For us to carry on being stars, we needed someone to work for us backstage, in charge of maintaining the steady tick-tock of well-regulated routine existence. But now it seemed that the stagehand was in open rebellion. This would never do.

'You . . . ?' False alarm. When Daiki peered through the spy-hole in the front door, the silhouette revealed there was not that of his beloved wife, it was Kaho Jojima. Why oh why?

'I'm awfully sorry. I must have given you a fright,' she said, accurately enough. Daiki unlocked the door and she tottered in. Clearly something was badly awry. For a start, she was dead drunk at six in the morning. She had probably fallen over in the street, for her beige coat was dirty and crumpled. She stood there in the hallway, not even bothering to take her shoes off.

'What happened?' I asked her. As I moved closer to Kaho, she crumpled her face up like a small child and burst into tears.

'Ken's gone,' she said.

'What's that?'

'He's left me.' Ignoring our dumb-struck expressions, Kaho's careworn face now broke into a weird smile, and she started quietly laughing. At last I found some words:

'You've had a bit of a quarrel, right? Well, anyway, why don't you come in and take the weight off your feet. Surely the two of you can kiss and make up?'

'It's different this time.' Bristling with impotent fury, she shook her tousled hair in all directions, then leant up against the wall and stood there silently shaking. Mantled in despair, she wouldn't even let me lay a comforting hand upon her shoulder.

'Anyway, please do come on in.' Daiki took her arm. Led by his powerful, warm, masculine strength, she wandered aimlessly into the room. Daiki took me aside and whispered in my ear. 'I think it'll be harder to talk with me around. Anyway, I've got to get off to work, so you look after her, OK?'

The moment Daiki was gone, Kaho burst into another flood of tears. 'Ken's run off on me hundreds of times – but this time it's for keeps. It's the end, I tell you.'

'I'm sure it's not as bad as you think.'

'Oh yes it is! It's all over: *finito*. And what a way to end it.' As though she was slowly immersing her body in cold water, Kaho very gingerly started to explain the recent turn of events. For a start, Kenjiro had found himself a new woman. She was a wealthy madam twice his age, a sugar mummy. Right away she'd rented a flat for him and sent around a removal company to clear all his stuff out of Kaho's place while she was out for the day. In just a few hours they'd removed all traces of him. 'I don't even know where he's gone,' wept Kaho. 'The flat's an empty shell. And to make things worse, the next thing is I get this phone call from an underling of the boss at a big production agency, asking me to come to a meeting at a coffee-shop. When I show up, he tries to give me some money to make me shut up and go away.'

I was all at sea. What business did big corporations have intervening in personal relations between a man and a woman? Kaho continued spitting out the words as though she were getting something dirty out of her mouth.

'You see, Rinka, he's going to make his major-label début, Ken is.' Something seemed to explode inside me. It wasn't a big explosion, however; more like the *phut* of a damp firework left over from the year before last. Kaho described how the underling had explained the situation to her in the coffee-shop, concluding by sliding across the table an envelope that contained a million yen. Not that she was to think of this as a pay-off to make her go away of course – it was far too modest a sum of money for that – but perhaps she would be thinking of moving house now that her domestic arrangements had been modified, in which case the cash might come in handy.

I sat there dumbfounded. As if I had just been informed of Kenjiro's death, scenes from my friendship with him flashed before my eyes. The Kenjiro we had known was gone. He had graduated. The bastard had been and gone and graduated from this world we shared and supposedly loved.

'He said that if I wanted some proper separation money I should get in touch and they would be happy to discuss the matter,' continued Kaho. 'But I couldn't face doing something that shabby. So I stood up, said nothing, took the bill for the coffee, paid for both of us and left the café. Of course, I left the money on the table, too.'

'I understand perfectly, Kaho. Quite right, too. What a star. Well done.'

'You should have seen the guy's face. I expect he thought I was going to throw a wobbly or something. But I just gave a little smile and stood up.'

'Fantastic, Kaho, absolutely fantastic.' The coffee I'd made for Kaho was stone cold by now, but she swilled it down in a single gulp, puffing and panting like a stranded elephant seal.

'I'm thirty-three now,' she said. 'I know I'm past the age when most people make their début, but I've still got one last chance.' Kaho appeared to have an audacious plan in mind to take her revenge on Kenjiro. 'I'm going to start by releasing my own CD – self-produced. I've got some money I'd been saving up to pay for

Kenjiro's next release. I can get the cash together right away. I'm gonna get a nationwide release, and I'm gonna outsell Ken.'

'What?'

'You should do the same. Or are you happy to be a health-spa star for the rest of your life? There are bigger markets out there, you know.'

'Well, yes, I suppose there are . . .'

'Ah, I feel great. I'll be much better off without Ken. I can't abandon my singing. I wouldn't commit a love suicide with a guy like Ken, but I would with jazz.' A love suicide with jazz? Music really is a devil, like those old bluesmen say. It's no exaggeration.

Since the history of the world began, I wonder how many tens of millions of people music has led into hunger, unhappiness and sometimes even death. It's scary to think of such a dangerous thing pervading our everyday lives, like water or air. If only you could see the harm music does to people in some tangible form, the government would have banned people from singing long ago. Hell, it's only a matter of squeezing a few sounds out of your voice; why is it considered so bloody cool? Singing's not even that different from talking, so why do people hold it in such awe? I had no satisfactory answer to this question, however. You can find reasons to explain why you like things, but there are no reasons to explain why certain things seem *cool*, whether you like them or not. So I just sing. And now Kaho, too, is going to sing – and Kenjiro, and David.

David: what would become of him now?

Kaho knew. 'He's going to be deported, Rinka. Someone from the sugar mummy's office shopped him to the immigration.'

'That's terrible.' I was outraged at the sheer heartlessness of it. Poor David. He'd always been anxious about his illegal status, always worrying that somebody might notice the black roots of his blonde-dyed hair. I could just picture the scene: the policemen barking questions, the defenceless David, head bowed, sitting there in silence. I couldn't bear to think of it. That bastard Kenjiro. Had he agreed to it?

'They're going to launch Ken's career in Taiwan. Apparently it's some kind of joint project with one of the Taiwanese production companies.'

Kenjiro, singing all over Asia. Uh-huh.

'C-cool!'

'Rinka? What are you going on about?'

I listened to the full story of the sensational plans for Kenjiro's début. And, guess what? I suddenly found that Kenjiro's voice, which until just now I wouldn't have given a flying fart for, was actually shimmering with glory and echoing in my ear. The guy actually had talent. Come to think of it, he'd always had that little something that set him apart from the rest – and I'd noticed that special quality, right from the days when he was still a hundred-yen singer. I always knew he had it in him. I'm like that. I can always spot talent. When I see a singer on television and think they're good, they always go on to enjoy fabulous careers. I've got an ear for it. Clever me.

I became immersed in myself. Before me I could see Kenjiro and all the other singing stars, so tiny that I could move them like around like chess pieces. Ah, what foolish things we people are.

'Oh no!'

'What's up?'

'Oh no.' Now that I'd let my thoughts surface as spoken words, I'd have to reveal all. 'If only I'd known, I could have got his autograph before everyone else. And also –'

'And also what?'

'I shouldn't have turned him down – at the love hotel in Uguisudani.'

'Rinka!' Kaho stared at me as if I were a complete and utter idiot. At length she seemed to run out of patience and went off home without another word.

'I see. And is Kaho getting over it?' Daiki was relieved that nothing worse had happened. He'd been worrying about Kaho all day and had even cried off from another session with the lads at the sushi shop. 'OK, let's see about supper. Would you mind popping out and getting some beer while I'm cooking?'

'All right.' I went to the supermarket to buy some cans of beer. It was just a short ride away, even on my rusty old bicycle that squeaked incessantly as I rode along. Left at the crossroads, zip through the alley between the pub and the laundry, and there it is: it's a very familiar route to me.

Into the shop; the booze is in a refrigerated cabinet at the back. My feet move briskly forwards, my hand reaches out and seizes a six-pack of the appropriate brand. Daiki likes domestic beer. I used occasionally to buy some of those fancy imported beers, attracted by their pretty bottles and labels, but he never showed much enthusiasm for them. To go with his beer he likes clams and smoked shad; when it comes to tuna, he likes it moderately fatty – actually, I'm gradually getting to share his tastes. We've already been together two years: sometimes it feels like *only* two years, sometimes it feels like *already* two years. Come to think of it, my love affair with singing is also in its second year.

As I came through the door on my return, the fax machine in the corner of the room was chuntering away. To my ear, the squeaking and rumbling of the fax is sweet, sweet music, for it generally means I've got a booking. The fax machine gave a final high-pitched squeal and relapsed into silence, leaving three sheets of paper lying on the carpet. I picked them up and took a look. All these jobs were going to involve travelling, but they looked like attractive gigs for all that.

> From Tsurukame Productions Inc.
> You have been engaged for the period September 21st (Sat) to 25th (Wed).
> Location: The Washington Baths Health Spa, Nagoya.
> Showtime: 2 p.m. and 8 p.m. daily.
> Each show to last at least 45 minutes and to be composed mainly of enka.
> Costume: Two outfits a day.
> Accommodation: On the premises (TV provided).
> Meals: Lunch and dinner provided by client.
> Transportation: Tokyo–Nagoya roundtrip bullet-train ticket provided.
> You are advised to set out from Tokyo station around 9 a.m.
> Sales of cassette tapes are permitted on the premises. (Please keep prices reasonable and refrain from hustling the customers.)

The fax had originally been sent by the client in Nagoya to my agency, the Tsurukame Corporation. The agency had passed it on to me. In this way do requests come in to Tsurukame from hot-spring resorts, cabarets and people planning events all over Japan. The agency has to divide up the work between the 120 artistes on its books, which is no easy task. The agency has to consider which artiste might be best suited to each job, which artiste is going to get on well with which employer and a host of other factors, yet, with a calculating capacity that would put a super-computer to shame, the people there make each decision more or less instantaneously, using a professional instinct honed over many long years. If they get it wrong, they can expect loud complaints, so it's a serious game they play.

'Supper's ready. Got some lovely traditional Japanese fare for you tonight. Let's tuck in.' Mr Wild is an excellent cook. The moment I heard those words of his, my stomach started rumbling and I threw the three sheets of paper aside in a childlike dash for the dinner-table.

'I'm starving. *Bon appetit.*'

'Hey, try not to chuck your food around. Don't eat so fast. Dear oh dear, for a supposedly elegant enka singer you have bloody awful table manners.'

I was so hungry that I was reduced to breathing through my nose because my mouth was full. I was making little snuffling noises through my nostrils, like an old bluesman on the saxophone or maybe more like the snuffling of a cat tearing into a bowl of food.

'You're an animal, you are.' Even Mr Wild was somewhat shocked at the spectacle.

First thing the next morning I ring up the agency to check a few details about the bookings on the faxes. I punch in the number and the telephone starts to ring. It rings five times, ten times, fifteen times. At last somebody picks it up, but there's a noisy crashing sound at the other end. Probably my boss, Mr Hirata, has dropped the receiver on the floor.

'Hello.' He finally comes on the line, with that characteristic note of barely restrained desperation in his voice. He always sounds out of breath, like a marathon runner who's just made it to the finishing line. 'Kazuki? Oh yeah, yeah, Rinka Kazuki, the new girl. With you now.'

Another thing about Mr Hirata's voice is a sort of sadness that seems to pervade his breathless speech. A marathon runner who's given it his all but hasn't managed to win the race.

'Yes, it's me. Thank you very much for everything you're doing for me.'

Tsurukame Productions has been in business for over fifteen years. In Japan they call this kind of showbiz-talent delivery company a 'box shop' after the roaming musicians who used to wander around Japan carrying their instruments in a wooden box. Mr Hirata runs the office in Minami-Aoyama with the help of a few girls to do the clerical work, but he nearly always answers the telephone himself. There must be something in his character that won't let him delegate.

'You got those faxes yesterday, did you, Rinka? I want all three of those shows done in kimono, please.' Kimono – how nice. I always think a kimono goes much better with enka than a Western-style dress. And, actually, I've just bought a rather gorgeous long-sleeved kimono from a second-hand dealer, so the timing couldn't be better. I'm so pleased that I want to thank Mr Hirata.

'Actually, I think kimono are really –' lovely, I was going to say, but before I can finish the sentence I'm cut off by a voice like a thunderstorm.

'You're supposed to be a professional. A pro, right? So just quit the moaning and wear it, *please*.' I'm too surprised to muster an immediate reply, but I pull myself together and patiently explain that I actually *like* wearing a kimono. I explain in a voice that is aggrieved, loud and clear – but not quite clear enough, evidently. Mr Hirata pays no attention at all to the content. Responding only to the aggrieved tone, he scolds me even louder than before.

'Oh, honestly! All the singers hate kimono these days. Such a bloody nuisance. The things they say. It's too heavy to carry around, it's too hot and sticky to wear, it's a hassle, it takes too long to change so I can't get home in time – God, I've had it up to here with silly little girls whining about their flaming kimonos.'

I make several valiant attempts to tell him that I'm not that sort of girl. My hand gets all sweaty, and the telephone receiver starts slipping around as I struggle to keep a grip on it. It's squirming around like an eel. The tighter I grip it, the more it squirms. It squirms, it slips and it slithers – just like the conversation. The two of us just aren't making sense at all. In Mr Hirata's mind, any utterance by a showgirl of anything other than 'yes' and 'no' is automatically considered to be a complaint or objection. The old man has no doubt spent years and years listening to people say things he really doesn't want to hear. In the depth of his disillusionment with the pronouncements of the singers he's managed over the years, he's kind of edited out all the content, treating everything they say as one rather irritating noise.

'Well, er, um, I'll just do my best anyway.'

At the sound of those words, Mr Hirata's tone finally softens. 'That job at the Red Leaf Festival,' he said, 'we were going to give it to someone who's been with us for about five years, but I thought I'd let you have a try at it. This is a test, OK? We've been getting some fairly favourable reports about you, so here's a chance to show us what you can do. As I think you know, these engagements pay the usual 13,000 yen per show. The client will pay your travel expenses.' He jabbers on and on, and then he suddenly flies into another totally unprovoked rage. 'And don't you go telling me that 13,000 yen isn't good enough in this day and age. You should hear the way they all complain about the money. Now just look here, there are plenty of people out there working in miserable part-time jobs for a few hundred yen an hour, I'll have you know. Compared with that, you girls are living in the lap of luxury. The lap of luxury, I said. Oh, just a sec, I've got a call on the other line.'

I can just see him, sitting there at his desk with a telephone to each ear. No doubt I'll now be left holding the line like an idiot. He's kept me waiting like that for ten minutes or more in the past, and when I do finally regain his attention he's perfectly capable of saying, 'OK, so that's understood', and hanging up on me. I'm used to this now, and I generally hang up at my end for the sake of the telephone bill. He's never complained about me doing that; I wonder whether he even notices.

On this particular occasion, however, I decide not to hang up, since he seems to be having rather an interesting conversation on the other line on which it might be worth eavesdropping. 'How many times have you let us down now? We can't look after you like a nanny, you know. Got that? Look, you show up late, you forget your scores, you forget the lyrics and the melody, you'll forget your own bloody name next. You're a disgrace to the whole bloody profession.' Click. That would appear to be the end of that conversation. But he turns out to have another caller on hold. 'I see. Well, as I told you before, that girl used to be on our books, but it's been several years now since she left us, so I'm sure you understand that my company really isn't in a position to take on her credit-card debt. Her current address? I'm afraid considerations of personal privacy prohibit me from disclosing it. Awfully sorry.'

At last he comes back to my line. 'Ha-ha-ha. Oh, dear me. Rinka, I know you're an honest, hard-working lass and I'm sure I won't have this kind of trouble with you, but really . . . You wouldn't believe the number of debt collectors who come and badger us over unpaid credit cards and loan defaults. I have to see all these sharks off, and you wouldn't believe what a pain it can be.'

There's really nothing I can say to that, and Mr Hirata rings off shortly after. But just before he does he has one more thing to tell me. 'Oh, by the way, Rinka, this is kind of important, so listen carefully and don't forget. As of now, you are officially twenty-two years old. All right?'

'Twenty-two?'

Click, brrrrrrrrrrr.

This is going to be tough. The gap between my stage age and my real age keeps widening. Now I'm thirty-four, but on stage I've gone from twenty-six to twenty-four, and now I've shed another two years. The first thing is to check my new Chinese horoscope sign. It's a favourite topic among the old folks at the health spas, and it's got me into trouble before. And when I'm feeling mellow from a nice hot-spring bath, I'll have to avoid carelessly humming some outdated pop song that doesn't match my stage age. Well, I could get away with old enka since they're in my job description, but I'd have to leave out songs by groups like the Pink Ladies, who were in the charts when I was a real teenager. I used to imitate the Pink Ladies' dance style when I was at school, and my arms and legs tend to respond automatically when one of their numbers comes on the radio. I'll have to watch out for that. I'll have to stop wearing sleeveless dresses, too, since they reveal all those little scars left by vaccinations they stopped giving children in the 1970s. What a drag. Why do I have to go to all this trouble to deceive the audience? Anyone would think I was a criminal or something.

Pop Idols and Their Hit Songs from the Good Old Days; *The Sixties and Seventies File* – these nostalgic song books are essential accessories for any singer trying to conceal her true age. Displayed prominently, they offer a handy explanation for the surprising depth of the young girl's knowledge of music that was popular before she was supposed to have been born. Meanwhile, I'm still cross with Mr Hirata for the way he treated me over the telephone. Just a few simple words about a forthcoming engagement, and he's managed to spread a dark cloud right across my heart. And for some time after he's hung up, this horrible feeling of disgust keeps lingering. I've had that feeling many times before, but I still can't get used to it. There was a time when I used to try to avoid it by pretending it wasn't there. Now that I *am* thinking about it, it seems to me that every time I get into an unpleasant conversation it feels as if a great black sadness has come over me, like a blot of Indian ink spreading across my breast. It might be just a word out of place from one of the bandsmen or from one of my fellow singers – any silly little thing. It used to be that when those nasty words came rushing into my ears, I just had to go to the toilet and wash my hands – scrub, scrub, scrub. I'd wash my hands so hard that they'd get quite red and raw. I never noticed until someone in the audience pointed it out to me when we were shaking hands after a show. I was quite surprised, as a matter of fact.

I managed to get out of that particular habit before it became completely pathological, once I became aware of the problem and started talking about it with a few close friends in the profession and writing about it in my diary. Now that I keep myself under close observation, I've quite calmed down and I'm fine.

You know, all too many people in the lower ranks of show business have let the profession completely take over their lives and destroy their souls. It's something I really can't stand. Practically every showgirl and MC I know has gone that way. When they talk to you, their eyes are always shifting restlessly around, as though they're looking for the day after tomorrow: arrangements, arrangements, arrangements; time, time, time. Their conversation is all arranged, and their lives are all arranged, too. Their eyes tell you that they've got it all sorted out. Their attitude says that there are no more surprises that could possibly interrupt their personal long-term forecast. When they speak a word, the spirit of the word isn't there. Body and soul have separated for good, and all they are concerned with is getting the next arrangement sorted out. They're like balloon people: soft, light things with nothing in them but air. Their ears are designed not to hear any thoughts given voice by other humans. Crackle and blaze. Chuck the lot of them on the fire. Roast them one and all, see the warped and empty pots amid the flames of the furnace. Look at their ugly swollen bottoms – they can't even stand up. They're rolling around in the alcove. You can't even put seasonal flowers in them. And while you look on, they are transformed into blunt instruments, shapeless things for hitting people over the head with.

One dream, too many people rushing into it. One by one they burst, all of their own accord. Poor old Mr Hirata. He's clearly had his nerves shot by having to look after these empty gourds for so many years. It's not his fault. He's a humanitarian, a guy who's full of the volunteer spirit. But beyond Mr Hirata I can always see a great sea of slime. Even while I'm talking to him, I can catch a glimpse of dozens – no hundreds – of slime people, squirming and writhing, and I can sense an involuntary scream of terror rising within me. And here's what the slime people say:

'I don't really want to do this kind of work. When I finally make it on to the big stage, I'll change my makeup and my wardrobe, and I'll have a completely new image.'

'What you see here is just a "temporary" me. The real me is going to be in action on television, climbing up the charts, 'coz I know I've got the ability to make it all happen. Ah, television. To appear on television. I can't stand working in those health spas with an audience of senile old grannies and granddads.'

Public opinion is rather dismissive of the likes of me. Just the other day I got a postcard from an old friend who was at school with me. Apparently she's married with kids these days. She'd heard a rumour from someone about my having become a singer, so she kindly sent me an encouraging note:

I hear you're travelling all over the place doing shows these days. Don't get downhearted. Keep on fighting. You carry on chasing your dream. Go, go, go! Something good is sure to turn up sooner or later.

Something good is sure to turn up – that was a bit of a shock. I'd prefer to think I was doing something good already. Another time, the boss of one of the health spas had this to say to me:

'No recording début yet, I hear. What, you're not interested in that side of things? Well, of course, there are a lot of singers who take that view, though I do wonder a bit about these singers who do it just for a hobby, you know?' A hobby. This is a job that I get paid to do, so is it really right to call it a hobby? Those guys who do the puppet shows in the parks, don't they have the right to make a living out of their art?

The audiences at the hot springs and health spas mean everything to me. However, I do sometimes think about my life the way I think about my shows: does it go down well with the audience? I want everybody to reassure me. 'Yes, you definitely are a happy person. I envy you.' What a luscious world that would be.

When I'm thinking about these things, my soul feels as if it's about to be torn apart. What do I really want out of life? Food to eat, plenty of sleep and my carnal desires thoroughly satisfied. If that's all there is to it, well, no problem – and yet, although my present lifestyle does conform to that old yearning of mine, to follow my dream and still have food on the table, somehow I still feel that my motor is idling, that I'm not really going anywhere.

The 21st of September duly came, and I headed off to the health spa in Nagoya. The night before, I'd been checking the weather on television. The biggest typhoon since World War II was supposed to be approaching Japan, and they were broadcasting updates on its progress at thirty-minute intervals. That was kind of worrying, but the day itself dawned bright enough, with strong winds but nothing too serious. For once I was without my trundle-trolley, having packed up five days' worth of stage-clothing – two shows a day, so ten outfits – and sent them off to Nagoya in advance by delivery service.

Arriving in Nagoya, I took the Higashiyama subway line, changed to the Tsurumai line and made my way to the Washington Baths.

On the first day I did a pretty good opening show and then headed for the waters. I'd been looking forward to this moment. This establishment had about ten different kinds of bath, and the first one I checked out was the outdoor rock pool. Sinking slowly into the warm mineral waters, I took in the gorgeous sunlit colours of the surrounding trees. Here and there the leaves had already turned from green to russet – it was a lovely sight to behold. Then I had a good soak in the sauna, before proceeding to the 'Akasuri Corner' for the massage I'd booked earlier.

Akasuri is a Korean style of massage, which involves very vigorous rubbing to peel off layers of dead skin and thereby uncover your hidden beauty and let the living skin breathe. Sure enough, my masseuse was a fat, middle-aged Korean lady, dressed only in the black bra and shorts that are like a uniform in her profession. The first thing she did was switch on a battered old cassette player she kept by the bed. The strains of Cho-Yon Pil singing 'Haste Ye Back to Pusan Harbour' in the original Korean came wafting through the room. Sprawled naked on the massage bed, I instinctively started to hum along. The massage lady was most surprised and asked if I could speak Korean. I hurriedly explained that I couldn't, but, being a professional singer, I'd learnt a few of the more famous Korean songs. She seemed pleased to learn that she had a singer for a client.

The Korean lady got down to work with her akasuri towel, rubbing my body furiously until little bits of skin started to come off.

I felt a faint, dull pain, but it didn't bother me much so long as I didn't pay it any attention. A little pain is a good sign that the grime is coming off nicely. I politely observed that Koreans always seem to be excellent singers. The akasuri lady said that she must be the exception that proved the rule. It's true, though. Every now and then you come across a singer whose voice is so lovely it really sends shivers down your spine. More often than not the owner of that voice turns out to be Korean, or at least half Korean. That Hiroshi Yumekawa, for instance – with his singing so passionate you might expect to see ectoplasm floating out of his mouth at any moment – he, too, is rumoured to be of mixed Japanese and Korean blood. What on earth makes Koreans so good at singing? I wondered out loud. The akasuri lady merely smiled and told me that if I ate plenty of spicy kim-chee every day I'd soon find my own voice improving.

It was fun to have a few jokes with her, but as the massage continued that dull pain gradually became harder to bear. It slowly settled all over my body, like snow settling on a landscape. Around my temples I felt a sharper pain, the kind you get if you bite on an ice lolly with a sensitive tooth. At last the massage finished and the akasuri lady stepped back in a glow of satisfaction.

'Look how much you've lost,' she proudly said. Turning over on to my stomach, I looked at the sheet I'd been lying on. It was covered with little white rolls of dead skin, like the little bits of rubber that come off an eraser. I was too embarrassed to come up with a suitable reply to her comment. 'Do come again,' the Korean lady continued and gave me a big friendly slap on my naked back. Her kind gesture left a tingling sensation all over me as I walked back to the outdoor bath. Catching sight of myself in a mirror, I turned my back and could see the red outline of her hand still clearly visible there.

When I came back on for the evening show, the Korean lady was sitting on the tatami floor, mingling with the audience. I was about to welcome her in person through the mike, but then I noticed her hurriedly putting a finger to her lips, so I changed the subject. She was even wearing the same kind of light bathrobe as the customers – obviously she'd skived off work to take in the show. I hoped she wouldn't get into trouble if her boss spotted her.

The show was a huge success, with many of the people who'd been at the matinée performance coming back for a second helping. Once I'd got them in the mood I made my usual imperious descent from the stage to give them a chance to show their appreciation in the time-honoured fashion. Four or five of them did, in fact, oblige with tips, and then I saw the akasuri lady also fumbling to fit something between her disposable chopsticks. I gladly accepted the donation and was slightly surprised to find that instead of cash she'd given me a little carnet of free tickets for the akasuri massage. No doubt it was an invitation to come back for more tomorrow. An involuntary little spasm of pain ran through my temples at the thought. Still, it was very kind of her.

The show ended and I returned to my room. They keep one of the guest rooms open for the entertainers to stay in, a little Japanese-style room with tatami mats. At mealtimes they bring you your food, and when you've finished eating you just put the tray outside the door and they take it away. You sing on your own, you eat on your own, you get ready for each show on your own, and in the end you go home on your own. There's nothing like the life of a travelling entertainer to remind you that you really are alone. When I say that, I don't just mean on your own as in not being married or not living with your family. No, I'm talking in more fundamental terms, like maybe it's too obvious to mention, but I am a single human being. You get born on your own and you die on your own, those are basic facts of life for anyone, but what about enjoying yourself on your own? There's no doubt about it, I did a really fantastic show tonight; the crowd loved it. But I have no CD out there, and at the end of the day I'm really just singing for my own pleasure – although perhaps that ought to bring some satisfaction to me personally.

A second night passed and a third. Gradually the pit of depression I'd dug for myself in the little room grew deeper. The nice Korean akasuri lady who'd cheered me up on the first day was replaced by a different woman on the second day, and I never got to see the first one again. I asked about her at reception, and they told me she only came in on Saturdays. Disappointed, I went back to my room.

I got out the futon, and although it was too early to go to sleep I lay down on it anyway. Wanting to keep my luggage to a minimum, I hadn't even brought a book with me. There was no telephone in the room, and although there were several public telephones in the lobby I knew I wouldn't be able to speak privately to Daiki or my friends because of the old people sitting on the sofa right next to the payphones. This was a roadside health spa out in the country, and there was nothing whatever to see or do in the area – and I do mean nothing, not even a shop. Just then I remembered the television I'd seen stored in the wardrobe, and suddenly sat up on the futon. Television!

It was an ancient set, and it looked broken. When I switched it on, however, it did respond. The picture was pretty rough, but you could just about make out what was going on. My heart jumped.

'Aha!'

There was a variety show on. Normally I would have thought it a load of silly nonsense, but for some reason on this particular occasion I felt exceedingly grateful for it. Somehow the feeble puns and crass anecdotes made the time pass easily, and when I happened to glance at the clock I was surprised to find that I'd been watching for fully two hours. I switched it off, turned out the lights and snuggled up in my futon with a nice comfortable feeling as I prepared to drift off to sleep.

'Thank you, God, for creating the television.' In my mind, I pictured myself kneeling before the square black box and bowing in gratitude. 'I'm far gone, I am.' Far gone, indeed.

Grieving for what I had become, I finally went to sleep.

This Nagoya job was a five-day trip – a very long one by my standards. I was worried about how Daiki might be getting on back home. I'd never taken a job that would keep me away from home for more than three days before, and when I signed on with the agency I told them I didn't want engagements of more than three days because I had a sick relative to look after at home and I couldn't get anyone to take over the nursing for more than three days. This time they must have forgotten about that, and I, too, had absent-mindedly agreed to a five-day gig.

Daiki doesn't like me going away for shows, and the longest his nerves can stand it is three days. After three days away I could just about put his troubled heart back in order, although not without expending considerable time and effort. And this time there would be five whole days of damage to repair. The day I finished the last show I was in such a hurry to get home that I felt sweat gradually spreading across the back of my neck as the bullet train headed for Tokyo. The last show finished at eight, and by the time I bundled myself on to the nine-thirty train, the accumulated days of hard work were making themselves felt, and I was in a state of complete exhaustion. Compounding this,

I found, to my great annoyance, that there was nowhere for me to sit on the train. I didn't have a seat reserved, and the non-reserved carriages were packed with luggage and people. In the aisles there were crowds of people, myself included, falling over each other in the desperate search for an empty seat. Cursing the office for being too mean to pay the little bit extra to get me a reservation, I adopted my usual strategy in this situation: squatting down in the narrow space between the last row of seats and the back wall of the carriage. One time I tried spreading out some newspaper in that little space and sitting on it. But I soon gave up on that bright idea when I realized that the whole area was crawling with tiny cockroaches.

I don't suppose anyone would believe just how many cockroaches make their home in those smart, high-speed, super-express trains. They're cute little things, whose main pleasure in life is to scramble for the crumbs that passengers drop from their sandwiches. They're not like the big cockroaches you often find in the kitchen – no, they're tiny things, each one about the size of a sesame seed. Just casually looking around me I could see about thirty of them right now. Occasionally, one of them would absent-mindedly wander into the aisle, there to be sent to cockroach heaven or wherever it is they go when squashed flat. Sometimes a particularly enterprising one would climb up on somebody's shoe, only to slide regretfully back to earth on discovering that there was nothing to eat up there. Looking down on these tiny creatures made me feel as if I'd become some kind of god, embarrassingly enough.

At last the train reached Tokyo. I changed to a local train and finally made it back to East Kawaguchi. I ran desperately through the streets back to the flat, as if I'd suddenly remembered that I'd left the kettle on. People I passed on the way looked at me in some surprise. What on earth was getting into me? My own pathetic behaviour brought tears welling up, and the street lights started to blur before me. Just got to keep running, running for one thing.

I want to be loved blindly.

I want to love myself blindly.

I hold the real me in both hands. I mustn't kill it. At all costs I mustn't do that. I continue to struggle, wildly, hopelessly, but of necessity. For this is the melody of my life.

7 The Dregs of Dreams

'Hey, Rinka, get this. Kenjiro's actually going to make his major début. He's going to be on TV next week.'

'Really? Are you sure, Kaho?'

There's a supermarket on the ground floor of our block of flats. I often bump into Kaho when I'm shopping for groceries there. After Kenjiro left her, Kaho moved out of their flat and into a room in this block, just one floor up from Daiki and me. She must have been feeling lonely. She quit her job at the massage parlour, and she was hell bent on relaunching her singing career. However, it takes time to find places where they'll have you to sing, and the net result was that she started slowly frittering away the money she had earmarked for her major début on everyday living expenses. In a situation like that you feel anxious if you don't have someone near by to share your troubles with. I firmly believe that people who understand one anothers' feelings should be there for each other.

There's only one small problem, however. These days I find Kaho unbearable. I wonder when I started feeling this way – anyway, it's all her fault. Since Kenjiro left her she's changed completely. Sometimes the words that come spilling out of those big fat lips of hers are simply unforgivable.

'Ah, Rinka. Would you mind showing me two or three of your scores? There are a couple of things I want to ask you about.' That was an odd request to make in a supermarket, but I dutifully toddled off to my room and came back with two or three of my show scores. She grabbed them out of my hands, clutched them tightly to her and made a rapid beeline for the photocopying machine in the corner of the shop.

'Hey, what do you think you're doing?'

'You don't mind, do you? I'll just run off a quick set of copies as study aids for these phrases I want you to teach me.'

'What?'

Then the penny dropped. All that stuff about wanting me to teach her phrases was a pack of lies. What she really wanted to do was copy my scores so she could use them herself.

'Hey, stop that,' I shouted at Kaho, grabbing her arm. All the housewives doing their shopping promptly turned to look at us with unconcealed curiosity. I released Kaho's arm. Perhaps it would be easier to discuss this matter in the privacy of my own room. I dragged her out of the supermarket and back to my place.

'What on earth has happened to you, Kaho?' I pounded the tatami mats furiously with my fists. Before my eyes was a pile of my precious song scores. Kaho didn't seem to appreciate the enormity of her crime, so I would have to spell it out for her slowly and patiently.

'But, Rinka, I knew that if I asked you properly for a copy of your scores you'd only say no. So . . . You know I'm having a real tough time these days just trying to make ends meet.'

'Kaho, this is *theft*.' It costs a lot of money to get someone to write up a decent arrangement of a song for you, and if you're an unknown, poverty-stricken singer it's a huge investment. But for that very reason a conscientious singer will take great care over selecting pieces and getting them arranged in a key that fits her vocal range and a style that fits her stage persona. Put it this way: for singers like me, our scores are our livelihood.

But not all singers are conscientious. There are some who would rather spend their money on stage finery. As for the music, a few quick photocopies of other people's scores will do fine. Bandsmen know all about them, so every time they play at somebody's show one of them is liable to take the first opportunity to nip out to the nearest convenience store and photocopy the songs. The shameless bastard will then sell them off cheap to some equally shameless singer. And as long as this continues to be the prevailing standard of ethics in the music industry, we unknown singers will continue to be thought of as a bunch of losers.

'But, Rinka, you told me you didn't actually pay for those scores yourself, right? I know all about it. You've got that dirty old man who charges other people but does it free for you because he fancies you, right? Didn't you say you'd saved yourself close to a million yen in arrangement fees because of that guy?' Kaho hurled more and more abuse at me and my scores. OK, I admit it, I get them for free off this guy, just like I get my singing lessons for free from Teruo Hikari. All that has nothing to do with love or sexual attraction or anything like that. But what was the point of trying to explain to Kaho about the spirit of music I shared with those guys? She'd never understand.

Making a mighty effort to repress the utter revulsion for Kaho that I could feel rising, I attempted a calm, rational explanation. Unfortunately, I was so exasperated that I could not prevent a few warm teardrops from trickling down my cheek as I spoke.

'All right, Kaho, let's suppose for the sake of argument that what you say is true. Well – don't you feel ashamed of yourself for trying to steal copies of these crappy songs that you say you despise so much?'

'You're pretty much stealing them yourself in the first place.'

'And, besides, these are enka songs. You hate enka. Supposing you did manage to copy my scores, what would you do with them?'

'You get more work with enka. You can't go around the health spas singing jazz. I need to get hold of some songs that will put food on the table. I want to keep the jazz separate from that. I want to do my jazz singing in a pure world of art, where I don't have to think about eating or not eating. So copies will do fine for enka.'

'Kaho, that is blasphemy against music.'

'Why's it blasphemy? I told you I'd be happy to die for jazz, yeah? I did tell you about the love suicide, right?'

'Frankly, Kaho, you and jazz can both go and hang yourselves from the nearest tree for all I care. You want to use enka like a box to stand on when you put the rope on, is that it?'

'Rinka, I'm sorry, but I do just hate enka.'

'Oh, I see. Well, there we differ. I may dislike certain songs, but I prefer not to dismiss entire genres out of hand. You know what you are, Kaho? You are a pathetic, miserable caterpillar. You're a weakling, and you'll never be true to yourself. I've had enough of you, Kaho. I can see it, real clear. Our friendship is over. We're through.' We're through. Hm, I had to admit the phrase had a certain playground ring to it, a failure that I regretted. Nevertheless, I propelled her firmly through the front door and slammed it behind her as forcefully as I could. I could hear her wailing on the other side, 'Stingy bastard!' Then there was the rapid clacking of her sandals disappearing up the stairs. For a moment I closed my eyes and leant against the door. It was just too pathetic. With friends like that . . .

She really had changed. An unknown prima donna who demanded everything for free: free music scores, free lessons, free this, free that. Introduce me to this agency, give me that telephone number, give me food, give me drink – gimme, gimme, gimme. She was the pits. Yet she'd once had spirit. When I gave her that 10,000-yen note out of my tip-money, she'd blown her nose on it, crumpled it up and shoved it back at me with a look on her face that was a challenge to battle. What had happened to that obscure but proud jazz singer I had once known? People are so fragile. The Kaho I used to know had got broken somehow. Instead, what we had now was just a pig that happened to have Kaho's face. Kaho – or, maybe, 'Gaho', like the snuffling sound pigs make when they're looking for food in the compost heap: Gaho the Pig. Got any spare jobs you can pass my way? Got any easy-money work you don't need? If you have, gimme, gimme, snuffle, snuffle, gaho, gaho, oink, oink. This pig went through life with her snout on the ground, like a human Hoover, always trying to suck up any goodies she could sniff out. She was one of the circus freaks you find on the fringes of show business: Gaho, the Human Pig.

The phrase fitted her so well that I gave a little involuntary laugh. Gaho the Pig, you are weak. Weak people have no place in my dreams. So fuck off, and don't come back, because I can't stand the sight of you.

Ah, here we go again. That old battle between wanting to dream and needing to eat. You can't write music without having a blank sheet of paper first. I won't kill my true spirit. Never. Where am I going? Just drifting, drifting endlessly on this sea that has no tides, never arriving anywhere. Not even picking up any sea shells. I appear to have become a jellyfish, floating oh so lightly on the waters of the sea.

I sleep deeply in the bus, my heart still heavy over yesterday's quarrel with Kaho.

'So. Here goes with the Red Leaf Festival.' The girl sitting next to me is smiling brightly. Although she's an enka singer, she's got this crazy close-cropped hair. But she used to be a model as a young teenager, and with her face it actually looks cool. She has an elegant, aristocratic nose, too. My biggest complex is about my piggy little nose, and I can't help stealing frequent glances at her elegant profile.

Titter. She's having a little laugh. Oh dear, has she noticed me staring at her? Flustered, I try to act like I wasn't looking at anything in particular.

'Sorry, Rinka, it's just that you've been asleep almost the whole time since we got on this bus.'

Shiomi Genkainada, the former model, has been in the business since she was sixteen. Even when she was little she used to win every amateur song contest in sight. She hasn't made the big début yet. Her mother, who also serves as her manager and is on the bus with us today, used to sing in the shows herself, and told her to start by paying her dues on the circuit. Shiomi's sales point is her passionate, uplifting style of singing. She will be top of the bill on the giant open-air stage at the Ose Red Leaf Festival, which is where we're all heading. Among the support acts are myself, Hiroshi Yumekawa, a couple of comedians who mimic showbiz personalities and a guy who runs a monkey theatre, along with five gibbering macaques who will be appearing in his dramatic presentation. We're all bouncing about together in the same bus.

'I was just thinking you must be a really nice person, Rinka.' Shiomi gave an innocent laugh. I saw what she meant. Everyone else in the bus was wide awake, and there was quite an air of tension as all the artistes and their managers and promoters tried to maintain strictly formal relations, reflecting their relative degree of seniority. And I'd just been snoring merrily through it all.

'Back from the Land of Nod, are we?' said Mr Hirata, as he came and sat on the foldaway seat between me and Hiroshi Yumekawa, a can of hot tea in his hand. 'That's all right, dear. You take it nice and easy.'

Mr Hirata was quite transformed from the man who'd treated me so brusquely on the telephone. Now he was ever so friendly towards me. The reason was very simple: during my stay at the health spa in Nagoya I'd taken the trouble to send him a picture postcard. 'Hope you're well. I'm sure you are, since we spoke so recently on the telephone. The autumn leaves are beginning to turn red here in Nagoya. You always seem so busy, but do please take good care of your health . . .' Just a conventional little note, really. However, according to Mr Hirata that was the first time in his entire career that one of his artistes had bothered to send him a picture postcard.

People change, just as everything in nature changes with the cycle of the seasons. Even an old log, rotting away in the winter, will put out new shoots when spring comes. I expect even Gaho the Pig will put out new shoots some time. She'll go back to being the brave and imperious Kaho of old, no doubt. I gave a little inner sigh.

The blazing red leaves went flowing past outside the window. While marvelling at the sheer life force of this display that covered entire mountains, I couldn't help worrying about Kaho. If only we could get back to the way we used to be. It was almost like praying. But, to be honest, the thought also occurred to me that I really didn't have time to look after Kaho right now. She would have to sort things out by herself.

'You know, I used to be handsome in my youth,' said Mr Hirata, and with a shy smile he produced a tatty old photograph from his pocket book. It showed a smiling youthful Adonis clutching a folk guitar. You could make out a microphone stand, too.

'President Hirata! You were a singer yourself.' I squealed with excitement, and he flushed crimson and laughed in embarrassment. He added that he'd actually put out a record at the time – just the one, mind.

'Well, in the old days, all you had to do was win one of those amateur song contests and you'd be making records in no time,' he remarked. 'Kind of different from how things are now. It's much tougher for singers these days.'

'These days a lot of the record companies won't make a disc for you even if you offer to pay them!' This comment came from a portly former sushi chef sitting just behind us. He was fifty-five and had made his enka-singing début this March with a comic song entitled 'A Tune About Tuna'.

'Yep, it's really hard to get a record out these days. That's why you just have to grab any chance that comes your way.' Sitting on the other side of Mr Hirata from me, Hiroshi gave me a little wink to accompany the comment. Just then Mr Hirata's attention was distracted by another passenger, and Yumekawa took the opportunity to address me *sotto voce*:

'I've been waiting for that phone call,' he said, in a husky whisper that would send shivers down any woman's spine. 'You're a cold one, you are.' I started. 'Don't leave me all on my own now,' he added. He tried to round off this persuasive gambit by flashing me a very flirtatious sideways glance, but unfortunately Mr Hirata was just turning back from his conversation with the person in the seat behind, and he caught the full force of Yumekawa's bedroom eyes. The boss was most surprised, and his eyes opened out like dinner plates.

'We know all about you and the ladies,' said Mr Hirata, 'but I didn't know you, er, swung both ways.'

'Ah, ah, um, it's not like that at all.' Squirming with embarrassment, Yumekawa hotly denied the charge.

Mr Hirata, delighted at the opportunity for a bit of fun, told Yumekawa there was no need to hide his true feelings in these enlightened times. 'I know you work for one of our competitors,' he said, 'but I must say I've always had a soft spot for your singing. I see . . . So that's where you get all that sexy oomph from. Well, well, the sand guy from Tottori never ceases to amaze.'

'Did you say "sand guy"?' I asked Mr Hirata, puzzled.

'Well, yes, Rinka, as a matter of fact I *did* say "sand guy",' said Mr Hirata, and triumphantly proceeded to explain about an embarrassing phase in Hiroshi Yumekawa's career, while the latter sat next to him in a cold sweat. 'You see, Rinka, being so young, ahem, you wouldn't know about this kind of thing, but there was a time when Nikkatsu, the film company, took to giving its stars nicknames, for publicity, you know. It started with Yujiro Ishihara – he was "the nice guy". Then there was Akira Kobayashi – they called him "the mighty guy" – and Joe Shishido, "the tough guy". And then along came another fine-looking young man, none other than Master Yumekawa who's sitting right here with us . . .'

'Please, please, President Hirata. Mercy, I beg of you!' Yumekawa was squirming in the death-throes of embarrassment. Clearly the nickname that his production company had thought up for him had not been a great success.

But Mr Hirata showed no mercy. 'They called him "the Monster Man from Tottori, Sand Guy Yumekawa"! Rather good, don't you think?'

'It wasn't my idea,' wailed Yumekawa. 'They wanted some name that would make people associate me with Tottori, but there's nothing famous at all in Tottori except sand. Those sand dunes are all we've got.' Yumekawa had his head hidden in his lap in an excess of shame.

The two comedians sitting behind us burst out laughing:

'That's fantastic, Mr Yumekawa.'

'It's not fair, you'll get more laughs than us.' Suddenly a sort of showbiz electricity ran through the bus as the comedians got going.

'You've got no right to laugh at poor Mr Yumekawa. With a brain the size of yours they should call you the pebble guy.'

'You can't talk. The best job you ever got in the theatre was being the sandwich guy!'

'Any more sand-guy jokes and you'll be the banned guy.' And so on. The bus was seething with laughter as the assembled artistes gave a generous round of applause. Thanks to the ad-libbing of these two underemployed comics, the tense atmosphere melted away in an instant to be replaced by that familiar exciting buzz when a crowd of people know they're about to have fun. It was that glorious moment when the hot, sweet butter of fun is about to descend from above like manna from heaven.

Naturally, everyone in the bus wanted a piece of the action. One passenger got up and gave a passionate performance of his forthcoming new release; another produced dozens of coloured silk handkerchiefs from his hat and sent them cascading across the seats. The monkeys were getting excited, too, and started swinging from curtain to curtain along the bus windows.

Shiomi Genkainada also got up and belted out an enka. No doubt she'd be wearing some splendid first-rate man's kimono on stage today – that being part of the look for young, female enka singers with close-cropped hair – but actually she came across really well singing in simple jeans and sweatshirt. I'd heard her sing this song before on a CD, but she sounded better live. Probably she'd only just learnt the melody when she cut the CD, and I don't think her voice had fully matured at that point.

Everyone got terribly excited and the whole bus was transformed into an impromptu stage. Even Shiomi's mother somehow raised her great bulk out of her seat and gave us an impassioned performance. Each artiste wanted to show the others what they could do, and the temperature in the bus was rising to a dangerous level.

I was the only one left out. I wish I had some original songs. I had never wished it so fervently. I'm just a hack singer, trotting out copies of other people's numbers. I want a song to call my own, and call it mine with pride. I want it. I want it. I stole a sideways glance at Hiroshi Yumekawa. But a duet? Thanks, but no thanks. If I'm ever going to make my début, I want to do it solo. I want a tune and lyrics that are so good they'll make me tremble, they'll make me forget myself completely when I'm singing that song. To get my hands on a song like that, I'd gladly abandon anything or anyone – parents and lovers included. Hm, don't overdo the theatricals, old girl! Starting to get overheated here; must get a grip.

The site of a scaffolding tower above the trees indicated that we had arrived at the festival site. Rehearsals commenced immediately. Although we were deep in the mountains, there were already a couple of hundred people there – tourists who'd hiked up in the hope of a free show, free booze and free snacks, officials from the local authority and so on – and they treated us to thunderous applause as they saw us climbing down from the bus.

'Thank you so much for coming all this way.'

Although we were only rehearsing, one old man got so excited that he got up from his seat and climbed on to the stage in hopes of shaking hands with Telepathy Okada, who was holding his breath at the crucial moment in his magic show. Okada had his hands full with top hats and rabbits and stuff and wasn't really in a position to shake hands with anyone. The other artistes observed his acute discomfiture from the wings and fell about laughing.

'We've got some interesting punters in the audience today.'

'Let's see how many of them we can get on to the stage.'

And so the comedians and the singers hatched a little plot. I had a little chuckle and went along with it. If we all did our damnedest to break down the psychological barrier between stage and audience, we'd soon have the makings of a really fine broth of emotion and excitement.

'Let's get them hot and cookin'.'

'All together now – give 'em the works.'

'Let's see if we can get some tips out of 'em.'

Then it was my turn to rehearse. Mr Hirata was standing just behind me, and he chose the perfect moment to give me a pat on the back and whisper in my ear:

'Go on, girl. Knock 'em dead.' It was just like being seen off by a favourite uncle. I swanned gracefully on to centre stage.

'Good afternoon. I'm Rinka Kazuki of Bolydor Records. I'm twenty-two years of age. This kimono is the very one I wore at my coming-of-age ceremony the year before last.' I overheard poorly suppressed laughter coming from backstage. As I feared, it wasn't going to be easy maintaining my new stage age. Never mind. The audience was watching from a considerable distance, and most of them seemed willing to believe. Right, here we go.

I hammed it up for all I was worth. I rolled my voice in that old-fashioned enka style, a hundred times a song or more. I made highly exaggerated gestures. I looked at them and talked to them as if I were some sort of megastar. I went real low on the low notes, growling out of the pit of my stomach, and on the high notes I went up clean and pure as a little angel. And do you know what happened? They started coming up on the stage to give me money – yes, even though it was only a rehearsal. Hey, I pulled in 7,000 yen, just like that. I could hear gasps of amazement coming from the dressing-room. The joy of it – I live for moments like that.

Anyway, the main event was almost as much fun as the rehearsal, and the Red Leaf Festival came to a suitably riotous conclusion. Afterwards, I stood there looking at the wreckage. Picnic leftovers were lying around in the seating, along with the odd abandoned baby shoe and crumpled programme, and the stage was grubby with the dusty footprints of the performers who had recently graced it. Here and there were odds and ends of showbiz detritus – fallen sequins, a rhinestone earring, a plume that had moulted from a feather boa – mingling with the dust and fallen leaves that were nature's contribution. Amid all this, a team of youngsters wearing staff jumpers was busily clearing up.

In the bus on the way home the peace was disturbed by explosive snoring sounds from all directions. The performers, the managers, the promoters, all had apparently succumbed to some sleeping spell and were lying around with their arms and legs hanging out of their seats, sleeping fiercely with their mouths wide open. In among them, a few people were still awake and talking in low whispers. When people in our line of business start talking in low whispers you can be sure the subject under discussion is serious and probably not very respectable.

I could just make out the hushed conversation going on near by between the look-alikes, a girl who made a living out of impersonating pop singer Seiko Matsuda and a guy who specialized in doing Hiromi Go. They were complaining about the poor standard of aftercare at some hospital or other. It gradually dawned on me that they'd been undergoing plastic surgery to make them resemble their models more closely. Their entire livelihood depended on maximizing their resemblance to people who had actually made it in showbusiness, and in the intensity of the enterprise they were more than willing to remake their own faces. Needless to say, they also had the hairstyle just right and spent many long hours perfecting the singing style and mannerisms of the two stars. Now that's what I call professionalism.

Pretending to be asleep, I carried on listening to their conversation, which I found almost moving. We singers can always give it up and go back to ordinary life if we want to. But what about these guys? There's no way back for them. They really are like kamikaze pilots with no fuel for the return journey. These are true outsiders, people who would never be understood by regular folk. I stole a glance at them: Seiko Matsuda, deep in conversation with Hiromi Go. They looked great. I shivered.

'Well, Rinka, have you had a think about that matter we discussed the other day? The suspense is killing me.' Sitting directly behind me, Hiroshi Yumekawa spoke in a voice so low that only I could hear it. In the seat beside me Mr Hirata was snoring loudly.

'Why's it got to be me? If I'm going to make a CD, I want to do it solo. So I'm sorry, but will you please give up on this one?'

'Are you sure? A good opportunity like that, and you're going to let it go? You're the one I want to do it with. Oh well, if you've got something better lined up I guess I'll have to give up.'

'I don't have anything else lined up in particular. I just don't feel like doing it, that's all.'

'Huh. Have it your own way. By the way Rinka, do you have a patron? Whichever way you choose to go, you'll get there a lot quicker if you get yourself a nice rich old man to look after you. If you're interested, I might be able to introduce you to someone.'

Just then, little Shiomi Genkainada cut into the forcefully whispered dialogue. She'd been quietly listening in, and now she gave a large, somewhat exaggerated sigh.

'I wish I hadn't heard that.' She gave another little sigh. In the seat next to hers, her mother-cum-manager was enormously and noisily asleep. 'So you're like that with all of them.' She sighed yet again. Yumekawa maintained an embarrassed silence. I couldn't think of anything to say in response to the girl's remark, so I, too, lapsed into silence and looked out of the window.

A light drizzle had set in at some point, and lots of red leaves were sticking to the damp surface of the bus windows, like appliqué. The homeward road was glowing in the light from the setting sun and was strewn with fallen leaves. It was almost as if they'd put out the red carpet for our triumphant return.

Why this beauty, at a time such as this? I gazed wistfully at the wonderful scenery. I still couldn't think of anything to say to Shiomi's reproachful lament, and the bus just drove right on, silent save for the snoring of those who slumbered.

Then there was a little hiss as Shiomi Genkainada pulled the ring-tab off a can of Coca-Cola. She tipped back her young white neck and drank with a kind of desperation until she'd drained the can.

She had the trace of a smile on her face as she finished drinking. Now she was laughing out loud, a dry laugh. And then Shiomi turned her liquid brown eyes, so beautiful it almost hurt to look at them, on Hiroshi Yumekawa. He immediately averted his gaze.

Shiomi may have skipped homework a few times at school, but she was basically an innocent girl who had just arrived in adult society. In society there are rules, and, she was now learning, there were even rules for people who lived outside the usual rules. But there was no textbook to explain this other set of rules. Even so, everyone seemed to expect her to know them.

'Don't you come over all innocent with me, young lady.'

'No, no, she really doesn't know the rules.' And they would wave the phantom rulebook in her face until she was sick and tired of it.

I wonder if Yumekawa's naughty suggestion was just the tip of the iceberg? Maybe, but I'm not the kind of person to believe everything I hear without evidence. Besides, even if I did believe every salacious rumour about the entertainment business, it wouldn't do me a bit of good. All that had happened here was that I had caught a glimpse of how sex and patronage could be negotiable currencies here at the bottom end of the showbiz world. Yumekawa and Shiomi: who'd have thought it? And wouldn't the public be delighted if the whole world of entertainment was like that. The world of showbiz thrives on envy, and people probably like to believe that it is infested with moral hazards: this star did something dirty; *that* star did something dirty; I'd have become a star myself only I refused to get my hands dirty; that kind of thing.

The people who benefit from the patronage system like to flourish the phantom rulebook as if it were an official pardon for their own behaviour. That's just the way things are, they say. And the people who get exploited get to think the same way. It can't be helped. That's just the way things are.

Well, I have one thing to say to all that. If you want to think that way, go ahead; if you want to act that way, go right ahead. But if the only way you can do something is by telling yourself 'this is what everyone does', well, chances are that what you're doing isn't right for you. And yet how seductive that way of thinking is. There are a thousand ways to entrap the human spirit.

It was seven o'clock in the evening by the time I got back to the flat. I hadn't had supper. I called Daiki on his mobile, and he said he was going out with the lads. I could hear the sound of construction machinery in the background. He was in a better mood than usual for a day I'd done a show, because it had been a matinée rather than the usual night-time affair. I suppose men generally tend to worry more if their woman is out and about after dark.

I didn't feel like cooking for myself, so I started wondering where to go for supper. There aren't too many places around my part of town where it's OK for a woman casually to show up on her own. While thinking about it, I started vigorously wiping the wheels of my trundle-trolley with a hand-towel. That's always the first thing I do when I get home from a gig. Those wheels have been rolling over asphalt, and so, of course, they're every bit as dirty as the sole of your shoe. Therefore, it wouldn't do to bring the trolley into the room in that state. Definitely not. Got to get those wheels nice and clean.

One time, in the early days of our relationship, I got into a row with Daiki – you know, one of those ordinary lovers' tiffs about who's going to leave whom, or not, as the case may be. I had quit my job at the hostess club because he told me to. But that was cool, because I wanted to quit that job anyway. The trouble was, now he wanted me to quit singing, which was the job I'd taken up in place of the old one. This time it was a job I was doing because I liked it. Also, he didn't just come straight out with it and tell me to quit. He just made his wishes apparent through various trivial gestures and signs that he probably didn't even notice himself. Eventually, I confronted him about it:

'I know that's what you're thinking, so why don't you just spit it out?'

'I really can't seem to figure out why I think that way myself. And if that really is what I think, it means I'm a really mean sort of guy.' At the time, Daiki's vagueness only infuriated me more, so I triumphantly interpreted his vague feelings for him. I told him he was nothing but a big, pathetic coward. He was scared that if he told me outright to quit my work, I would turn around and say that if he wanted me to quit, he'd have to keep me and feed me out of his own pocket. Right from the word go he'd been going on about how much he loved me and all that, but his feelings didn't actually extend as far as paying my living expenses.

Remembering that old quarrel of ours, I felt the remorse rising once more. What silly things I'd said. Somehow even my hand cleaning the trolley wheels responded to my inner feelings, giving the wheels an extra thorough polishing. There: squeaky clean.

How did Daiki respond to that tirade of mine? Hm, if I recall correctly he thought for a while and then said that, believe it or not, he really did want the two of us to stay together – permanently. He wasn't a rich man, but he confidently believed that he could make enough for the two of us. But he felt that being a full-time housewife just wasn't me. He was irritated with himself for his inability to put his feelings into words, but that was what he thought. That was how we'd ended up with our present living arrangement, and to keep the arrangement going there were some thoughts that were better not put into words.

I gave the wheels one last, brisk wipe. Very good. It was very good that Daiki and I had cleared the air and made our positions clear. Now all we had to do was battle with our own feelings.

'Hm, nice and clean.' I gave the trolley a satisfied little pat, then lobbed the blackened hand-towel into the wastepaper basket. I pinch the hand-towels from a certain karaoke parlour. It's one of those places with private rooms, and I sometimes rent a room there all by myself to practise my singing. They always give me one of these hand-towels along with the wireless microphone. You're supposed to leave the towel in the room when you finish, but somehow the towel always ends up in my handbag. I use them first to wipe the table, then to wipe the floor and, finally, to wipe the wheels of my trundle-trolley. One go is enough to make them coal black, at which point I chuck them away. It feels really good.

'I know. I'll go to Hiro-zushi.' Suddenly remembering the smiling face of that street-fighting sushi master, I cheered up and got ready to leave.

*

'Well I never, it's Rinka. Been a while, hasn't it? Finished singing for the day, have we? I've got some nice crab in today.' It was a hearty greeting. There were already seven or eight customers chatting and laughing in the little shop, including a few show people. I sat myself down at the far end of the counter and ordered a beer. It was the first time I'd come in on my own, and the master put an extra glass at the place next to mine, assuming that Daiki would be coming in to join me shortly.

'I'll have some clams and smoked shad for starters,' I said. 'I'll try some of the crab a little later.' I had a go at ordering in the same nonchalant style that Daiki always used. I felt oddly nervous.

'Coming right up.' It was nice to hear the sushi master respond to my order the same way he always responded to Daiki's. I smiled and helped myself to a sip of beer.

'Good *evening.*' Wouldn't you know it. Hardly had I picked up the beer glass, when the curtain over the entrance was pushed aside and Gaho the Pig made her entrance. Worse still, she was on her own, like me. 'Great to see you, Rinka.' She sat down next to me. The master concluded that this must be a girls' night out, smiled cheerfully and turned his attention to making sushi.

'Well, it looks like I've finally found myself some work,' said Gaho the Pig. 'How about you? Still getting by without a patron?' She poured herself some of my beer without asking if it was OK and raised the glass for a toast. I wasn't going to raise my glass to that pig, however. I picked up a bottle of soy sauce that was standing on the counter and clinked it half-heartedly against her glass. Avoiding eye-contact, I turned my back on her and gazed apathetically towards the television at the other side of the shop. Water off a duck's back. Ignoring my display of sullen indifference, Gaho the Pig mentioned that she was starving hungry and started busily tucking into my *hors d'oeuvre.* I wearily decided I might as well initiate some conversation.

'Mr Hirata's being really nice to me these days.' I told her about the picture postcard and how the boss and I had been getting on so much better since then. I wondered how Gaho would react. At first she looked puzzled, smirking with one cheek only, but gradually her expression relaxed.

'Rinka, you really are fantastic,' she said. 'Still doing that kind of stuff. Amazing. Hey, I didn't know people still did things like that.' Maybe if I talked to her long enough the old Kaho would come back. I would purify her. Feeling as if I were chucking one bucket of cleansing water over her after another, I told her a whole string of amusing stories, along with plenty of gestures. But washing her down and wringing her out proved to be incredibly tiring. She just sat there nibbling at the sushi, saying nothing, only listening. Was it because I didn't really like her that I started to feel she owed me some kind of response for providing all this entertainment? Surely not. The one thing I couldn't forgive in this woman was her laziness. She didn't have the energy to love herself. Her talk about 'living for the sake of her dream' was just an empty slogan, and she didn't even seem embarrassed about it.

'Oh, I just remembered,' – at last she'd thought of something to say – 'you know I told you Ken was going to be on TV? Well, it's tonight. Why don't you come and watch it with me?' She giggled. 'Ken's gone, but it'll be nice to see him again – even if it's only on TV.'

I guess it's easy to love somebody else – after all, you can always stop loving them – but loving yourself, now that's a permanent job. You can't rest for a moment. There are all sorts of demons waiting to possess you the moment you take a breather from loving yourself.

'By the way, Rinka, I've got something to tell you that I think will be of interest. How would you like it if you had a guarantee of a certain number of singing jobs coming in every month, regular as clockwork? That'd be pretty relaxing, yeah?'

I just knew this wasn't going to be worth listening to, and I made it crystal clear that I wasn't interested. 'Actually Kaho, thanks to Mr Hirata's efforts, I'm doing OK now. Not that there are too many places left that still do shows these days, what with so many cabarets closing down, and the recession generally. Even so, he always manages to get me at least five shows a month. So I'm just about getting by, thanks.'

'It's great that Mr Hirata's doing all that for you, Rinka. But you really ought to have some other way of getting engagements, too, you know.'

'I don't like two-timing. If you work for two different agencies you have to use two different stage names, and you're always worrying that somebody might find out. It's not worth the stress. It's much better to have a trusting relationship with just one agency.'

'I'm not talking about another agency, Rinka. All you have to do is subscribe to this newspaper.' The newspaper that Kaho put on the counter before me was published by a certain religious sect. I was astonished.

'Kaho! Is there nothing you won't do to get a bit of work? This is a religious cult, right? Are you telling me you've been and gone and joined it?'

Gaho gave an expansive smile. 'No, silly. Just give me a chance to explain, OK? I haven't joined – this is just an expedient. An expedient to make my life a little more stable.' She spread the newspaper out in front of me. There were a number of mug-shots of celebrities dotted around the page. She pointed them out one by one.

'Look, Rinka, it's X, that guitarist you like; and Y, that actress. They're both members. I don't know how serious they are about it, but they must be fairly serious about it to let them print their photos in the paper. You wouldn't go hungry if you got in with these guys. Because there are lots of high-ups from the entertainment companies in it as well. And people do help each other out, you know. It's the way of the world. I mean, you're getting a bit of help, too, right?' True, I am getting my song arrangements and lessons for free, and sometimes a fan will give me some stage clothing as a present, and I do depend on tips for my livelihood. True, too, that I claim to be with a record label that doesn't really exist, when in fact I've never made a CD in my life. All in all, my life involves an awful lot of hokum and humbug. Still, one has to draw the line somewhere.

'Kaho. From this day forth, I really do not want to have anything whatsoever to do with you. I admit I'm a bullshit sort of person, but there's something about your particular kind of bullshit that I just cannot abide.'

Gaho the Pig reddened and flew into a rage. 'What the hell are you going on about? What's the big difference between you and me? I'm just trying to help. Just being nice, trying to help you get some more gigs.'

I did not flinch. Instead I shouted back at her, loud enough to make the sushi chef look up from the squid he was slicing with a look of some concern. 'That's a lie, Kaho. You think it doesn't look too cool, doing something like that for the sake of your career. And you're too scared to get mixed up with some weird cult on your own, so you want to get someone to do it with you. Am I right or am I right?'

Gaho the Pig fell silent. Bull's-eye – but her body language still tried to deny it. She sat there, head in hands. Glancing up, I noticed that several of the other customers were settling their bills and making ready to leave, possibly having tired of our noise. The few remaining customers were staring at us with evident unease. I could feel their eyes drilling into my back.

Totally bewildered, Gaho the Pig started crying. 'Everybody's doing bad things all the time, aren't they? Why's it always me who gets the blame? What's the matter with you, Rinka? You just want to make me quit, yeah? Because more work for me means less for you. That's what it's all about, yeah? Your theories are all nonsense.' She grabbed my shoulder in exasperation. I pushed her arm away roughly and screamed at her:

'Shut up! You just don't understand. I'm talking about *the spirit of the stage.*'

There was a sudden burst of noisy applause behind my back. I turned around to see a little cluster of worn-out middle-aged men and one woman. I hadn't recognized them at first in their ordinary clothes, but they were the magicians who had shared the stage with me at the Red Leaf Festival earlier that day.

I staggered up the stairs, stumbled into the darkened apartment and collapsed on the floor without even switching on the lights. Daiki wasn't home yet. Completely exhausted, I lay face down on the sofa, sobbing quietly to myself. The latest quarrel with Gaho had seeped into my heart like an ineradicable stain. I want to be nice to people. If only I could simply accept every person I met, how easy my life would be. I wouldn't have to suffer like this. But sometimes, for the sake of my self-respect, I just have to keep away from people. When I'm with her, I have this uncomfortable feeling that I'm going to be infected with something nasty.

The telephone rang. Daiki? I sprang to my feet to answer the call, preparing a bright telephone voice a couple of tones higher than usual to conceal the fact that I'd been crying.

'Hi, it's me.' It was Kenjiro, that old pal of mine who used to understand the spirit of the stage. What with the happiness of hearing his voice, and the nostalgia for the old days, and the thankfulness that he happened to have called while Daiki was out of the house, I was in raptures.

'Ken-chan! Where are you? What are you doing? Come on, come on, tell me.'

'Ha-ha-ha! You're like a puppy, Rinka. Down, girl. I've been thinking I want to drop by and see you one of these days. But first, let's meet at eleven o'clock tonight – on television!' He was ringing up to tell me about his television appearance. Come to think of it, it had been less than two months since his sudden disappearance. And here he was, about to appear on the telly. What an incredible rate of progress. Evidently the bedroom favours really did work wonders. I wanted to ask him how he'd wangled it, but it was a bit difficult to know how to broach the subject without appearing impolite. I was still wondering how to go about it when he started telling me the whole story of his own accord.

'Rinka, I'm having an affair with this amazing old girl. I asked her how old she was and she said forty-six. That's the same age as my mother, you know.' This sponsor of Kenjiro's was the president and chief producer of a major production company. She'd made stars of several young talents already – and apparently Kenjiro was just her type.

'Ken-chan. Mind if I ask you a slightly odd question?' I spoke in a lower tone. Kenjiro giggled as if he'd been tickled and asked what the question was. 'Do you love her?'

Even by my standards it was a pretty strange thing to ask. I just wanted to see how he'd answer. Would he say, 'Of course I don't bloody well love her? Don't be ridiculous, she's just an ugly old cow with a load of dosh'? And if he said something like that, would I hate him for it? Somehow I thought I probably wouldn't. I might be quite pleased, actually. But the answer that I got from him was unexpected:

'I want to love her.' And then, with an underlying chuckle in a voice full of confidence, he started to explain the situation. 'I think you'll understand when you see me on TV, but this old lady's a really interesting person. She senses what my attractive features are, and she brings them out. I feel this new power inside me, and whatever we do it feels so right. I tell you, every day is just so much fun.'

'Wow! Incredible. That much fun, eh?' Still the same old Kenjiro, I was pleased to note.

'Please,' he added, 'let's carry on being friends.' It was the same line he'd used on me at the love hotel in Uguisudani, with that look of deep seriousness on his face. Such a charming guy. I do like him. 'But don't be too jealous. I've always liked you. Rinka, you're the only one I really love. Uh, heh-heh.'

What? There appears to be some weird misunderstanding here.

'Er, Kenjiro, Daiki will be back any moment, so I'll let you go.

I'll make sure I don't miss the TV show, OK? Oh, and tell me how to contact you, will you?' I wrote down Kenjiro's new mobile number and hung up. At that very moment I heard a car pull up down below. Apparently Daiki really had come home.

'What's all this? You haven't even switched the lights on.'

Having left the lights off when I got home, I'd only switched on the one in the living-room when Kenjiro called. I heard the sound of Mr Wild putting his bags down in the hall. I made a dash through the darkness in the direction of the sound. I bumped into his huge frame and fell over, but I got straight up again and sprang on to him, clinging on around his neck with both feet off the ground.

'Whoa! You're just like a little puppy dog, you are.' That took me aback somewhat. It was exactly what Kenjiro had just said to me, and I felt slightly guilty that I'd just been talking to him.

Daiki started to peel off his dirty work shirt while he spoke. 'Hey, Rinka. There was a phone call for you today, from the credit-card company. They couldn't make the transfer from your bank account this month because there wasn't enough money in it. So you've missed your payment. What are you playing at, young lady?'

'Oops, sorry. I did get the warning letter, and I was just thinking it was about time I paid up. I didn't think they'd actually start telephoning. What a fuss.' I'm always late with my credit-card repayments. More strictly speaking, my economic arrangements are based on the principle that I will delay payment until the last possible minute. After all, collecting overdue debts is part of a credit company's job, isn't it? Just as dealing with noisy hecklers is part of a singer's job. So I don't see anything wrong in making them wait for their money.

'I know what you're up to,' said Daiki. 'Delaying payments, juggling debts, robbing Peter to pay Paul. No good will come of it. Oh well, you chose to live this way, so I suppose it's none of my business.' Still grumbling, Daiki closed the bathroom door behind him. The last grumble had a bathroom echo to it. Then I heard the shower come on, and I was on my own again.

Hey! Eleven o'clock. I realized I was about to miss Kenjiro's television appearance and ransacked the room for the remote control. The television was already on the right channel. The programme was called *Asian Sensation*. Hang on a minute, though, wasn't that an amateur talent contest? I thought Kenjiro was already a pro. Would he really be on a show like this? Yes, he would. Even as I was puzzling over this, the contestants were being introduced. There were six of them, carefully selected through a series of preliminary heats held all over Asia. And there was Kenjiro, right there, in among them. Tonight was the Grand Final.

Every bit as absorbed as if I were in the contest myself, I held my breath and watched the drama unfold.

8 Squealing Wheels

'I am contestant number three. My name is Kenjiro Yoshii. I am twenty-six. I will do my very best today. Please favour me with the honour of your attention.' Please favour me with the honour of your attention? I'd never heard Kenjiro talk that way before. He'd certainly cleaned up his language, and someone had modified his voice to make him sound as if butter wouldn't melt in his mouth. I struggled to suppress a laugh as I watched him introduce himself.

'I was born in Vancouver, Canada, but my family moved to Japan when I was four years of age.' Canada? Vancouver? What a load of rubbish! 'Tonight, ladies and gentlemen, I intend to sing my heart out for you – and show you the true heart of Japan.'

Dressed neatly and modestly in jeans and T-shirt, the televised Kenjiro looked like a very fine young man indeed. If you listened very closely you could detect faint traces of the effort made to suppress his coarse everyday speech – the H in heart was just a little too self-consciously aspirated, for instance. Still, he had clearly worked very hard to project a crisp, bright image, and the hard work had been rewarded. He was a man transformed. I had to laugh: Canada, Vancouver, the heart of Japan – it was just too funny. I was in stitches. The guy was going to kill me.

The contestants finished introducing themselves. Of the six of them, two were from China, with one each from Taiwan, Malaysia and India and Kenjiro from Japan (and Canada). The winner would get to make a CD that would be released all over Asia, with live performances throughout the region.

'I get to win it – you'll see. The whole thing was recorded three days ago. But it wasn't fixed – honest! I really did win it fair and square.' That's what Kenjiro had told me. His new promoter had bent over backwards to turn his act into a sure-fire winner and had entered him in this contest as a calculated gamble aimed at generating publicity for him.

'And now, ladies and gentlemen, please allow me to sing, for your diversion and delectation, "Man of Japan".' The Kenjiro who now appeared on stage was transformed once more. This time he was dressed in a stylish men's kimono. This was too much to bear. I was rolling around on the floor, laughing till the tears flowed down my cheeks. Kenjiro, who came into this world loving the style of Elvis Presley, had discarded his tight white trousers and his rhinestone-studded jacket for something very different. He'd come over all enka.

I stared at the screen with increasingly intense fascination. Actually, the glossy, sapphire-blue men's kimono was a classy item, and it happened to suit him very well. The navy-blue sash was smartly tied, making him look a very fine specimen of Japanese manhood as he gripped the microphone in one hand and struck a dignified pose. From somewhere behind him came the strains of an electric guitar played in the coarse, persistent manner that seems to be *de rigueur* with enka sung by men. The sound welled up around Kenjiro's legs and waist, and, almost as if disdainfully avoiding it, he took a step forward.

> HaaaaaaaaaaaAAAA! Ho ... HO!
> (Yoshaa!)
> HaaaaaaaaaaaAAAA! Hohoho ... HO!
> (Aah, dokkoi!)

The song started with the sort of cries that fishermen make when they're hauling in the nets. It was an original melody, yet it was pervaded with nostalgia. About a third of each chorus consisted of bold cries of 'yo, heave-ho' and the like.

On the staircase behind Kenjiro, a couple more gorgeous young men had appeared, dressed in festival tunics, and they echoed Kenjiro's lusty cries. On the screen a subtitle read 'Chorus: Kai and Daichi'. One name meant sea and the other land – very elemental, I must say.

One thing that kind of impressed me was the coordination of the movements. As well as singing out his 'yos' and his 'hos', Kenjiro would also join Kai and Daichi in their refrain of 'Yoshaa', and he'd be striking the same pose as them, too, although he couldn't see them standing behind him. Just watching them was enough to make me start fidgeting – I wanted to join in. These days this kind of performance is considered old-fashioned and corny, so you never get it in pop songs, but I had to admit there was something oddly fascinating about the spectacle.

> The sea . . . the wind . . . the sky . . . the mountains
> The leaves . . . the stars . . . the flames . . . life
> And what am I?
> I am a MAN!

That was about it for the lyrics. You couldn't get much simpler really. But it was a very expressive performance from Kenjiro, his voice dynamically scaling the octaves to produce an effect that was curiously moving. Had he really been this talented? He should have been an enka singer all along.

'Hey, this is good.'

The look was right, too, really rather dashing. A man's *kinagashi* kimono is properly worn with a low-slung, half-width sash, tied smartly below the waist. In front, the sash goes just under the stomach, so a guy with a figure like Kenjiro's, who doesn't have a lot of meat in the underbelly region, has to bolster the sash with an extra belt of cotton underneath. Around the back, the sash passes just above the buttocks, thereby accentuating the man's backside in a manner that is really rather delightful. For me, stealthily observing the bottoms of men wearing these stylish kimonos used to be one of life's little pleasures. Sadly, however, the only men who wear them these days are elderly enka singers, whose rears tend to be somewhat too saggy to offer a really tasty feast for the eye. This was not the case with Kenjiro's televised bottom, I am pleased to report. It was delightfully pert, a real revelation.

'What's all this? Hey, isn't it that guy I nearly beat up in the street? What's he doing singing on TV all of a sudden?' Daiki had stuck his head out of the bathroom door to see what all the commotion was about. His hair was still covered in shampoo. 'You were laughing like crazy, so I thought I'd see what was so interesting on the box. Wow, this guy is really amazing!'

On screen, there was a momentary silence. With a dramatic flourish, Kenjiro whipped off his kimono and hurled it away.

'What? Oh my God!'

The surprises just kept coming. Now Kenjiro was revealed in just a white loincloth, barefoot and clutching a pair of giant drumsticks. His taut, bronzed skin had been slathered with some kind of glistening oil that turned his lean, muscular frame into a shimmering vision of virility. Truly, it was magnificent to behold.

Now he and his two acolytes bared their shiny white teeth and started beating on massive *taiko* drums. There was no tune as such at this point, no more than a faint memory of the instrumental line lingered in the rhythm of the drumming, while the three men whirled like leaves in a hurricane and wildly attacked the drums, dancing like crazy as they did so. It was a wonder they didn't drop the drumsticks they were moving so fast. The beating of the drums grew more and more intense, and gradually the rhythms of the three came together in perfect unison.

Tremendous.

As the excitement mounted, I felt something swelling up from inside me that I just couldn't hold in. I'd had that swelling-up feeling before, listening to Kenjiro sing his 'uh-huh' song in the old days. The difference was that in those days it was a feeling of revulsion swelling up inside me. This time it was the thrill of raw emotion that suffused my body. This was great. This was brilliant. Bravo!

The drumming came to an end, the song came to an end. He stood there quietly for a moment, his back turned to the audience. The camera zoomed in on his back. A dragon! Yes, he'd even got a magnificent fire-breathing dragon tattooed on his back. Of course, it was only one of those temporary jobs that they do with body transfers, but what the hell. It was extremely stylish. Hats off again.

The audience erupted. They rose from their seats as one and engulfed Kenjiro in a thundering whirlwind of applause. The camera roved lasciviously over the frenzied fans in the stalls and the circle: their pupils were dilated, the veins were standing out on their necks and they were screaming themselves hoarse with excitement. It was almost scary.

The camera returned to Kenjiro. He stood there, bathed in sweat, not bothering to wipe it away, beaming radiantly:

'You make me most happy.'

Kenjiro, you were fantastic. Time and again, I applauded him from the bottom of my heart. Even Daiki was impressed – sopping wet and with only a towel for modesty, he had been drawn from the bathroom into the living-room by the extraordinary spectacle.

'Well! That guy really is something.' Talking in excited tones, Daiki and I agreed that Kenjiro was bound to win. And, sure enough, just as he'd said, he beat off the competition easily, registering the highest score of the night by far. It was a triumph. Apparently the whole elaborate concept had been thought up, right down to the finest detail, by this amazing sugar mummy of his. Clearly she had a very shrewd grasp of showmanship. I was suitably impressed.

Somehow the whole experience filled me with happiness. As I went to the kitchen to make a cup of tea, I felt as if I were walking on air. I was so light-headed I thought I'd bump my head on the ceiling. One of us minor people had just become major. Things like that always make me happy – maybe it has something to do with all the bullying I got at school.

The following day I looked up the address of Kenjiro's production company and sent him a floral tribute. I felt the occasion called for something a bit special, so I splashed out on a really gorgeous bouquet. Mind you, I expect he got plenty of bouquets far more spectacular than mine that day.

Today, as ever, the chosen ones are anointed with the blood of living things whose life has been cut off. From now on Kenjiro would be deluged with offerings of cut flowers, and each one of the sacrifices laid at his altar would have some hidden motive behind it, as he himself went on the block in the world's most pitiless auction: how much for those eyes, how much for that smile, that throat, how much for each of those gestures? How much happiness would it bring Kenjiro in the years to come, having a value attached to each and every part of him like that?

'That woman is the pits. When I hear her singing, I want to throw up.' The contemptuous words that came floating back from my memory were said to me one time by an old gardener at a hotel where I was doing a show. He was doing some pruning in the front garden as I arrived, and I happened to get into conversation with him. Apparently, when he was younger, he'd been employed by a certain very famous enka singer. One day, while he was trimming the ornamental trees in the grounds of her mansion, he discovered some little living things that were weeping – baskets of flowers from her fans that she'd abandoned on the lawn.

'There must have been a dozen or more of them, just lying

there. She hadn't bothered to water them. She'd chucked them out just like that. Beats me how she could do it.' He spat the words out. 'I don't suppose you're like her now. But if you ever hit the big time, I dare say you'll do the same as her and think nothing of it.'

'Don't be silly. I'm never going to be that famous. Look, if I ever get even one flower from a fan, I'll press it, frame it and put it on the mantelpiece for keeps.' I laughed it off at the time, but ever since that conversation I get this sad feeling inside me every time I see that particular singer on television. It probably wasn't her fault at all. Maybe one of the maidservants threw the flowers out while she was away from the house for a few days. But, even so, this incident with the abandoned flowers has permanently tarnished her image for me.

Apparently this famous singer did a lot of years barnstorming around the country like me before she hit the big time. You might say that in her desire to escape from the misery of the touring-show life she'd jumped straight into a world with a different kind of suffering, for those who achieve celebrity are always under pressure to look like good people. I only hope Kenjiro doesn't suffer the same way.

One time I had a bitter experience of my own involving flowers. I had a ticket for a recital by a very famous male singer, and I splashed out 30,000 yen, no less, on a really magnificent floral tribute, big enough to be displayed in front of the auditorium on a special metal stand with my name on a card attached to it. I really went to town on it; I even took the trouble to select flowers that were mentioned in his songs. But when I arrived at the concert hall I discovered that, although the glorious bouquet had been delivered as ordered, there had been some terrible mix-up and the name of a certain well-known songwriter had been attached to *my* bouquet. Worse still, the card with my name on it had been attached to a far inferior bouquet in the 10,000-yen price bracket. Since it was clearly a mistake, I immediately pulled off the two name cards and switched them around.

However, when the recital was over and I passed the floral tributes on my way out, the card with the famous songwriter's name had mysteriously returned to my bouquet. I naturally made enquiries and received the following distressing information from the florist. Apparently it occasionally happens that some very eminent person in the music world sends in some flowers that are really far too cheap for one of his class. It is extremely embarrassing for the singer giving the recital to have such a bouquet on display at the door. He worries that members of the audience who inspect the floral tributes will be surprised to see what a low opinion the great maestro has of him. So, in order to keep up appearances, the great singer's assistants are detailed to reshuffle the name cards on the flowers so that the embarrassing inconsistency between status and appearance may be removed.

I like flowers. I like giving them and I like getting them. But, unfortunately, when you get to the very top of the showbiz world, flowers become transformed into bargaining chips in a rather nasty kind of trading system. I wonder how Kenjiro, when he comes back from Taiwan, will get on in this world that cares for nothing but outward appearances.

And what about me? Am I made for the big time, or am I fit only for the provincial barnstorming circuit? Which kind of suffering am I better suited to bear? I don't have what it takes to get into the big time anyway. Still, I would at least like to have an original song to call my own.

One day, while I was thinking along these lines as usual, a rather disturbing proposal came my way from my old pal, everyone's favourite master of ceremonies, Moody Konami. He wanted to introduce me to a potential sponsor. 'Rinka-chan, would you mind meeting this guy just once? For me?'

Why this sudden interest in me? No doubt it was because of Kenjiro's sudden rise to stardom. Strange chain reactions happen in the entertainment world. When one guy hits the big time, all his friends and acquaintances start wondering when it's going to be their turn. And it's not just the artistes themselves who get all excited; people who know them a bit start getting ideas in their heads. It's about time we gave so-and-so's career a push.

Seated in the changing-room of the I Love Yu health spa in East Omiya, Moody briefly told me about the man he had in mind as a possible patron for me. 'He's not a bad guy really. He's been running this company, Mitsuboshi Construction, for well on thirty years now. He's made a fair bit of cash, but his only hobby is playing chess, which means he doesn't really have anything to spend his money on. So he's looking around for some kind of constructive investment. A venture business, if you like. He won't make any trouble for you – he's a very serious kind of guy. The only kind of playing around he's ever done is with board games, for heaven's sake. If you see him and you don't like what you see, all you have to do is say, "Check out, mate," and go off home. Though I dare say he'd feel pretty "board".' This with a dry, apologetic laugh.

Beguiled by Moody's characteristically persuasive style, I started to think that maybe I should at least consider the proposition. 'If we play our cards right, it can be done without me having to have a "special relationship" with him, can it?' I put the question as delicately as I could. If this was about sex for money, I wanted no part in it. However, Moody soon put me in the picture: 'Don't be silly, dear. Of course he'll be expecting all that as part of the deal. Unless you tried something really radical – I don't know, introduce him to your starving family and appeal to his humanitarian instincts? Nah, you'd have a better chance of getting into Tokyo University, frankly.'

'Just a second, Moody. Show me that list.' All through the conversation Moody had been surreptitiously glancing at a green leather-bound notebook, and I was dying to get a peek at it.

'No talking to anyone about this,' he warned, as he flashed me a very brief look at the open page of the notebook. It was a list of names of businessmen; presidents and directors of all sorts of companies. A lot of them were in construction, but I also spotted firms that made cardboard boxes, personal seals, customized toiletries – towels with the name of your restaurant on and the like. There was something so blatant about that collection of names that I felt nauseous at the sight of it. Moreover, Moody wasn't showing me the whole list. He had his hand over one side of the page, doubtless concealing some information on the results of his matchmaking activities for each businessman and the names of the girls he'd set them up with.

'You can't get enough legitimate work, so you do this kind of thing all the time,' I suggested.

He admitted it surprisingly frankly. 'I get a little commission for making the introductions. It's not a lot, honest, unless the deal actually goes through, of course. In that case I have a bit of a payday. Anyway, will you just see the guy? I can see you're going to turn him down anyway – plain as the nose on your face. Not that it matters to me.'

The kind of deal this guy had in mind didn't stretch to a recording début with a major label. The best I could hope for was a self-produced CD on one of the small independent labels. I had a bad feeling about the whole thing. No doubt the pinnacle of the showbiz world has plenty of dangerous moral pitfalls, but even near the bottom you can still fall far enough to severely bruise your conscience if you're not very careful.

Anyway, I said OK. Moody brightened up and suggested we

meet the guy right away. Perhaps he thought that if he left it a few days I might change my mind. Actually, that's exactly what he was thinking.

'It's no good giving women time to think about stuff,' he remarked. 'Their mood changes every day. It's their biorhythms or something. You've got to get in quick, that's the key to success. Yep, old Moody Konami knows how to cut a deal. Done it a hundred times – but you don't want to know about that.' He gave an overly hearty guffaw and slapped me on the back so many times it hurt. He had the bad habit of demanding approval for his own jokes. Somehow, though, I was quite carried along by Moody's noisy, joking seduction, and before I knew it, we were on our way to the meeting place.

Four o'clock in the afternoon. It was the quiet period between the morning and evening shows. We'd just have a chat and a laugh with this guy for an hour or so and we'd be back at the health spa in plenty of time for the evening show at eight. Moody drove me to the rendezvous in his beloved Toyota Celsior, and as we purred along I felt for all the world like some useless princess in a cheap drama. We arrived at a little roadside restaurant off a stretch of motorway, and sat down there to await Prince Charming.

He showed up right away. He bustled into the restaurant, looking restlessly around him, his manner suggesting a nervy, fussy personality. He was a small, thinnish guy, and I reckoned I could easily beat him if it came to a fight. Moody had made him out to be stinking rich, but you wouldn't have thought so from his clothing. He was wearing grey slacks and a standard-issue salaryman shirt, with a conservative dark necktie and a pale-green cloth waistcoat.

'Yeah, I know, I know. But according to the previous president, you know, eh? Ah, ha-ha-ha.' He surely knew we could see him, but he just stood there in the entrance to the shop, yakking away on his mobile phone. The way he said 'eh' at the end of sentences reminded me rather strongly of Mr Hirata. He gave off the whiff of a middle-aged man who'd put in a lot of vigorous hard work.

'Ah, there you are. Sorry about that.' He came over and sat right down with us. For some reason, although this meeting was supposed to be all about me, he never even looked at me. Instead he focused on Moody and launched into an interminably long conversation that had nothing to do with anything. I had already surveyed the guy in great detail, and now there was nothing for me to do but sit there, bored out of my skull, devoting myself to such activities as idly poking at the ice cubes floating in my orange juice with my plastic straw crinkling up the paper wrapper the straw came in to make it look like a caterpillar and dripping orange juice on to it to make it wiggle, the way children do.

At long last Moody brought the meeting to order. 'Ah, by the way Mr Mitsuboshi,' he said, waving a hand in what was roughly my direction, 'about her.' At last he started to introduce me, at which the guy seemed most surprised, as if he'd only just this moment noticed me sitting there. His eyes went big and round.

'Oh, well, well, well. How nice to meet you.' I hung my head in sullen silence. This was hopeless. Every little gesture the guy made suggested intense, guilt-ridden lust. 'I'm going home,' is what I would have said if it had been just the two of us. But I couldn't very well walk out on him in front of Moody, So instead:

'Delighted to make your acquaintance,' I said, trying to give a shy smile by way of greeting. I'm sure it was a very tense, twisted kind of smile, but I needn't have worried about him noticing anything wrong, since he made not the slightest move to look in my direction.

'Moody and I have been the best of friends for some ten years now, haven't we, Moody. Go on, Moody, tell her about that funny thing that happened one time when we were playing chess together.' Apparently he didn't say 'eh' at the end of his sentences except when he was talking business. With that, his one attractive feature faded away.

'Oh, yeah, that was a funny one. You see, Rinka, Mr Mitsuboshi here is a terrible scatterbrain . . .' His name wasn't really Mitsuboshi. Moody was calling him by the name of his company, as people sometimes do in Japan. The name means three stars, although I wouldn't have given him even one myself. Anyway, prompted, Moody launched into a rambling account of some silly episode. Being a pro to the roots, Moody is perfectly used to turning the most trivial incident into a comic performance. The way he tells them, even the dullest person is transformed into a unique character, starring in an amazing story. Maybe that's why stuck-up businessmen find him a handy chap to have around.

'Honestly, you should have seen Mr Mitsuboshi's face at that moment. I remember thinking, it's at times like these that a man really needs the inner confidence to hold his ground.'

The man listened to Moody's highly dramatized account of this incident with apparent satisfaction, looking at Moody's extravagant gestures through half-closed eyes. Personally, I had not the slightest interest in what the old geezer may or may not have done, but at least I was getting through the interview without having to make eye contact or talk to him, so I felt somewhat relieved.

But not for long. I was concentrating on Moody, who was sitting next to me, but when I briefly glanced at the guy, seated opposite Moody, I realized something rather alarming. While I was listening to Moody, he was taking advantage of my distraction to very thoroughly check me out. Oh, those dirty, slimy eyes; his gaze dripped sticky desire. To top it all, he had no idea that I could see right through him. God, he was the pits. I've heard it said that one guy in ten is a charmless, dirty old man with no redeeming features – well, this one was definitely in that category. You could imagine him telling tasteless, dirty stories, casting a chill over all who listened.

'Go on, Moody, tell her about the time it was a rainy day and I fell into that puddle, will you?' Incredibly, he was still merrily requesting anecdotes, and meanwhile his eyes crawled all over me. Again and again they lingered on my legs, my stomach, my shoulders, my breasts, like a pair of hairy tarantulas slowly crawling all over me.

It was a snug little restaurant, designed in log-cabin style and dimly lit. The background music was cosy pop-songs by Yuming. How many beers did the guy order? We had ordered some mushroom pasta, but he didn't touch it, and it was still sitting on the table, stone cold. I gave a deep sigh. I fear he even incorporated that sigh into his filthy little fantasy, for I distinctly heard a little glug as he swallowed his spit.

I, too, started to fantasize. Before me stands a nice glass of merrily fizzing soda water. I grasp it in my hand, stand up, and empty the contents over the top of his head in a single, sharp movement. Soaking wet, he still can't grasp what's going on; he blinks in stupefaction. This is an exorcism. In quick succession I throw a second glass of soda water at him, then a third . . . Perhaps my fantasy trumped his, for his eyes abruptly returned to normal. He fished in his Dunhill briefcase and pulled out a book. Written on the cover was *The Four Pillars of Psychic Knowledge*. Apparently we were in for a spot of fortune-telling.

'Rinka, you were born in 1974. That was the Year of the Tiger. Your lucky number's eight, your lucky colour's white and you were born under Saturn. Now I was born in 1935, the Year of the

Boar. My lucky number's two, my lucky colour's black and I was also born under Saturn. Now, let me see. Oh, I say! It says here that we are very compatible indeed. We'll have to set this thing up. The stars never lie.'

'Maybe not, but I lied through my teeth when I said I was born in 1974, which may somewhat affect your cosmic calculations, baby,' was that I longed to say, but it's not a good idea to let anyone know your real age, so I kept my trap shut.

'It's also a very auspicious day today,' he continued. It's *Taian* – the luckiest day on the Buddhist calendar, and it's also *Kitsujitsu* – the luckiest day on the Shinto calendar. This could prove to be a very good day in both our lives.' He seemed to be getting all excited, without any encouragement from me. The next moment he was making what sounded suspiciously like a speech at a wedding reception. 'There's such a thing as an auspicious day to set out for the future. You're still young, and you mustn't waste that youthfulness. You'll do very well if you get to know a person like me. There's such a thing as karma between people, you know.'

Once again the devil had taken possession of him. I returned to my fantasy, splashing more and more soda water in his face. Take that, and that.

You know, I met quite a few different types of men in the days when I worked as a club hostess, but I never came across a man quite as infantile as this one. In a hostess club there are various unwritten rules about what kind of fooling around is OK and what kind is not. The guys who showed up wanted to look cool if possible and behaved accordingly. But the showbiz world, I now realize, is different. Out here, there are no rules. This is the anarchy zone. That's why you end up coming face to face with reptiles like this guy. What a crap paradise.

He had drunk too much beer and was getting carried away. Having treated us to the sermons, the speeches and the astrology, he came to the *pièce de résistance*: the dirty jokes – and very horrible they were, too; even Moody couldn't raise a laugh. Couples sitting near us got up and left, turning our corner of the restaurant into an isolated little stage for this guy and his one-man show. He ran out of blue material eventually, but there were still a few chess metaphors left in his bag of tricks:

'I expect Konami's told you I play chess to professional standard. I like to "mate early", you see, and I've "pinned a few queens" in my time. I always try to "thrust right through the middle", and I don't mind "sacrificing a few pawns *en passant*" to get what I want – if you get my meaning?'

I gave a vexed little sigh. 'Sir, faced with this overwhelming display of skill, I have no choice but to resign.' I flicked the salt-cellar over on its side and rose to depart. He was taken somewhat by surprise.

'Oh, so you know chess? That's another thing we've got in common. We're the perfect couple. I can see my "knights" are going to be pretty busy from now on.'

I picked up my handbag and turned towards the door. Moody hurriedly pulled on his jacket.

'Ah, sorry, Rinka, you're quite right. We need to make a move or we'll be late for the evening show.'

The guy also stood up to leave. 'Time to go time, I suppose.'

Emerging from the restaurant we found a rather disgusting young flunky waiting for the guy in the car park. A presidential fashion accessory, apparently. He can't have been much over twenty, and he had his hair done in the latest fashion. His bronzed skin said tanning salon rather than beach.

'Hope you've had a fruitful meeting, Mr Mitsuboshi. Ah, is this the young lady you mentioned? Very nice, if I may say so.' The youth had picked up on the guy's mellow mood and seemed to have concluded that the deal had been done.

'Isn't she? Rinka here tells me she likes Italian food, so fix us up with reservations somewhere nice next time.'

'Yes, siree.' Mitsuboshi reached for a cigarette, and the flunky had it lit for him in a second. He was so quick on the draw with the presidential lighter that I had to check him for gimmicks. Deferentially lighting customers' cigarettes is part of every club hostess's job, and I retain a slight interest in that kind of thing from my own days in that profession. It turned out the youth had the boss's special lighter hanging from a leather thong tied around his neck like a pendant. It merged so neatly with his overall surfer-boy look that I hadn't noticed at first. It's amazing the lengths to which people will go.

The guy exhaled some smoke and spoke reflectively, as though speaking to himself:

'Showbiz people, they're just beggars, really. Heh!'

Our eyes met. And thus the tryst came to an end.

Back in the Celsior Moody put his foot down, lip quivering with suppressed anger as he took us back to the health spa at dangerous speed.

'The patronizing old bastard. Calling us all beggars. He'll pay for that. I'll not be seen dead with him again in public.' In his excitement, Moody was starting to lose his grip on the steering-wheel. I found my face twitching with fear as I tried to calm him down.

'It certainly wasn't a very well-timed comment,' I conceded, 'but he'd already said so many horrid things by then that it didn't really make much difference to me.'

'Look, Rinka, I'm sorry. No, really. Putting you through all that. I won't send you to any more filthy old bastards like that, I promise. I'll find something better for you.'

'Please, don't bother.' Since I took up professional singing, I'd been helped out several times by Moody Konami. He'd shown me the ropes. I'd gone along with him on today's matchmaking mission out of a sense of duty. Now, however, I felt the debt had been fully repaid.

'Moody, that surfer boy who was hanging out with the old guy, what is he? A comedian? A singer?'

'That kid? He's not in any kind of showbiz. He's just some flash Harry who's trying to flatter his way into Mitsuboshi's good books 'coz he hopes the old man will set him up with his own shop one day.'

'Shop? What sort of shop? A bar of some kind? A variety store?'

'Dunno, actually. He's got some kind of dream, I suppose.' He's got a dream, but he doesn't want it to end up being just a dream. Perhaps there was something not so bad about the youth's single-minded pursuit of his shop. Compared with the stress of living each day in a bored mood of resignation, maybe it's better just to devote yourself to the pursuit of some ambition, regardless of the cost. Once you've decided to do that, you can just get on with enjoying your life without making a big fuss about things. That seemed to be the young flunky's approach, and I found it almost admirable. Maybe, contrary to conventional wisdom, men are actually better than women at enduring humiliation.

'Ladies and gentlemen, thank you so much. You've been a lovely audience. My name is Rinka Kazuki, and enka singing is my life. And now for my final number . . .' That night I gave a truly pas-sionate performance at the health spa. The meeting with the horrible old man had left a black footprint on my heart, but, although the experience had left me feeling insecure, at the same time it had somehow increased my love of humanity, and that feeling had communicated itself to the audience magnificently.

'Rinka-chan! You're all right.'

'We'll be back for the next show.'

'Good luck, love.'

In my emptiness I wanted the company of people, and they wanted me.

My phrasing was a bit of a mess that night, and so was my appearance. I overdid the theatricals, bustling around the stage in such agitation that they must have struggled to follow me with their eyes. Yet the power of my inner rage helped me to sing with unusual intensity, and with ease I broke down the barriers between stage and audience. We were as one.

When I got back to the dressing-room I found Moody Konami, still in his lamé stage suit, hastily vacuuming the floor.

'What's up, Moody? You don't have to do that. It's my job.'

'If I get the cleaning done first, you'll be able to get home quicker. After what I put you through today, it's the least I can do.'

'Thanks, Moody. But please don't feel bad about this afternoon.' I took a deep breath before continuing. 'I'm glad we did it.'

Moody blanched. 'What? You surely don't mean you seriously –'

'Intend to shack up with that dirty old man? No, Moody, that's not what I mean.'

'Phew, you had me going for a moment there.'

'Sorry to raise false hopes.'

'No, no, Rinka. I wouldn't want to set you up with that bastard who called us all beggars. That would give me no pleasure at all.'

'Is that so? Well, thanks. But no more "sponsored dating" arrangements, OK?'

'I got it. Next time I mention setting you up with some guy, I'll be talking about a smart young man who really wants to marry you, not a dirty old man looking for a bit on the side.'

'You silly old thing. You know perfectly well it'll never happen.'

'Oh yeah, I was forgetting. You can't cook, and you hate housework. You'd make a lousy wife.'

'Oh, you are awful.'

We both had a good laugh.

'Mind you, I did think that if no one at all would take you on I might take you on myself. Though it might be kind of tough on you, having to sing all the kids to sleep.' Moody's wife had walked out on him some years ago, leaving him with the kids. He was just joking, of course. I've never been any good at lullabies anyway.

'People don't still sing lullabies to their children, do they?'

'Ah, you youngsters just don't understand.'

'I'm not as young as I used to be, Moody.'

Thanks to Moody's assistance with the chores, I should have got home nice and early that night. But it wasn't to be. Amazingly, when I walked out of the stage door, I found a small crowd of *fans* lying in wait for me. They were in a state of some excitement.

'It's Rinka-chan.'

''Ere she comes.'

'Quick, you, get that camera out.'

In a flash I was surrounded by a dozen or more elderly folks up from the country who'd been at the show. They wanted to have their photographs taken with me, shake hands with me, get my autograph and all that jazz. I came over all shy.

'Rinka Kazuki! Oi'll remember that name, Oi will.'

'Good luck to you. 'Ere, take this from me.'

I was showered with presents. It was all stuff that they'd bought at the health spa's souvenir shop, planning to take home with them: packets of health tea, steamed buns, body shampoo with essence of aloes, hand-towels and travel-wash kits. Still, it's the thought that counts, and to me this display of impulsive generosity was deeply moving. I'd been in the business for two years, and this was the first time anything like this had happened to me.

Unfortunately, however, I tarried a little too long with my crowd of admirers, and missed the last train on the Musashino line. I wound up stranded in the street in front of South Urawa station just after midnight. South Urawa may not look too far away from central Tokyo on the map, but in this sector of the Tokyo outskirts the stations are a long way apart. If you carelessly forget about that and get a taxi into town, your wallet will sustain serious damage. On one occasion I took a taxi for just a couple of stations along the Musashino line, and it set me back 6,000 yen. So I knew I was in serious trouble here.

I had an idea. I'd get Daiki to come and pick me up. I rang him up. He was in, but as usual on days when I had a singing engagement, he was in a grumpy mood. His voice was sullen and what he had to say wasn't very friendly:

'Who the hell do you think you are, ringing at this time of night? I was already sound asleep. I've got to get up at five o'clock in the morning and get to the building site, you know. You can bloody well make your own way home.' It was sickening. I'd taken this kind of thing from Daiki before. Usually I just soak up the punishment in silence, but this time I decided to answer back:

'Now, just a minute. You can't leave an innocent young girl hanging around in front of a station at this time of night. What if some guy tries to pick me up? Come and get me.'

'What do you mean "this time of night"? It's only just gone twelve, you know. And who is this innocent young girl you mention? Don't tell me you've forgotten your real age. Or is this the girl that time forgot? Do me a favour and act your age, you silly old cow.'

'Shut up, you old fart. I'm still twenty-two in stage years, you know. You're only as old as you feel.'

'Well, if you feel so young and frisky, why don't you just get your trainers on and sprint home, eh?' And he hung up on me. Evidently I would be requiring a taxi. Unfortunately, I didn't have the price of the fare on me. In front of the station a long queue of people who'd also missed the last train had already formed at the taxi-rank. I had a little think and decided that my only option was to find some people to share the fare with.

'Excuse me, everybody, I'm heading for East Kawaguchi. Is there anyone going the same way who'd like to share a cab?' I hear that in South Korea and the like, it's perfectly normal for strangers to share a taxi, but here in Japan people are still kind of shy about it. No one responded to my call, so I tried the more personal approach, walking down the line and asking people individually. I succeeded in digging out two men and one woman who were willing to share. Fortunately they were near the front of the line, too, so I was able to jump the queue. Leaving the long and near-motionless line of people behind us, we sped off almost immediately.

'Well, well. You know what? This is the first time I've ever shared a taxi.' One of the passengers was a shy young man in his twenties. Probably some kind of junior salaryman. Next to him in the back seat sat an elegant middle-aged gentleman whose hair was just beginning to show signs of turning silver. He laughed at the young man's comment, and replied, 'You, too, eh? I've never done it before either, but taxis are so fearfully expensive these days that it's a sensible thing to do, really.'

In the front seat, a plump little office girl, just past twenty, I'd say, with slightly drooping eyes, tittered in amusement. 'It feels funny, doesn't it, riding with strangers? I'll be getting out at East Urawa. Where are the rest of you going?' Her eyes flitted in my direction, so I replied first:

'I'm heading for East Kawaguchi.'

The two men chimed in directly.

'I'm going to Takenozuka. It's a lot of money for one person, so this is a great deal for me.'

'I'm for Nishi-Arai. That's the furthest of all. I'll be last out.'

'How much is it going to come to, anyway?'

'I think it'll be just a shade over 2,000 yen a head. Or will it be more than that? What do you think, driver?'

The driver, indicating his displeasure at all the talk about the excessive cost of taxi fares, gave no reply. The middle-aged gent thought he hadn't heard and asked him several more times, but the driver ignored the question completely and casually turned up the volume on the radio. The man seemed quite shocked at this calculated display of rudeness. He said nothing, but you could see the confusion on his face. Inwardly, I couldn't help laughing. My long association with cabaret bandsmen meant that I was quite used to being totally ignored by bitter old men, and it actually made a refreshing change to be reminded that some people are still taken aback by that kind of behaviour. It was a nostalgic reminder of how I used to be myself when I first got into showbusiness.

An uncomfortable silence enveloped the taxi. The young salaryman tried to break the ice by giving a brief introduction. Turned out he worked in the sales department of a certain food manufacturer, and he'd got stuck at the office doing overtime today. It was a very commonplace tale, but his bright manner brought a perceptible thaw to the atmosphere. He followed up his opening gambit by asking the middle-aged gent what line of business he might be in.

'I'm involved with the electrical industry,' he said, somewhat enigmatically. We all had to guess the precise nature of his involvement with the electrical industry, like in one of those quiz programmes. At last he put us out of our misery. 'Actually I work for a company that installs the lighting systems in convenience stores and the like. It's not a line of business that people know a lot about.'

Oh really? Well I never.

The time was passing pleasantly enough. The middle-aged gent modestly opined that his kind of work was really of no consequence to the rest of us and invited the young office girl, sitting there primly with a briefcase clutched to her breast, to tell us about her line of business. Another round of the quiz game got under way.

I got slightly excited. It would be my turn next. What would I say? As a matter of fact, I'm a professional singer. They'd be surprised, no doubt. Pleased, maybe. But I haven't made any CDs. Shows? Oh, mostly health spas and similar. Well then, why don't we go along and watch next time? All three of us? What a splendid idea. Well, perhaps that was being a little too fanciful.

I forgot to listen to what the office girl was saying about her work, but it must have been very funny, because the two guys were laughing fit to bust and were talking noticeably louder than before.

Here it comes, my turn to talk. But just then the atmosphere in the taxi went all stiff again. All three of them went silent, and they weren't even looking at me. Then suddenly they started talking about baseball and sumo wrestling and stuff. It was like they'd changed channels on the television or something.

How come no one asks about what *I* do for a living? I was taken aback. Very much taken aback, like the middle-aged gent when the taxi-driver ignored him. Why? Why, for crying out loud?

We got to East Urawa, and the office girl with the drooping eyes got out. 'Goodnight, all.' She glanced momentarily in my direction, then held out a couple of 1,000-yen notes to the men in the back seat, but they would only take one.

'A thousand will be plenty.'

'Really? Are you sure?'

'Sure we're sure. Go on, put the other one away. I've got a soft spot for young ladies.' There was a round of good-natured laughter, and then the taxi sped off once more.

After the droopy-eyed office girl got out, the atmosphere in the taxi reverted once more to a frigid silence. The two men couldn't very well talk to each other and completely ignore me, and they appeared to be furiously searching their brains for some way to bring me into the conversation.

Can't think of anything to talk about, eh? Well I'm damned if I'm going to help you out after what you did to me just now. I used to think I was the same as everybody else. Maybe I was wrong. Maybe there's some huge difference. What could it be?

When I was about twenty, I was still the same as everybody else. OK, I guess I was a bit more showy than your average girl, which people sometimes found slightly intriguing. 'Are you involved in the entertainment industry in some way?' they would ask, half in fun. But, with the passing of time, I realized, the fun half of that question had clearly been disappearing. And so to the present day, in which people carelessly neglect even to ask me about my work. I don't know why. I don't suppose I'll know why to the day I die. Could it be something to do with my clothing and makeup, I wonder. Is it out of synch with those of other people? I stole a look at my appearance reflected in the taxi window. Night had turned it into a black mirror, and my white face was reflected in it like the moon. I was wearing a leopard-skin-print trouser-suit with matching hat. Admittedly it was a little on the gaudy side, but I had bought it during the daytime, from the kind of place where regular folk buy their clothes – the respected Marui Department Store, no less.

I recalled another of Mr Wild's complaints. When I arrived home from a show and went flying to his arms, he would sternly order me to go and wash my face before he'd give me a kiss. 'Do me a favour, kid. This isn't the kabuki theatre.' Well, when you're on the stage, there's a lot of glare from the lighting and the audience is seated a long way off, so inevitably your face gets blurred. Naturally, I have to put on a certain amount of makeup. Eyes, mouth, eyebrows – well, OK, I guess I do it lay on pretty thick over my whole face. I suppose you could even say I slather it on. Slather, slather. If I don't put plenty of effort into my makeup I somehow feel that everything, even me, could just fade away like foam.

After a few warnings from Daiki, I took more care to get my stage makeup off before returning home. But, you know, makeup's funny stuff. It sort of seeps into you, and there comes a point where somehow your face seems like it's caked with it even after you've washed it off.

Riding the train, walking the street, wherever I go I can spot them, the slather people. They live in among the regular people, unnoticed by most folk but not by me. Takes one to know one. Day after day I slather on the greasepaint in the dressing-room. I'm sure every contour of my body is well slathered. No wonder people are surprised when they see me. I know – I'll soften the lines by feathering them into the background a little more, like Yumekawa and Shimako Sado do. Like in those posters of theirs.

The taxi threaded through the night until at last we got to East Kawaguchi. The two male passengers had atrophied into silence, but the moment they heard me tell the driver that we were nearly at my getting-off point they started shifting and stretching in their seats like workers realizing that their long-awaited tea-break was about to begin. The moment I'm out of the taxi, they'll get that liberated feeling and their conversation will bloom. I felt betrayed. Who was it who had the bright idea of sharing a taxi in the first place? Me. They had blithely ignored the hero who had made the whole event possible.

I felt my anger rising. The taxi arrived in front of the station and came to a halt. I got out, ostentatiously clicking my high heels on the road, and heaved my trundle-trolley out of the trunk. The door of the taxi was still open, but I slammed it shut with an imperious flourish. I'd decided I wasn't going to pay my share.

'I haven't got any money. Sorry, guys.' The two men made no attempt to look me in the eye. They just sat there stiffly like dummies. The pathetic jerks. I set the trundle-trolley in motion and set off for home. At that point the taxi-driver poked his head out of the window and called out to my rapidly receding figure:

'Good luck, darlin'.' Those unexpected warm words hit home and stopped me in my tracks. I looked over my shoulder, and there was the driver, grinning broadly enough to reveal the few teeth he had left in his head.

'You're a singer, ain't ya?'

Taxi drivers always know. Maybe they have the knack of spotting the slather people. Or maybe they can hear us, hear the drifting, the slip-sliding, the squealing wheels.

9 Birth Elegy

December comes, and you start to see girls wearing kimonos on the street. By January you see them everywhere, as traditional events like New Year shrine visits and Coming of Age Day demand the wearing of traditional clothing. We enka singers have to devote extra care and attention to our stage-clothing at this time of year because the audience grows used to the sight of pretty kimonos. We have to wear something that looks sharp enough to draw a clear line between ourselves and all the ordinary girls in kimono.

With that in mind I set out one day in early December on my winter pilgrimage to the specialist kimono stores of Tokyo, but nowhere could I find anything that might set me apart from the crowd. So I started thinking that maybe I should look for something more Western in style – a line of thinking that took me back to Uguisudani, to a clothes shop located just around the corner from a retro-style dance hall. But the ball gowns on sale for social dancing were all far too expensive for the likes of me.

It was no good relying on others. Resolving to make a dress for myself, I headed for Okadaya, a huge six-storey emporium in Shinjuku that specializes in dressmaking and stage materials. This place is an Aladdin's Cave of lamé and spangles and all things shiny, wigs and hair extensions, furs and feather boas, greasepaint and rouge. Each floor has its own theme, and all are packed to the gunwales with everything an entertainer's heart could desire. Every time I go there I'm liable to bump into people I know – travelling magicians, strippers and so on – looking for props for their shows.

Aha! As I walked around the fabric displays an image started to take shape in my mind. I bought a job lot of black lace and headed for home.

With a cabaret show in Chiba coming up in two days, I was determined to make myself a really flashy kimono in the limited time available. You'd be surprised how simple it is to make one up. All the joins are nice and straight and you just need a clear eye and a steady hand. In the kimono workshop at school we used to have competitions to see who could sew up a kimono quickest, and some of us could do it in less than thirty minutes – hand sewn, you understand, no machines involved.

I wanted to get the rough shape of it cut out and pinned by early evening, since I was expecting Daiki to come home around six. If he caught me absorbed in the task of making a stage costume there'd be hell to pay. He'd go straight into one of his moods.

The heavy tailor's scissors gleamed dully in my hand. I attacked the black lace, slashing in all directions. The scissors cut through the material like a leaden ship making its way uncertainly through a black oil-slicked sea. Wearing a kimono made of this high-class French lace, I ought to look pretty stunning. If I added a beige lining, it would give the impression that I had nothing on under the lace, so it ought to be a fairly sexy look, too. I wouldn't bother with any lining in the sleeves. I reckoned that the audience would be able to see my arms right through the lace under the stage lighting. When I put the kimono on, I'd drop a few ten-yen coins into the sleeves as weights. Lace obviously doesn't weigh as much as silk, and if the sleeves flap around too lightly it can look cheap. An enka singer's arm movements tell a story, and this kind of little detail makes all the difference.

I would wear a gold *obi* with it. The broad belt would be offset nicely with a green lamé support and drawstring. I'd put my hair up as high as it could possibly go, and hold it all together with a single peacock feather in place of the usual hairpin. There'd be no earrings, and certainly nothing as undignified as high heels – no way! I would stick to kimono orthodoxy and go with the white socks and *zori* sandals. That would really bring out the daring concept of the black lace kimono. I had it all figured out.

Just then I heard a sound at the front door. Glancing up at the clock, I saw it was already well past six. Mr Wild was back from work. In a panic I shoved the pinned-up material and the tailoring kit into a paper bag like a dustman clearing away rubbish.

'Hi,' he said and gave a smile. 'Today was mess-up day at the building site, so I didn't have to work that hard. Did work up quite an appetite, though.'

'Er, what's mess-up day?'

'Oh, well, that's the day when we have the final inspection to make sure we haven't messed anything up. Just a bit of building-site slang.' Building-site slang, eh? Cool. Wish I could use it, but there's no such thing as a general inspection in the world of travelling shows. Our work is like building a house and then knocking it down again in the space of an hour.

The next day, however, alone in the room once more, I wasn't so sure. So, I'm going to be under general inspection this evening. Hope this isn't going to be my own personal mess-up day . . .

The black-lace kimono is completed and ready to be unveiled here at the Chiba branch of the Knockout Cabaret, on the eastern outskirts of Tokyo. Today's main event will be Hiroshi Yumekawa singing his brand-new release for the first time in public. I will be the support act, getting the audience warmed up for my good friend Hiroshi.

'Laydeeez and gennlemen. Opening tonight's Golden Show, we present for your delight and delectation, the tiny songbird of the world of enka, live on stage, the lovely, the talented, the one and only Rinka Kazuki!' As the MC's mike reverb echoed away, a great hubbub arose from the audience. You could see right through the black-lace kimono at my arms and legs. I had fixed the lining below the waist to make it look as if I was wearing some kind of miniskirt under the kimono, but since all the lining was beige, not unlike the colour of human skin, it looked from a distance as though I had nothing much on at all under the kimono.

I had hoped to make an impact, but I hadn't expected the uproar that now ensued. Catching the mood, the lighting man put a stronger spot on me while the sound man turned up the mike. Well, all for the best I suppose. I could see the hostesses starting to chatter enviously about my fantastic outfit and to speculate as to which famous fashion designer might be responsible for it.

> I fix my eyes upon the rain-swept top deck,
> But they are blinded by my overflowing tears

Singing passionately, I glanced left and observed a crowd of several dozen men jostling up against the side of the stage, fixing their eyes on *my* top deck. What is going on here? I can't believe this is happening.

'Go for it, baby.' The guys lining the stage looked like a real bunch of gangsters. They were all waving their disposable chopsticks, carrying tips. I didn't like their eyes, however. They stared at me intently, trying to figure out whether they really could see right through the lace, and also calculating my age, evaluating my looks and generally inspecting the goods in as much detail as possible.

'Oh, er, thank you very much.' I took the tips with as much grace as I could manage. Mostly they were the usual thousand-yen notes, although for some reason a few of the men held out betting tickets for the horse races in their chopsticks. There was also one old guy who rather adroitly held a hundred-yen coin between his chopsticks. Every time a song started or finished, he'd rise from his seat and make his way to the stage to present me with another hundred-yen coin. Evidently he wanted a thousand yen to buy him ten close looks at me rather than just the one.

'Whoaar!'

'Fwaaar!'

Every time I tried to ask the MC to do something about the situation, my voice would be drowned out by the lusty catcalls of the bandits. They hadn't had this much fun in years, and they wanted to make the most of it. These guys were wild animals. I gulped nervously. Chiba is an unfashionable, semi-rural suburb of Tokyo, but some parts of Chiba have a bad reputation. Come to think of it, I had seen some funny-looking posters stuck up in the dressing-room and corridors:

> You may have been told that drugs can help you to lose weight,
> but don't be fooled.
> Heroin, marijuana, LSD, etc., are all very bad for the health.
> Please refrain from using them.

I eventually retreated to the safety of the dressing-room, weighed down with an almighty load of tip-money. Suddenly, I felt a twinge of concern about Hiroshi Yumekawa. The audience was seething with lust, and now they were about to discover that the night's main event was going to feature a singer of the male persuasion. Uh-oh, this could turn nasty. Maybe it was already too late. In mounting desperation, I rushed to the wings and took a peak at the stage. There was Yumekawa, bathed in the pure white stage lighting. Just as I'd feared, he was being loudly heckled. Portions of fried chicken and balls of crumpled paper were flying through the air all around him.

'Fuck off, fancy pants.'

'Get stuffed.'

Poor old Hiroshi, my heart went out to him. But there wasn't a lot I could do other than watch events unfold and pray for his safety.

'Fuck off! You're spoiling my drink.'

'Get him off!'

'Off, off, off!'

'Don't worry, mate, I've got a job for you at the building site!'

Freezing, freezing,
With these blues,
With these freezing-cold blues.
Oh, oh, oh . . .

You had to admire the guy's professionalism. He didn't flinch for a moment. In the middle of all the abuse, Hiroshi carried right on singing the blues – and with feeling. Today, as ever, the song came welling up from his inner soul like the boiling waters from a volcanic hot spring, passionate enough to shake your very soul.

'Cool . . .' I stood there quivering with emotion. 'Man, you are so cool.' Yumekawa glanced sideways and caught sight of me watching from the wings, now back in my ordinary clothes. He seemed pleased to see me, and flashed me a little grin.

'And now, ladies and gentlemen, the sand guy from Tottori, Hiroshi Yumekawa, presents, just for you, his brand-new single, scheduled for nationwide release this coming March.' The MC – who was in fact a waiter at the cabaret – did his best to cut through the noise of the heckling, standing centre stage with a massive smile plastered across his face. The drum-roll commenced its familiar accompaniment to events of gravity and significance. The artificial air of tension thus created had some effect: the noisy heckling of the Chiba bandits was reduced to a subdued grumbling.

'OK, it's the moment you've all been waiting for! I give you Hiroshi and Miko with "Rumba for Two". Oh yeah!'

The band struck up with a lively rumba rhythm and Yumekawa walked calmly back on stage. At the same time his duet partner, 'Miko', came bouncing on to the stage from the opposite direction, smiling fit to bust.

It was Kaho!

I stared slack-jawed as the detestable Gaho the Pig answered Yumekawa's greeting of 'Hi there, Miko!' with a cheery 'Hi there, Hiroshi!' What the hell is going on here?

Rumba for two, rumba together.
Yeah, yeah, do the rumba, baby.
[He] You're the only girl who can rumba with me,
[She] You're the only boy who can rumba with me,
[Together] So come on, baby, and rumba, rumba, rumba with me!

Gaho the Pig was dressed in white to match her partner. It was a frilly, girlish one-piece, and she was behaving in a modest, demure manner that went with her character like salt in coffee.

Oh, lordy. It's that song Yumekawa told me about when we met at Teruo Hikari's place. The one for the rigged competition. The one for the Cinderella début.

'Ladies and gentlemen, allow me to introduce the enchanting Miko. This is the young lady selected from thousands of hopefuls in a nationwide audition to be my partner in the duet you have just heard. Another big round of applause, please, for Miko!' There was a smattering of applause. The sight of something female on stage had placated the assembled bandits to a degree.

'I thank you most sincerely.' I recoiled at the sound of Gaho the Pig's artificially ladylike voice. All the frilly white dresses and elocution classes in the world couldn't conceal her true nature – which was about as elegant as a hippo. It was horrible to behold.

At the same time I guess I also felt a sense of relief that Gaho had started to get some proper singing work – and to be honest, a slight twinge of regret that I had turned down Hiroshi Yumekawa's invitation to do the duet with him. Hey – that could have been me. Then again, it was only the kind of regret you might feel at losing out in a lottery where the top prize was a designer head scarf.

'We can't put Yumekawa back on stage solo. The crowd won't like it.'

'We'll just have to ask Miko to do the second half.' Right behind me, a hurried meeting had been convened by the MC and some of the other cabaret staff. The band started playing Yujiro Ishihara's 'Thank You Once Again, Night Mist'. I think Yumekawa was supposed to be singing this number, but they'd let the band do it as an instrumental to protect him from the booing. The bandsmen saw this as their big chance to show what they could do, and were playing their hearts out. The song opens with a rather beautiful breathy saxophone solo, and the cabaret sax man was doing a good enough job of it to restore the crowd to good humour. They started treating the band like a karaoke kit, supplying their own drunken vocals.

In the wings, on the opposite side of the stage, I could see Kaho nodding to the MC and then rushing off backstage. It would appear that she had agreed to act as Yumekawa's emergency substitute for the second half.

'The first number I will sing for you is entitled "Butterfly". I've always wanted to be a beautiful butterfly of the enka world, but I guess I'm just a humble caterpillar at present.'

Just a damn minute. That's one of my lines. Word for word. Has she been taping my show, the bitch? Feeling deeply suspicious, I listen to the opening of the song. It's supposed to start with a haunting violin solo, but the cabaret band doesn't have a violinist, so the intro is being played on the piano. Ah, that familiar despairing melody, hinting at life about to collapse into ruins.

Hang on, that's a little too familiar. That *is* my score, no mistake about it; a straight copy. How did she do it? I definitely tackled her short of the photocopying machine that time she was pestering me about the scores.

I stood there in shock, trembling all over. Just then I noticed the alto-sax player glance my way with a faint look of embarrassment in his eyes. He was a bit of a bad lad, this sax player; he used to be one of Kaho's customers in the days when she still worked as a prostitute, and he made a fair bit of money out of setting girls up with singing jobs in clubs and charging them a commission. A real creep. Come to think of it, he was sitting in on the band at another club I played at last month. I'd figured out a rather nice programme that night, which included a medley, one chorus each of 'Ballad of the Man of Kawachi' and 'Summer Cicadas', followed by 'The Sound of Waves' and 'Love's Autumn Leaves'. Gaho the Pig was now singing the same songs, in the same order.

I sensed a distinct possibility that the alto-sax player had popped out during the interval that day, nipped over to a nearby corner shop, photocopied the lot and then sold them to Kaho – possibly to other singers, too. Shit.

You know, the Rinka Kazuki show has a good reputation within the profession. I quite often see other travelling enka singers in the audience when I'm on stage. I don't know them personally, but you can spot the type a mile off, even in their daytime clothes. Besides, who else takes notes while listening to sentimental ballads? Imitation is the sincerest form of flattery, and this unspoken compliment from my fellow artistes is the one thing that gives me a real sense of pride in my work. I owe it all to Mr Iwatani, who has provided me with some thirty masterly enka arrangements, all at no cost to me. These all-important arrangements were now being performed without me being on the stage.

Kaho Jojima, you will fry in hell for your sins. Oh ye gods of music, take those songs away from her!

Right before my eyes I could see her big red rubbery lips, like slabs of cod roe past their sell-by date, befouling those lovely sounds made just for me. Her white one-piece diffused the gaudy stage lighting in all directions as she turned from white to blood red, from red to a deep, diseased blue. Kaho spinning on her heel; Kaho's blubbery lips, laughing; the sax player, standing up to take his solo.

It was only last week that I had received a missive, self-consciously entitled 'A Hopeless Love Letter'. It was from Mr Iwatani, the sixty-year-old man who wrote all my lovely arrangements, and now, as the anger and disappointment at Kaho's treachery welled up within me, I recalled those bitter-sweet lines from the old man:

> I know this is a hopeless love letter, but please read it anyway. I understand that word has got around about my writing arrangements for you free of charge and that this has led to some unpleasant rumours, for which I am deeply sorry. But the undeniable fact is that I love you, Rinka. Or, to be more precise, I feel a profound fellow feeling for you and your love of music.
>
> How your eyes shine whenever we meet to discuss our musical arrangements! When I first saw those eyes, I knew I could never take money from you. Please do not be alarmed at this letter. For I

am content just to commune with you through the medium of music.

I am embarrassed to have taken such liberties in writing this letter to you, but these are my honest feelings. When you have finished reading this letter, please throw it away.

K. Iwatani
23 November

Mr Iwatani used to figure out his arrangements in his head while working as a security guard. Now he has a new job, winding metal rope into coils on the night shift at a factory. He never complains about the mind-numbing work or the pitiful wages; somehow he finds time to carry on with his music. Even his long-suffering wife, who shared the ups and downs of life with him for so many years, finally lost patience and walked out on him a while back.

I remember his hands, placed on the table in the coffee-shop where we used to meet to discuss arrangements. I don't know whether it was some kind of work-related injury, but each one of his fingers was crushed fat and flattish like the head of a snake. A wave of sadness always runs through me when I recall those broken, ink-stained hands. Shows, music, that sweet fruit with its rough and bitter-tasting rind, he had accidentally put in his pocket. And the result was a sound that had a manly strain of pathos to it that was his and his alone.

> Today, once more, my swelling feelings
> Vanish with the sinking sun at dusk.
> How many dreams have washed away with the years?

Only someone with a little body, singing her heart out, can really bring out the sweet melody of 'Love's Autumn Leaves'. The sight of Kaho standing there with her graceless bulky figure and her big sullen face, butchering Mr Iwata's bitter-sweet arrangement of this beautiful love song, was too much to bear. If I was going to stop her, now was the time.

'Hey, Rinka?' Dressed in my day-time clothes, I marched on to the stage and grabbed the microphone out of the Pig's hands. The members of the band were thrown into confusion at the sight of it all, and Kaho herself was all of a fluster. The bandits in the audience didn't notice. They hadn't been listening to Kaho's hastily mugged-up enka anyway.

Beloved one, fly to me.
Even living in love,
There is no tomorrow
For one such as I.

Having seized possession of the microphone, I thought I
might as well carry on with the song. I only managed a couple of
lines, though, before an outraged Kaho swiped the mike from my
grasp. I grabbed it back; she grabbed it back again.

At long last the audience began to buzz. A few people were giggling. It was nine o'clock, peak time for the cabaret. The place
was packed, and the staff were too busy rushing around serving
all the customers to notice anything untoward happening on the
stage.

'Give that back. It's *my* mike.'

'Shut up, you lousy thieving bitch! If you want it, you can damn
well have it.' I hurled the microphone at Kaho's feet. Emitting ear-
splitting squeals of feedback, it bounced off the stage and rolled
away.

Aiiieeeee!

The hostesses and customers squirmed in their seats, hands
clasped over their ears. The racket finally alerted the waiters to
the situation, and they started shouting to each other about
whose job it was to go up on the stage and do something about it.
The MC was howling in total confusion.

'Envious are we, Rinka?' The scent of battle had got to Kaho, and
she instantly shed her thin veneer of ladylike decorum and revealed
her true character, that of an overgrown teenage delinquent. She
stood before me, hands on hips, showing her white teeth in a leer
of victory.

'You're just jealous of me, aren't you.' She really thought I
envied her because she was going to release her silly CD. Everything about this woman was gross – even her misunderstand-
ings.

'Wrong again, shitface.' In the heat of the moment, I slipped
into Kyushu dialect. Uh-oh. Down, everyone. I'm gonna knock
her block off. I tightened my fists, glaring up at Kaho. Unfazed,
she gazed down at me in utter contempt. It did give me pause for
thought, the huge height difference between the two of us: this
giant woman was nearly six feet tall, and I was the tiny songbird
of the world of enka. How could I hope to bring her down? Not by
a frontal assault, surely. What to do? My fists trembled slightly,

just like Kenjiro that time he stood face to face with the giant Daiki.

'Come on, girl, show 'er who's boss!'

'Cat fight! Cat fight!' The bandits were all shouting out in unison. Some came crowding up to the stage to get a better view of the action. The bandsmen held on to their instruments and feigned indifference, but their eyeballs were about ready to pop out on stalks. They were holding their collective breath and making little expectant gulping noises.

At that moment, the MC came rushing breathlessly on to the stage. Seeing that he was about to grab me by the arm, I hurriedly switched tactics, picking up the fallen microphone and clearing my throat.

'Ladies and gentlemen, please accept my most sincere apologies for the regrettable situation that has just developed.' At once the MC's tense facial expression relaxed a degree. Kaho glanced at me as though I were the world's biggest idiot. Her shoulders rocked in silent, sneering laughter.

'What, is show time over already?'

'Bummer. No punch-up after all . . .' The Chiba bandits' eager expressions turned to looks of disappointment.

'I am very sorry indeed.' This time I turned to Kaho and gave a deep, deep bow. Her feet came into vision. She was wearing very high-heeled stage stilettos. Why, those heels must be all of four inches. I gave a wicked little smile. I wasn't really admitting defeat, no way. That was just a tactic.

'Have some of *that*.' I didn't really shove her that hard, but on those wobbly heels of hers Kaho immediately lost her balance. She gave a comical little dance, teetering around like a puppet on a string, then toppled backwards, arse over tit, straight into the orchestra pit. With a shrill scream of horror, she went to ground between the keyboards and the guitar, dragging a few bandsmen down with her in an almighty cacophony of crashing musical instruments. That should teach her a lesson. The bandits responded once more:

'Woo! Yee-hah!'

'That's the spirit!'

'Go for it, little 'un!'

But Kaho wasn't finished yet. She picked herself up from the wreckage and glared at me like a demon from hell. It occurred to me that I, too, had high heels on, almost as high as hers. As she came menacingly towards me, I hastily crouched down, took them off and flung them aside ready for the fray. But before I had time to stand up properly, she was upon me. With a blood-curdling cry, she kneed me in the lower stomach. For a moment pain swept through my body and I thought I was going to puke. But the moment passed: she still had the stilettos on, and that robbed her of the firm footing you need to deliver a really destructive knee in the stomach. Besides, my stomach muscles are pretty tough from all those hundreds of hours belting out enka. Winded only for a second, I regained my balance and lunged straight at her knees. This time I got both my hands around the back of her legs and hauled both of them off the ground with a single mighty heave. Same technique: same result. She gave a shrill squeal and went over again, arms and legs flailing in all directions.

The bandits were delighted and laughed like hyperactive children.

'This is great.'

'Go on, do it again.'

'Get in there. Finish her off!' They were laughing and yelling and stamping rhythmically on the cabaret floor. The din brought the whole place to boiling point, stirring me to ever greater excitement. However, the next time Kaho picked herself up off the floor the MC got to her before I could, and he hauled her off to the dressing-room. At that moment, a sonorous amplified voice filled the auditorium.

'Go for the hook! Straight to the body! Body, body, uppercut! So, you'd mess with me? I'll get you for that!' With a barrage of lines in the hard-boiled style of Yujiro Ishihara, Hiroshi Yumekawa stepped on to the stage. Almost as if it had been arranged beforehand, the lighting man picked him out with the pinpoint spot. With a cheesy grin, Yumekawa delivered the punch line:

'You want trouble, then come and get it!' The place suddenly fell silent. Yumekawa turned to the band without bothering to switch off the microphone. 'Are you ready, boys? Then let's go.' The bandsmen started hastily turning pages in their scores, and the drummer kicked things off with a determined solo. The song was 'Stormbringer'. Yumekawa sang it with gusto, a gusto that instantly communicated itself to the assembled bandits. The cabaret came back to life again; audience and stage merged and became one. Yumekawa lifted his voice with great enthusiasm; almost certainly he'd never experienced such high levels of tension at a show before. Exactly as originally planned, he launched into a medley of Yujiro Ishihara songs. The bandits of Chiba lapped it up like puppies.

As for the staff, they were totally cool. When the fight broke out, Yumekawa had apparently had a quick word with them. They would treat the whole ugly affair as if it were part of his stage show. Nothing to worry about; leave it to me. This was typical of the man. He loves to put on a theatrical performance – in fact, he once told me his dream was to top the bill at the famous Koma Theatre in Shinjuku.

As for me, I felt a tad deflated to find that my fight to the death with Kaho had been reduced to a single scene in somebody else's drama. On the other hand, Yumekawa's quick thinking saved me from being drummed out of the profession, so I suppose I should be thankful to the guy.

However, some time after the event, when I had almost forgotten about it, my stage-fighting antics did have very serious consequences for me.

Kaho – no, I have to go back to calling her Gaho the Pig, although even that is too good for her – Gaho the Pig took a terrible revenge on me and promptly went into hiding somewhere.

'Some woman rang up my wife and calmly told her all about you and me living together. The wife tried to laugh it off – probably just some practical joke, she said. But I'm a bit worried about her psychological state. Seems she's started getting into some weird religious cult lately. What a drag.'

Last week, Daiki had been driving through the neighbouring district when Kaho spotted him and flagged him down. She wheedled him into giving her a lift home, and during the ride the cunning bitch started up a conversation about how funny it is that people's photographs on their driving licences always make them look like criminals on wanted posters. She managed to persuade the unwitting Daiki to get out his own licence and show it to her. His home telephone number was written on the licence.

I really should have told Daiki about my fight with Gaho the Pig. But it was too late for regrets now. For a few days I would have to get out of the flat, taking all my possessions with me, so that Daiki could show the place to his wife. What a drag, indeed.

'All I have to do is give her a quick look at the flat, and I'm pretty sure she won't want to poke her nose in any further.'

'I see. I guess that's the only thing for it, then.'

'I've already fixed up one of those short-term weekly rental places for you. It'll just be a week, at the most. I'll come and get you in a week, with the light truck from work to bring all your stuff back.'

'What a pain.'

'Don't get upset about it.' Actually, to tell the complete truth, I was secretly rather curious to check out life all on my own. I could concentrate on my show without having to worry about what anybody else thought about it. That wouldn't be too bad – hey, it sounded like paradise. My eyes moistened at the very thought, and Daiki's face blurred over as I talked to him.

'One week of complete chastity. It'll probably be good for both of us. We'll come back to each other stimulated and, er, fresh.'

'Oh, how you do go on.'

Maybe it was only going to be for a week, but a week was a long time for a lusty fellow like Daiki. A twinge of anxiety that he might have it away with some other woman while I was out of sight did briefly cross my mind, but things were already under way. He showed up at the flat with some of his workers, and they cleared all my things out of there in next to no time.

'Your possessions consist almost entirely of clothes!' Listening to gripes such as these from Daiki as we drove along in the truck, I was taken, along with all my worldly chattels, to a place a considerable distance away.

It only took one evening to set up my little castle at the temporary lodgings in Tokorozawa, Saitama Prefecture. This temporary move brought home to me that, just as Daiki had pointed out, the components of my daily life consisted almost entirely of items related to singing and shows. There were ten clothing boxes with denim finish, all of them packed with dresses; feather boas, gloves, clothes, props and paraphernalia filled another seven cardboard boxes. And, the *pièce de resistance*, seven beautiful long-sleeved kimonos, another twelve short-sleeved ones and twenty-eight sumptuous *obi* belts, all in a gigantic paulownia wardrobe. Of course, I also had a whole bunch of clothes for everyday use. I didn't have a single kitchen utensil or a single book – unless you count all the enka songbooks and back numbers of enka magazines. I also had three hundred CDs. I had to admit Daiki had a point. These things did not suggest a regular, respectable sort of lifestyle.

But I really enjoyed having that stuff around me; and I wanted someone to tell me, 'That's all right. It's you.' When I want that kind of encouragement, the person I call is Kenjiro. He's had a big hit with 'Man of Japan', and he's quite a star in Taiwan these days, but we still have the same frank, open-hearted relationship as ever.

'Oh good, Ken-chan, you're back in the country. Got time to meet up?'

'I'll be right over. You're where? Tokorozawa?'

'You can't come here, Ken. I'm on my own and I don't trust you with your wicked ways.'

'No need to worry. I'm with my singing teacher. He's the guy who writes my songs. We'll just pop over to your place and have the lesson there.'

'Still acting on impulse, I see.'

Amazingly enough, Kenjiro arrived at the flat just ten minutes after I put down the telephone.

'Ta-daa! Surprised? When you called, we happened to be at a petrol station right near here. The maestro's Mercedes was feeling a little thirsty, see. Wasn't it, maestro?' The man Kenjiro called his maestro was a greasy, middle-aged fellow. He gave a little titter and passed me a business card on the fat palm of a hand the stubby little fingers of which suggested a man incapable of thinking other than in broad generalities. He had a forceful way of looking at you and a mouth that suggested he probably liked to have a few drinks. His whole appearance was that of an unhealthy gourmand.

'Would I be correct in reading these characters as Reiji Gosaka?' I enquired, politely inspecting the business card.

'Yes, indeed. Delighted to make your acquaintance. I've heard all about you from Ken here. My ear's still buzzing.'

'What do you mean, maestro, your ear's buzzing? It's not like I talk about her all the time.' The two of them seemed to be on decidedly familiar terms. The relationship didn't really feel like one between a singer and his teacher. It was more like they were best pals. I found myself feeling a bit dubious about them.

'Um, what sort of thing does he say about me?' I felt a bit awkward about intruding on this sort of private joking relationship they seemed to have, but I thought I ought to contribute to the conversation anyway.

'Well, Ken's always boasting that he's got this really naïve, innocent girlfriend . . . Hey, stop poking me.'

'Gotcha, gotcha! I'm butting in, like it or not.'

'Lay off, Ken. Anyway, as I was saying, apparently the two of you went to a love hotel in Uguisudani, though I don't quite know what happened after that . . .'

'Maestro, please! That's more than enough. Do me a favour . . .'

'Heh-heh-heh. Sorry. Making all this fuss the first time we meet.'

Giving them a look close to disgust, I found myself distracted by a memory from the past. When I was younger than I am today, boys quite often tried to pick me up simply by calling to me in the street. Usually there'd be two of them. If I agreed to go to a café with them, they'd start joking around with each other just like this, and before long I'd be wanting to go home and leave them to it. Another thing about those teenage pick-up teams was that they were much too insensitive to notice that you were getting tired of their company. They would just go on and on with their unfunny in-jokes. What was a girl supposed to do in a situation like that? Smile cheerfully and let them get on with it? There came a moment when you just had to yell at them, 'Give me back my time!'

However, while I was absorbed in these recollections, the pair of time-wasters currently invading my space had cunningly sat themselves down on the floor and started their singing lesson right there in my flat. The sheer impudence was unbelievable, but for some reason I couldn't bring myself to hate them for it. Instead I pottered off to the kitchen to make the tea.

'I keep telling you, you've got to put more of your sloppy, irresponsible character into that phrase.'

'Hm. That's a tough one.'

I was surprised to find that they were doing the lesson right here in this empty room, without a piano or any other equipment. The lesson consisted entirely of discussion on how best to put the lyrics over. Gosaka was an entirely different man now; his face showed an intensity terrible to behold, and he spoke the lines with feverish excitement. The menacing atmosphere was thankfully offset by the comic effect of Gosaka's roly-poly appearance. He sat there like a big teddy bear. He wore these old-fashioned braces rather than a belt – perhaps because they don't sell belts big enough for someone his size – and they made him look even more ridiculous. Somehow it made you feel less scared of him.

Gosaka's lesson was out of this world. Even just reading out the lines of songs, he had an amazing power of expression. He had a brilliant voice, too. Apparently, his father had been a professional storyteller, and Gosaka himself had enjoyed speaking in rhetorical style from early childhood.

'You're a singer, too, I gather,' he said to me. 'Why don't you join in the lesson?' I accepted the invitation. The song was called 'Rambling Gambler', and it was supposed to be Kenjiro's next single. Like 'Man of Japan' it had words and music both by Gosaka, and also like 'Man of Japan' it was brimful of spirit. Both songs had a simplicity about them that made you admire them whichever way you tried to look at them. They were so simple and clear that no ordinary adult could have written them. Something about them pierced the soul. It was no use trying to analyse them; you just had to take them for what they were – expressions of pure sentiment. The purity made you admire them despite their simplicity. These songs were so pure and innocent that they could have been written by a child.

'You've got a nice voice, Rinka.' I'd just been about to start praising Gosaka, but he beat me to the draw. I shyly remarked that if I sang well it was all thanks to the excellence of the song. To which Gosaka responded, in a voice so loud I thought my ear drums would burst, with a lengthy, passionate account of the intense personal struggle that went into getting that song written. 'That's why it's so good. Of course it's good, after all that. I've got better ones, though. Just a moment. Do you have a cassette player here?'

As it happened, my proper tape deck was at the mender's, and all I had to hand was a clapped-out piece of junk that I bought ten years ago on sale at a discount warehouse. I got it out of the stored luggage anyway, and by the time I'd located it Gosaka had already nipped out and come back with a tape from his car. Even that short journey had left him puffing and panting, and taking his shoes off on his way back into the apartment seemed to have tried his patience to the extreme. A creature of impulse, he'd trampled all over my shoes and knocked over the umbrella stand on his way in. It was as if a small whirlwind had visited the apartment.

'Here we are, here we are. Listen to this one first. This one. Fantastic, eh? Ha-ha-ha! How about those airplane noises? Vrooom!' Gosaka forgot all about Kenjiro's lesson and launched into a presentation with full commentary on his unpublished works. Kenjiro sat there listening in silence, smirking smugly all over his face. The one with the airplane sound effects was called

'Rainy Day, Terminal B'. It was still at the demo stage – a rough and ready recording he'd made himself. He hadn't even added a vocal line yet; it was just the backing track. Even so, you could tell it was a fantastic song, a really moving piece of music.

'What d'you think? Pretty good, eh? That background effect with the jet engines – I recorded that myself, you know, at a real airport. I took a little tape recorder with me, sneaked out of the building and ran over to where this airplane was standing on the tarmac with its engines running. Actually I nearly got run over and killed. The security guards arrested me and gave me a two-hour lecture about my irresponsible behaviour . . . Aha, here comes the next number. Now this, you'll find, is a very different piece.'

He played us one song after another. Each one had a truly astounding originality about it, and not one would have sounded out of place at the top of the charts. I couldn't believe it. Here was this guy I'd never even heard of before, sitting on the floor of my room, using my tinny little cassette deck to play a series of songs, virtually unheard by human ear, each and every one of which would put to shame the top-selling composers and lyricists in the land. Out they came, just like that, one after the other, a string of pearls. Did things like this really happen to people?

After he had played us his masterpieces, Gosaka sat there in great good humour and said something that really blew me away:

'You know, Rinka, I have a feeling that you and me are going to hit if off together. Hey, Kenjiro, what say we look after Rinka as well?'

Kenjiro opened his mouth blankly for a moment. 'Er, look after . . . ?'

Gosaka thrust out his mighty paunch and explained in a low voice. 'What I mean, of course, is that we'll arrange Rinka's début the same way we arranged yours.'

'What? Ha-ha, here we go again.' When Kenjiro laughed and said 'here we go again', he didn't mean that Gosaka was just fooling around and liked to kid singers that he was going to launch their careers. No, what he meant was that this was Gosaka's style, making really big, serious decisions on impulse. I nearly fainted. Could it really be that simple?

Début. Officially, of course, it was my great aim in life, just as it is for any singer. But until this moment I hadn't really wanted it for real, not from the bottom of my being. Now, however, the word had a lovely ring to it. The difference, of course, was that now I was crazy about this guy's composing ability. These songs could be mine. I swelled with pride at the mere thought.

Gosaka, perhaps sensing the impact his words had made, smiled broadly. 'If you like those songs I just played you, feel free to pick one of them – whichever you fancy. But, to tell you the truth, I want to write an entirely new song, just for you. One that will be perfect for you.'

'A song that's perfect for me?'

'Yep. I want to call it "The Great Drum of Life".' Ohmygod, he even has a title for it. He's already started work on it. What a guy. 'La la la . . . oom-chakka-chakka-cha . . .' He's got a rhythm and a tune on the way as well. I can't take my eyes off him. 'OK. This is what I call a flourish. Boom, boom! And kacha-kacha-ka on the edge of the drum . . . Hey, get me a piece of paper, quick! I've got to write this down. Anything will do, but hurry up.'

I brought him a memo pad. Gosaka practically tore it out of my hand and set to work on writing down phrases, frowning intensely as if the end of the world could interrupt his labours at any moment. Believe it or not, this song, too, was a masterpiece. It had all the basics of a good ballad – rhythm, phrasing, sentiment, the bread and butter of enka – but it also had a lyrical beauty to it that was better than the finest strawberry jam.

It turned out that Gosaka and I were kindred spirits. In the end we stayed up all night talking about music and life. At some point Kenjiro got tired and went off to sleep in my bed, from where we could hear his noisy snoring. During the wee hours of the morning, Gosaka started to open his heart to me and tell me about his chequered past. He'd had an unimaginably sad life. He had a criminal record with four offences. He didn't tell me the full details, but apparently it all stemmed from an incident in which someone had been making trouble for his lover. Gosaka had gone to her aid, but somehow he'd gone too far. There was a fight, and the affair ended up in court. Did he actually kill anyone? Several times I was on the verge of asking, but I just didn't have the guts. Anyway, he served a long prison sentence, during which he was driven almost insane from worrying about this woman. He tried to end his suffering by attempting suicide, repeatedly slashing his wrist with a fragment of an aluminium table knife he'd stolen from the prison canteen. These days he deliberately wore a silly novelty wrist watch, because it had a wide strap that concealed the scars, but he only had to shift the strap a fraction and there they were – a number of nasty-looking marks.

There was nothing I could say. I just wept, silently – I only hoped that the tears I shed might fall upon the parched soil of this man's heart and bring a little moisture to it so that something might grow there again in future.

Then he told me about his family, who had stood by him through all his troubles. He showed me photographs of his children and talked about them. Reiji Gosaka was a man with a past, but he also had plenty of present-day troubles: he was up to his neck in debt and continued to live in a reckless, extravagant manner. This had brought him a bad reputation. Plenty of people acknowledged his talent, but nobody wanted to use his songs. Singers and producers just didn't want to have anything to do with him. Even so, big-name singers would occasionally be sent to him – on a clandestine basis – for lessons. He mentioned several names, including a certain young enka star blessed with overwhelming vocal power, and a certain pop singer who was currently right up there at the top of the profession. I didn't really know whether to believe Gosaka, but at any rate he claimed to have coached these singing stars.

Gosaka had one of those rather suspicious-looking business cards, with all sorts of posh-sounding titles attached to his name, all at companies I'd never heard of. All in all he was a dubious kind of guy, I could see that, but I could also see that for all his shameless self-promotion he did have a genuine gift for song-writing that was very, very special. I would love to sing some of his songs, but what exactly would it involve?

The life of a travelling singer who has no original material gets gradually tougher and tougher. I'd been told that quite a few times by other artistes I'd worked with on the circuit. Perhaps, indeed, I had just about reached the limit of what I could achieve on the road.

'I'm up for it.' I was surprised at how easily those words popped out of my mouth. 'Come on, Mr Gosaka. Let's make some really good songs together.'

His face lit up. 'Really? You're up for it? Well, all right!'

The two of them went home around dawn. Left alone, I tried to sleep, but the intoxicating sense of anticipation, that I was about to spread my wings and fly into fresh new skies, wouldn't leave me. I lay in bed wide awake until early evening, songs glowing on my lips.

*

That was the start of an almighty struggle.

Gosaka had plenty of talent, of that I was sure, but as a human being he was a complete and utter mess. His behaviour was enough to leave me feeling quite faint at times. He had a very uneven temperament, laughing one moment and crying the next. He would forget appointments. When he was in a good mood he'd be kind and considerate, but the moment he slipped out of that mood he'd throw his weight around like a madman and say things that could really be very wounding. He had a pure love of music but no financial sense at all. Behind the scenes he was always getting involved in shady frauds and con tricks in his reckless pursuit of funding for musical projects.

Just being with him for a couple of days as he pursued his crazy path through life was enough to leave me completely exhausted. However, the music on the demo tape that he played in my flat and later on the stereo in the Mercedes was undeniably in a class of its own. I wanted those songs badly enough to beg for them.

'Oh, what fun we're having,' I heard him say. 'I haven't laughed like this in years.' Pure as a child, this man would take the statements of others at face value; quite a rare type these days.

The first time I got into the Mercedes with him I had a word with him that was designed to ward off any thoughts he may have had of trying some monkey business.

'When I was a kid, there was this pervert who messed around with me. Ever since then I've been no good with men. Just the other day a guy tried to chat me up, and by the time I realized what I was doing I was waving a knife at him.' I fumbled in my make-up bag and pulled out a little fruit-knife with a 'Hello Kitty' motif. 'This knife, I always carry it with me for self-protection. Cute, isn't it? Look.'

Gosaka's face showed an expression of raw terror that still makes me laugh to recall it. 'Hey, hey, don't be silly. Put that thing away, *please*. You'll do yourself an injury. Well, really.'

The way I see it, there's no such thing as a purely platonic relationship between a man and a woman. If a man spends time with a woman whom he likes, sooner or later his mind will drift towards wickedness. And just supposing I did make the mistake of becoming this man's woman, he would undoubtedly want me all to himself, the way men do. He wouldn't want to launch me on a career that would put me in front of huge crowds of other men: the début would never happen. Mind you, there are plenty of girls who see it the other way round and use the interest men have in them to further their career. But, for better or worse, I'm not that kind of girl.

As these thoughts rambled through my mind, the Mercedes was passing through Tsurumi at high speed in the teeth of a cold winter wind. Gosaka laughed. 'Rinka, I hear you sometimes appear at the cabaret in Tsurumi. Once you make your recording début you'll have to stop playing crummy places like that, OK? And the same goes for the health spas.'

'What?'

He wasn't finished yet. 'You say you're no good with men, but I wonder. You don't strike me that way. You can tell that type at a glance, and you're not that type.'

'Er . . .' Look out, Rinka, here comes trouble.

'It's all very well putting on that vacant expression, but there's a surprisingly passionate character lurking in there, I can tell. If you got involved with a man, you'd get pretty *deeply* involved, I'd say. I wouldn't be a bit surprised if you had something pretty serious on the go right now.'

So what if I did? It was none of his damn business. For once, I was brave enough to voice my inner thoughts. Gosaka promptly flew into a rage.

'Of course it's my damn business, you damn fool!' There was the sound of screeching tyres and the smell of burning rubber. His angry hands were shaking on the steering-wheel; his eyes were dilated and his lips trembled; deep vertical lines appeared on his forehead as his face knotted in rage: a terrifying sight. Then he regained his composure.

'Oh well – it doesn't really matter. Even if you were living with a guy like that, we'd just move all your stuff out one day when he's not around. Then drop in and explain the situation to him later. Done it dozens of time before.'

'Eh?'

'You have to get rid of any boyfriends before you try to get into big-time showbiz, Rinka. You have to have a pure, clean body when you enter those waters. I mean, think about our side for a minute. We're serious about this business; we've got families to support. Say we launch a new singer on her career, and she's still got this guy on the side. She secretly goes out with him to a bar or someplace. The moment the other customers see her, it's "Hey, look! It's so-and-so, the singer. Do us a number, go on." The next thing you know, our new talent is singing for free with a bunch of amateurs and we producers look like a bunch of monkeys.'

'I–I see.'

'Then all it takes is for the guy to get some grudge against the production company. When some guy thinks he's madly in love with a woman, you never know what he'll start thinking or doing. He'll show up at the office and make a scene. It's happened before. And having to worry about that kind of thing is a great big pain in the neck. See what I mean?'

Up to a point, yes, I did see what he meant. But the need for love – linked as it is to sexual desire – is a basic human instinct, like the need for food and sleep. I was born a woman, and if I'm not to be allowed to love, you might as well just kill me and have done with it. What he was proposing sounded no different from the tragedy of wild animals cooped up in cages at the zoo. I gave a deep sigh.

'So, I'm going to have to live like a nun.'

Gosaka stiffened and pouted in a comical gesture of exaggerated shock. 'Silly girl. I'm not saying you can't have your bedtime fun. You go right ahead and get your kicks. All I'm saying is you've got to be a bit careful who you choose to do it with. You need to find a boyfriend who's in the same business. Like Kenjiro, for instance – not a great example, I know. You see, people who are in the business will keep their mouths shut. They've all got their own little secrets, so it's in their own interests to keep quiet. And if you really can't bear the frustration, I'll take you to Hawaii. At the firing ranges over there, you can shoot away all day – with real bullets. Haa-ha-ha! That'll soon get it out of your system, eh? Oh, but I was forgetting – you're no good with men, right? Ha! You're a one, you are. It's great fun talking with you. Ho-ho-ho. Oh, dear me.'

Gosaka took me out the following day, and the day after that, and earnestly taught me everything I needed to know about the world of big-time show business. We'd sit down over coffee at a family restaurant, and he'd sketch intricate diagrams on the back of a paper napkin, showing the mutual connections between the singer, the production company, the composer and the record company. Time and again he'd follow the lines with his ballpoint pen, glaring at me with a face like Satan himself and shouting at me like crazy if I didn't seem to be following.

'This stuff really matters – I have to drum it into you loud and clear. Because there's a certain smell about you . . .'

'Oh, sorry. I did have some garlic with my spaghetti . . .'

'That's not what I'm talking about. I'm talking about the smell of *trouble*. Somehow or other, you're going to make problems for us. I've been in the business a long time, and I've got a nose for it. Now listen up. Next week I'm going to take you to visit the president of a big production company – and when I say big, I mean you'd jump out of your cotton socks if I told you the name. He's already had a listen to your demo tape; and he says he's interested. So this is it, Rinka, the point of no return. If you've got cold feet, now's the time to quit. Don't start kicking up a fuss about things once we've already struck a deal and make me look like an idiot, OK? Oh dear, I'm quite worn out.'

Back at my flat I had another listen to the demo tape I'd recorded for Gosaka. The songs were all covers, but I guess I was putting a fair amount of feeling into it. Whenever I listen to my own singing on tape, there's always something that strikes me as not quite right. It bothers me and I want to wipe the tape and have another try. Sometimes I think I'll never quite be satisfied with my singing. Once I got that contract, would I just carry on recording stuff that didn't sound quite right, putting it on to CD anyway and sending it out to the big wide world?

I suddenly realized, as I sat there worrying about it, that my concern was based on a powerful inner conviction that I really was going to make that début. I was surprised at myself. But then, what was I going to do about Daiki? I wouldn't dream of dumping him for the sake of my career.

Or wouldn't I? Come to think of it, I'd had quite a few other boyfriends in the past. In the throes of passion we said all sorts of stuff about how we loved each other to death, but then along came some other guy and it turned out to be surprisingly easy to forget about the one before. Relationships always break up sooner or later – maybe it would be no big deal if this one happened to break up a little sooner than if nature were allowed to take its course.

I'm clinging on to the edge of a cliff. Far, far below, I can make out great waves crashing against the boulders. It is a mighty sea – and deep enough to make me shudder. I give a loud gulp. 'Time to jump,' I hear a voice saying, somewhere. No way. I might die. I ooze cold sweat, and feel it dripping on to my arms. I think I'm starting to get dizzy. If I don't concentrate the mind, my body will fall of its own accord. What to do? Well?

Well?

*

Every time I saw Daiki's face flicker before me, my heart filled with hatred. The overflowing hate for him was the fuel that lit my fire, the fire that made me sing. And little by little a thought took form in my mind that was cruel enough to chill me to the marrow: if only Daiki would die. Imagine his life, snatched away by some disease, some great force that he was powerless to resist, that took him clean away from the land of the living. After that, there'd be nothing for it but to devote myself to song. If only some such irresistible force of nature would settle my destiny for me, there'd be no need for all this anguish.

What idiotic thoughts. Well, anyway, I just wish things could be straightforward for me. You only live once, they say. There aren't many times when you feel you could really do anything you set your mind to, and that thought merely drives me deeper into sorrow.

Gosaka had already started to restrict my activities. Not only was my mind dominated by doubts over the sacrifices he wanted me to make, but he was also starting to chip away at my personal freedom in everyday life. He telephoned incessantly. Where are you? What time will you be getting back? What time do you go to bed and what time do you get up in the morning? Even with the telephone line between us, I felt his oppressive presence. I started wondering if he was making enquiries about me elsewhere, to see if he could detect the shadow of a man somewhere in my life.

Then one day, I got a call from Daiki. Making up an excuse to fool Gosaka, I slipped out.

'I can only get away for an hour or so today I'm afraid, I've got an appointment.' That was my clumsy opening gambit in our conversation. It took place at a coffee-shop near the building site where he was working.

'That's all right. I've got to get back to work in a little while myself. I was just wondering how you were getting on, like. Wanted to see your face.' The moment he said that, tears started falling from my eyes. They trickled down my cheek before I could stop them and fell like big raindrops on to my breast, soaking into the orange sweater that I'd put on today because he'd once said it suited me. Taken aback, he promptly supplied the wrong caption for the scene before him.

'I'm sorry. Maybe there was no need to go to all this trouble.

Look, I know it sounds like an excuse, but I thought it would be better to sort things out properly this time, precisely because I want you and me to stay together long term. But it looks like all I've managed to do is hurt your feelings . . .'

My tea had no sugar in it, but I stirred it meaninglessly anyway. I spoke without bothering to wipe my tears away. 'You haven't hurt my feelings at all, Daiki. I just want to carry on being in love with you, that's all. That's all right, isn't it? There's nothing the matter with me, really.'

Daiki's face brightened and he smiled. 'It's nice of you to say that, but I can see you're taking it hard. Don't worry, though – it's already Day Four, right? Another six days or so and then we can go back to our usual life together. I really am sorry I've put you through this, honest. Now, let me see – I'll send a removals van round to your place on the 22nd. Make a note of it. I was going to borrow the light truck from work, but we're very busy these days, and I don't think they can spare it.'

The 22nd was the very day Gosaka had earmarked for us to meet the president of the production company.

'Um . . .' My lip quivered. It was now or never. 'Actually, Daiki, I was thinking that this might be a good opportunity for us to try living apart for a while. I don't mean us splitting up or anything, I just thought maybe we should try a different sort of set-up.'

Daiki's face clouded over at once. 'Don't sulk like that. I told you I'm sorry about messing you around this time. I won't do it again.'

'Well, um, that's not really what I mean.' Time to jump. Now's the moment. Hanging off the edge of the cliff, I released my grip.

'The fact is, Daiki, I'm going to make my recording début.'

'What's that you say?'

'Tantantara! It's finally going to happen – probably.' Giggle. 'I know it's hard to believe, but it looks like I'm going to sign up with a really famous production company.' I was floating in space. Now I was afraid of nothing. No matter how I might struggle, I was definitely going to fall now. Having come this far. How would he reply? 'Don't do it. They'll just make a fool of you'? It didn't really matter what he said. But since this was the end of the affair, I kind of wanted to feel him pull on the rope and try to drag me back. Just one little tug, to show he cared. But after a brief silence, he simply said:

'Congratulations.'

'Eh?' I couldn't believe it.

But then he said it again:

'Congratulations. What fantastic news.' He drank the remains of his cold coffee and stood up. His face was drained of life and white as paper. Uh-oh. I'm falling. I'm falling...

Daiki stood at the cash register, swaying slightly. I went scurrying after him like a field mouse and tried to put some rope in his hand to see if he was ready to play tug o' war.

'Is that all right then, Daiki? What do you think?'

'That will be 1,057 yen, please.'

'Say something, Daiki. You're mad at me, right? Don't get me wrong – I'm not trying to break us up, you know.'

'Two thousand yen. Shall I take it out of that?'

'OK, OK, you win. I quit. I'm not going to make any CDs, I promise!'

'And here's your change: 943 yen.'

Daiki said nothing, and walked out of the shop with a face like thunder. I followed him out in hot pursuit. Nothing for it now but tears.

'Please, please, forgive me. The touring was getting me down, that's all. I just wanted to find some place where they'd treat me properly and let me get on with my singing. But it's all right, it doesn't matter any more, the whole damn thing can go to hell.' If only I really meant it. Maybe if I just chanted it often enough, like some magic spell, the belief would slowly spread across my heart like some kind of dye. If only.

But now Daiki was speaking. 'Don't give up on your début. You don't want to go back to singing in health spas, do you? There's no future in that. It's because I believe that you've got the talent that I always wanted you to quit the cabaret circuit. If you could make a proper début and try your luck on a major label – well, that'd be fantastic. I'd be a proud man myself, being one of your ex-boyfriends.'

'What do you mean, *ex*-boyfriend? You'd still see me, wouldn't you? They'd keep an eye on me for a while, I expect, but I'd get away from them somehow. You'd still come and see me, right?'

'Yeah. Sure. I'd come and see you.' Daiki's face was all twisted up, as if he were about to burst into tears. He looked away from me immediately. Just like him.

'I'll postpone the début as long as I can,' I said. 'So do send the moving company round on the 22nd just as planned. Whatever happens in the long term, I'm coming back to you, OK? I'll come back, and we'll live together, for a while.'

'All right. Whatever.' He walked briskly off to where his car was parked, not once looking back, even when he uttered his parting words, 'I got it. That's what we'll do.' He got in the car and shut the door with a bang. The engine started up and white smoke from the exhaust rose into the air like mist.

I'm standing on the street corner, embraced by the stinging cold of the chill night air. With every breath I take, warm memories seem to seep from my body.

It's all right, there's nothing to worry about. He said we'd see each other again. But then, why didn't he give me a lift to the station?

I didn't want to lose sight of the car, made small by distance, now waiting at some traffic-lights. I stared unblinking at the indistinct red smudges of the car's rear lights. I wanted somehow to murmur my true feelings before those lights disappeared from view. But like tiny midwinter shooting stars, they dissolved into the darkness.

I squatted down with both hands on the tarmac and cried like a baby.

The 22nd came around, and the van that Daiki had said he was going to arrange never showed.

That night I climbed into Gosaka's Mercedes and he drove me to the new production company. All I remember about the president – a portly, middle-aged man of fair complexion with sagging jowls that reminded me of fatty bacon – is the way those jowls wobbled every time he spoke. Gosaka made up for my tongue-tied silence by rattling on solo, and he got the president into such a good mood that he took us to dinner at the Akasaka Prince Hotel in a chauffeur-driven car. After eating in a swanky traditional-style Japanese restaurant we went up to the shot bar on the top floor and dallied there for an hour before returning to the offices of the production company.

'Well, Rinka, I think we made a reasonably good impression there. I'm pretty sure they'll be getting in touch again. Thanks for sticking it out.' Back in the Mercedes Gosaka was in excellent humour. He kept humming old enka songs, and he'd glance at me for approval after each one. Then he'd laugh out loud.

Back home, overcome by weariness, I collapsed on the bed, still wearing the smart woman's business suit I'd chosen for the meeting. I didn't even switch the light on; just lay there looking out of the window at the starry night sky. Apparently I was born on a starry night like this. My mother used to tell me how she lay there on the hospital bed, gazing out at the star-spangled heavens, hour after hour after hour, praying for my happiness. It's been quite a while since I wrote to my mother. I wonder how she is these days. I wonder if my father managed to get that new job he was talking about. Since I started on the singing, I haven't really been able to send money home. I hope they're eating properly.

How many years has it been, I wonder, since I left my family? It's another starry night, and I am about to be born again – a happy event, to be sure.

Somehow I drifted off to sleep, leaving the gas fire on. The temperature in the room went far too high, and as I lay there bathed in sweat I was assailed by a succession of terrifying nightmares. The stars of the show were myself and a living guitar.

The guitar was soft and rubbery and about the height of a human being. I touched it, and it proved to be covered with a thin layer of some soft, downy substance. It was breathing. I swallowed nervously. The two of us were alone together in a poky little cell. There was no escape. Just as if I'd been locked into a cage with a wild lion, I was gripped by raw terror. It didn't seem I could talk to it, and there was no knowing when it might come at me.

Then the monster started to emit a weird electrical sound, a kind of deep electric vibration that seemed to come from the depths of the earth. I tried to run, but it even had my legs trapped. Bound hand and foot by the monstrous sound, I could not move. The guitar-shaped monster started shaking its whole hideous flaccid body in a nauseating dance of triumph that brought it wobbling closer and closer to me. Some viscous, pulpy kind of mucus was dribbling off it.

The electric sound moved to a higher pitch, a wailing, a screaming, a squealing that was somehow familiar. Wasn't it one of those hackneyed melodies that keep cropping up in enka? That depressing distortion, rampaging heroically through an otherwise orderly system of sound. Obeying my inner conditioning, I cleared my throat in the exaggerated manner of a singer who hears the opening bars of the next number. I moistened my lips with my tongue, and then the moment was upon me. I stood up tall and took a deep breath. I opened my legs slightly, tautened the muscles of my lower belly and held that pose.

If you're really going to make a ballad work, you've got to grab the audience by the throat from the very first note. I burst into magnificent song. The guitar responded by lunging forward and toppling down on top of me with all the force in its monstrous body. I took a terrible blow on the back of my head and fell to the ground, twitching convulsively, still smothered by the thing's bulk. Now my whole body was soaked and defiled by the unearthly slime that it exuded, my clothes long since dissolved in it. I struggled frantically. Tangled up in the tiny prison cell, I writhed in naked agony. The guitar distortion assaulted me with mounting ferocity. At length my spirit was exhausted, and my limp body was at the mercy of the terrible instrument.

I jerked myself upright, breath coming fast and ragged, enveloped in the sweltering tropical heat of the pitch-black room. I had sweated myself close to complete dehydration and it was a struggle to stand up on my trembling legs. I tottered unsteadily to the window and somehow got it open. In a moment the room was purified by an icy December gale that came howling into the room. Afflicted with a splitting headache, I staggered to the bathroom, turned on a tap and drank from it desperately.

If all the people in the world wanted to be professional singers, the human race would definitely perish. It's just as well there are only a few people who put to sea in this clay boat, singing loudly, receiving flowers. The boat's overcrowded as it is, which is why so many people drown, so many suffer sickness of the spirit.

I rolled over in the empty bath and squatted in the middle of it. I'd left the tap running, and cold water was seeping through my hair and clothing. Had to open my eyes; had to cool down my head. How long had I been in this state?

I should have torn off the calendar pages of my drive towards happiness more carefully. True, I was a fool who always hated living an orderly, regular lifestyle, but even my foolish days had at least been marked off at regular intervals by the calendar. Now even that seemed to breaking down. My hand had wavered and I'd accidentally torn off one page too many, and somehow I'd turned into this person, crying her eyes out and rolling around in an empty bath in the middle of the night. I don't understand what is going on any more. What am I? Where am I? *When* am I? Is weeping in the bath really some kind of stop on the road to a future drenched in happiness?

I had gone far over the maximum permitted volume of emotion, and out of the excessive depths of my sadness and my fear a rather pleasant liquor gradually started to ferment, unbidden, in the pot inside my skull.

Hee-hee-hee. Laughter came welling up from within. Oh, dear me, what a completely stupid woman. Drunk on my skull-pot liquor, I started to sing loudly, right there in the bath:

> If you're a singer and your parents die,
> You won't be there to see them.
> If you're a singer and your boyfriend dies,
> You won't be there – no way, no way.
> The guy in your songs, well, he ain't no good.
> When his wife and kids see him, they say 'Who are you?'
> It ain't no good what you're doing right now,
> Stop what you're doing and stop right now.
>
> Only room for a few on the boat made of clay
> Only room for a few I say (way-hay!).
> It's overcrowded and it's starting to sink.
> Knock the others on the head and drop 'em in the drink.

The moonlight came beaming through the window, and winter trees cast skeletal shadows on the bathroom wall. The skull-pot liquor was a little too strong, and it called up a phantasm, something that really shouldn't and couldn't exist, yet there it was, gliding across my line of vision. A pair of *zori* sandals, like the ones I wear on stage but made of shiny glass. It occurred to me that I'd like to take a closer look at the vision, and it obligingly reappeared. The two sandals were neatly lined up together, and they were shimmering and transparent as water. They were sitting there invitingly on the bathmat. I stood up, climbed out of the bath and slowly slipped a foot into one of the sandals. It took to my foot perfectly – in fact it almost seemed to cling to my skin. How beautifully comfortable it was. There was no feeling of tightness or friction where the thongs went between my toes – it just shaped itself around my foot like jelly and breathed gently in and out to accommodate every movement of the foot.

I put my other foot into the second sandal. This time the thong suddenly tightened of its own accord before I had even got the toes all the way in. Just then in the distance I heard the sound of a human scream. Startled, I tried to take the sandals off. But they were already stuck firmly to the soles of my feet, and would not come off, however hard I struggled. On the contrary, the more I struggled, the deeper the soles of my feet seemed to sink into the sandals. I was attached to them like the prey of some gigantic predatory sea anemone.

Must call someone.

I was struggling inside my illusion. I hurtled out of the bathroom and paced around the living-room. Every step I took brought another human scream to my ear – *gyaaa, gyaaa, gyaaa* – the cry of a newborn child, or a man's howl of grief, or parents weeping.

When I came to, I found that I had gone back to sleep where I had fallen on the bed. I had left the heating on, and the room was tropical once more. This was hell. I staggered to my feet, tottered unsteadily to the window and somehow got it open. Once again, the icy December gale came howling into the room.

So that hallucination just now was another dream after all. Somehow I had been involved in a double layer of dreaming. I looked at the clock and it said 8 a.m. The world outside my window was already up and about. Must get changed. I touched my clothes. They were soaking. For a moment I thought maybe the glass sandals weren't a dream after all.

Don't be silly. It's only sweat. One by one, I took off all the pieces of clothing clinging unpleasantly to my skin and threw them on the floor. The wet button-holes on my blouse had shrunk, and it was very hard to undo the thing. Irritated, I tore it open with brute force and bared my breast. The buttons went skittering across the floor, making a pleasant little sound like popcorn bursting.

What I now understood was that I would never achieve happiness by singing songs. There was a time in my childhood when I believed that a prince on a white charger would come for me some day. But all too soon I came to know the pleasure of associating with real men. It was the same with songs. Once I'd tasted the pleasure of associating with them, I enjoyed being one of the people with scales on their skin. But concealed within the songs was an alleyway that led somewhere more terrifying than anywhere men could take me. Only when I got lost up that alley did I see the true shape of the songs – a slimy, grotesque, obscene thing that was alive – and realize that any involvement with it would lead to misery. If I was going to quit, now was the time. Ah, thank God I'd seen the light. I took off the underwear clinging to my wet body and flung it aside; once I had nothing left to take off, I gently closed my eyes.

Behind my eyelids, an afterimage of the glass sandals came floating lazily up from somewhere. I promptly reached my hand out to them, slipped them off both my feet, and flung them to the floor. SMASH. In the image before me, they shattered into a million pieces. Tiny gleaming fragments danced in the air like dust, and I gazed at them in fascination for some time; I felt them pricking at me as they came pattering down on my skin.

And with that, it was all over.

At last I understood. In my brief career on the cabaret circuit I had indeed been singing to people and sneaking off with money for it, but I had never truly been a singing woman in the full sense of the word. A true singing woman is like a miko, a Shinto shrine maiden who surrenders herself to the gods and speaks in tongues. She totally abandons herself to the song, the message. In contrast, people who wrap themselves in worldly love are not cut out to sing. They are the stuff of songs. Some women are born to be singers of ballads; others are born to be the subjects of the sentimental lyrics of ballads, and ne'er the twain . . . A truly great singer will never be happy in love – that's the oldest cliché in the world of Japanese showbiz. I had managed to get the love of a good man, and it was wrong of me to long for the love of songs as well. It was right that my love for the songs should go unrequited.

And then, one day, the songs had turned their faces towards me. It had been a terrifying, hellish moment. The songs had reached out to me, offering to turn me into a singing woman, and they had embraced me. The first thing they did was to take away the man I loved. What would they want next? They would gobble up the things that made me happy, one by one, until at last they turned me into a fine singing woman. Thanks very much, for taking a fancy to me. Thanks but no thanks. Sorry. Not for me.

However, it was already getting very close to showtime.

10 Space for an Angel

'You know that agency you've been using, Tsuru ... Tsuru ...'

'Tsurukame Productions?'

'Yeah, that one. Well the president of the new production company rang them up the other day to ask them to take Rinka Kazuki off the books there, because they'll be handling your engagements from now on. Nothing can stop us now, Rinka. We're on our way. Cheers!' Gosaka raised his brimming glass of red wine, and I raised mine to meet it.

'But, of course, you already had bookings scheduled for the next couple of months. Well, apparently Mr Hirata, the boss there, said he'd arrange for substitutes to handle all your engagements after New Year. Good of him, eh? Apparently Mr Hirata is delighted that you're going to be making your début.'

We were having a little celebration at a steakhouse in Yotsuya.

'You'll officially be put on the books early in the New Year, for good luck. You say you can't find a good place to move into, but you're just paying over the odds so long as you stay in that weekly apartment. In the New Year, we'll move you into the production company president's house. Seems he's got a spare room he can let you have. Splendid, eh?'

Somehow, my life seemed to be spinning out of control. I had no money to hand, yet here I was, about to become party to a huge gamble. Time and again Gosaka pulled out his huge engagement diary. I cowered in front of it like a terrified little furry animal.

'You're finally going to release your very own CD, Rinka. The title will be "The Great Drum of Life". We'll start laying down the tracks right away.' Gosaka gave me a thudding pat on the shoulder. 'This is the birth of a new professional singer, Rinka. The kind of singer whose CDs sell for a thousand yen a throw. No more need to tell fibs about your record label – you'll be a proper recording artiste. No need to milk the audience for tips any more. You'll be able to hold your head up with pride and enjoy all the money you'll make from your appearance fees.'

The following day Gosaka departed for Taiwan, there to join Kenjiro at the press conference to promote his new release, 'Rambling Gambler'.

I was wondering how much longer I could stay in the weekly apartment. Daiki did all the paperwork, so I really didn't know. These places have card-type keys like hotels, and, apparently, if you're still in one of them when the contract expires they have some automated system that disables the key.

My head felt as if someone had poured concrete into it. My throat was so inflamed that I could hardly swallow my own saliva. I'd gone and caught a cold – something that every singer dreads. It really messes up your professional life.

I had 'The Great Drum of Life' right there in my hand, but I also had this terrible headache – it felt like being bashed over the head repeatedly. Not quite the great drum I had in mind.

Without Daiki to provide for me, I actually couldn't feed myself properly, and my health had broken down immediately. At a time like this, if I called up the new production company they'd probably send somebody rushing over to help me, but I didn't want to do that. I felt miserable enough to try ringing up Daiki. But all I got was some meaningless recorded message. Perhaps he'd quit the apartment.

A tiny little boat, all at sea, anchor gone, drifting between huge waves: that was my boat. It drifted weakly, feebly seeking the great drum, whose rhythm could faintly be heard from far away.

For several days the cold got no better – in fact, it got steadily worse, and I developed a fever.

Then came a day when I had urgent business: Christmas Eve.

I awoke with my body feeling like a slab of rock and slowly got myself out of bed. I crawled weakly around the flat, getting my show-gear ready with agonizing slowness. Catching a cold really is disastrous for a singer. Some just lose their voices completely and have to cancel the engagement. Luckily, I am spared that – I can still hit the notes, even the high ones – but if I do fight through the illness and do a show, terrible after-effects await. I have to put five times as much effort as usual into voice production, and that puts a lot of stress on the jaw. Making the mouth open wide when it really doesn't want to results in pain running through the jaw after a show that is so intense that it makes me want to roll around on the floor. But this is where you show them what you're made of. I only had a few more shows to do at the cabarets and health spas, and I wanted to treat them all with due respect.

I loaded up the trundle-trolley with a suitably Christmassy kimono – bright red with white trimming – and went rattling off on a wobbly train to my engagement at a health spa in Utsunomiya, a provincial town north-east of Tokyo.

The show starts in the usual way. I stand on the stage, tottering on my pins. Never before has a kimono felt this heavy to me. It's as if I have another person riding piggyback. I took my temperature this morning, and the thermometer said 39 degrees centigrade. Breathing hotly, I greet the audience. Luckily I always speak with exaggerated slowness on these occasions, so the audience doesn't notice anything unusual tonight.

'My name is . . . Rinka . . . and I hope . . . you enjoy . . . the show.'

I give a passionate, fevered, performance. The song list is no different from any other show. Yet for some reason, the audience gets into the mood of it before I do myself, as they did on one other occasion.

'Kazuki! Rinka!'

'Go for it, darlin', you're doin' great!'

I'm still telling the same great lie, claiming to be on the books of Kink Records.

'Thank you very much for your kind support.' I get fresh vigour from the audience. All the things I've learnt, about staging, attention-grabbing gestures, vocal phrasing – all those things are mere accessories. This is magic. At this moment I am being loved by the songs. All I'm doing is standing here, opening my mouth, and it just naturally, sort of –

'Rinka!'

'We'll never forget you!'

Like a sea coming to high tide, slowly, slowly, this cauldron is coming to the boil.

'Everyone's got a place in their hearts called their home town. I'm going to sing you a song from the North Country, but I expect when you listen to it you'll be transported to the place where you spent your own childhood. Listen, if you will, to "The Plains of Tsugaru".' It's a song of farewell, sung by a Tsugaru man's wife who has to look after the children alone while he spends the winter months away from home working as a migrant worker.

> When the spring comes, darling,
> We know you will surely come back,
> With bags full of presents
> Hanging at your side.
> We'll surely be lonely,
> But don't worry, we're used to it.

I'm buffeted by a veritable thunderstorm of applause. If I carry on being loved by the songs like this, Rinka Kazuki will undoubtedly become a star. If I just continue to have the courage to become unhappy, I'll lose a lot of things that mean a lot to me and rush straight up to the summit. That's what it means to love the songs and to be loved by the songs, to commit a love-suicide with the songs. But, surely, I can't make the decisive move. I'm thirty-four, it's too late. I've taken a careless nibble at the happiness of life, at life's sweet taste. I'm disqualified.

People in the audience are openly sobbing. All because of my songs, with the magic in them. Every single face is looking straight at me. And in among them, I see *that* face.

'Well done. Brilliant.' There he is, furiously clapping his hands. 'Daiki!'

It's the last number. And it's a very fitting number to close out the show, 'Osaka Rhapsody'. Here comes the intro, light and jaunty, pregnant with sadness.

Daiki has come to see the show. He's seen me at my very, very best.

I decorate the springy rhythm with a voice clear as a bell. Smiling in all directions, I descend once more into the audience. I drop a low whisper as I pass his place:

'Let's go home together, you and me, Daiki.'

At last the curtains come down, as I bow deeper than I've ever bowed before. The lighting guy and the MC come rushing up, as if they've been waiting for me. Their eyes are wide and round and they're gabbling about the show: Why the special effort? What a triumph! I pay no attention. I go dashing out of the dressing-room and into the foyer.

Daiki.

The place is crowded with people who've just been enjoying the show, wandering slowly out of the auditorium in their muu-muus. They soon spot me rushing around in my kimono, and in a moment I'm surrounded by noisy fans.

'It's Rinka Kazuki!'

'Please, let me shake your hand.'

Hasn't anybody seen him? A young man in working clothes, with a sort of square-shaped face, who was watching the show.

'Now you mention it, I do recall someone like that. Why, is something the matter?'

'Heh-heh, Rinka fancies 'im, I reckon. Oh dear, oh dear.' They're laughing their heads off about it, and I'm getting shoved and jostled by the crowd. I've got to get out of here.

The fevered atmosphere is as thick as concentrated juice. For me, having just this minute come off the stage, it's murder. And all the weariness that I forgot in my excitement while I was up there comes flooding back, like the anaesthetic's worn off. All the pain that I somehow dispelled comes rushing back to gather once more within me. My throat and my jaw are throbbing and squealing in a melancholy chorus of pain. This is it: the limit.

Still in my crimson Christmas kimono, I dash out on to the street, dragging my trundle-trolley behind me. An icy sidewind slams into my cheek, a staggering blow. The wind pierces like frozen needles, carrying snow off into the black of the night. Everywhere is white; how pretty. The tall trees lining the streets, twinkling kindly with their Christmas lights, stand there in silence, wearing flossy white caps. The lights beaming forth from the health spa dance around busily. No doubt Tony, the resident comedian, will be on stage about now, wearing his Santa Claus out-fit and handing out biscuits and presents to the lonely members of the muu-muu tribe.

Let's go back in there. I'm going to get a present, too. I take two or three determined steps back into the light shining out from the building, feeling the crisp crunch of the snow beneath my sandals – but I can no longer endure the pain in my head, and I have to squat down on the snow.

'God!'

'It's the enka singer. She's collapsed.' Tony the clown, still dressed in his Santa outfit, comes rushing out from the main entrance. Yamamoto the Mysteron, who does palmistry, is by his side.

'We've got to get her home.'

'It's all right. I know where Rinka's living these days.' Tony picks me up and carries me over to the Mysteron's Mercedes.

'I'm . . . I'm so sorry.'

'Don't worry about it. We have to look after each other at times like this.'

The Mysteron, dressed in his sky-blue robes and still with his Ray-Bans on, puts his foot down and drives off like a maniac. It's terrifying.

'Er, could you . . . slow down . . . just a little?' My tearful entreaty makes no impression. The Mysteron swerves down a backstreet, wing mirrors brushing the telegraph poles.

'Don't you worry, Rinka darling, you ain't gonna die. Or shall I just check? Here, let's have a look. Uh-oh, you don't have a very long life line . . .'

'For crying out loud. Stop looking at my palm and concentrate on the road. Just keep your eyes looking straight ahead. *Please.*'

'Oops, sorry 'bout that. I'm awfully forgetful these days, you know. All right, er, what did you just say? Oh yeah, eyes straight ahead. I've got it now. No worries.'

Yamamoto the Mysteron makes his living by calling members of the audience up on stage and reading their palms, while making a lot of sarcastic jokes. He's a guy who naturally likes to have a laugh. Now, however, he falls silent for a moment.

'White Christmas, eh?'

'Yep.' There are people frolicking in the streets, people swaggering along clutching bunches of flowers. The Mysteron's car drives on in sullen silence, stopping occasionally at the traffic-lights.

No doubt the ghosts of Christmas past are running wild through the hearts of the two entertainers. Christmas is a time of year when people like us have a lot to reflect upon. Ding-dong, the bells reproach our wasted lives; the fancy ribbons are red as blood. Ever since I was a young girl, my boyfriends have always been people who have somewhere else to go to at Christmas.

'You know what? All those years I still had my wife with me, I never did give her a present, not once. Couldn't see the point. Some people just don't get it, you know? I was such an insensitive husband . . .' The lights turn to green, and the Mysteron's Mercedes speeds on once more. 'I was so busy trying to please the audience, I somehow forgot all about her. It was only after I'd lost her that I finally noticed. But it's too late now.'

The car screams around a tight curve like a whinnying horse, and at last we're in familiar territory. Familiar, yes, but this is not where I'm living these days. It's where I used to live with Daiki. I can see East Kawaguchi station.

'Now then, Rinka, which way to the abode? You were living somewhere round here with that guy, right?'

'Er, it's all right, you can let me off right here.'

'But you're not well.'

'No, really, I'll be fine.' I brush off Yamamoto the Mysteron's attempts to stop me and hastily get my luggage out of the car.

'OK then. Take care now.'

The car drives away, and I'm left standing pointlessly in the snow. I start staggering towards the old flat, although I know it is empty and Daiki doesn't live there any more. The rumble of the trundle-trolley is muffled by the snow as it leaves a double track behind it.

What is the point of what I am doing? I know there is nothing waiting for me where I am going. Still, I've always pressed forward, believing in something, just like now. I've enjoyed making my way through this snow-bound road, and that is good enough.

I stagger on at crawling pace through the darkened street, until at last I am almost in front of the familiar block. At which point a man comes walking towards me.

Daiki?

I am so surprised that I cannot speak a word.

'I heard that trundling sound. I thought it might be you, so I came out to see. And sure enough, here you are.'

I'm panting white breath and I pull a miserable face.

'Come on, I'll carry your bags. You'd better stay here tonight.'

I stumble into the room. My field of vision spins crazily around me, yet I realize that the room is quite unchanged save for the absence of my things.

'Have you been here, ever since . . . ?'

'Yes, indeed. Come on, you'd better get changed into this.'

'The telephone?'

'I thought you might casually ring up, so I had the number changed. Tsk, it's quite a job getting out of this kimono. Hey! You're running a temperature, aren't you?'

'Er, what about my apartment in Tokorozawa?'

'I know, I know, you couldn't get into it, right? The contract ended today. I knew you wouldn't be able to get in with the card key, and I thought you'd probably come over here.'

'No, I didn't know about that. Um, so, does that mean it's OK for me to come back here?'

'Don't be ridiculous.' Daiki looks away. 'I planned on never seeing you again. But it occurred to me that I didn't have a single tape of you singing your songs.'

'Wh-what?'

'I wanted one to listen to in the car. But I didn't have one. One of the guys at work happened to have a calendar with an advert for the entertainment at that health spa, and I saw your name on it.' Daiki presses the button on his cassette deck. Music comes out of it. It's the Rinka Kazuki show, as heard earlier today at the health spa in Utsunomiya. 'I've been listening to it all evening. You really do sing very well, you know.'

'Daiki!' I forget all the awkward details and fling myself at him.

'Tut! And what do you think you're playing at? Don't get carried away now. I haven't forgiven you yet. Even if you *are* going to tell me the début's off.' Is this his way of saying that he might forgive me if I do call off the recording? I start shaking violently and I can't hide it. Everything seems to be closing in on me. But what am I going to do about Gosaka and 'The Great Drum of Life'?

'Actually, that's exactly what I want to do – call it off.' My mouth moves faster than my heart. The words pop out and I throw away one of the drumsticks of the Great Drum of Life. 'I'm going to stay with you, Daiki. And I'm going to carry on singing at the cabarets and health spas.'

And so, in a fleeting moment, as casually as if making a joke, I throw away the other drum stick and the whole drum itself. Now I feel right. But the very next moment, I hear something deeply shocking from Daiki.

'Ah, perhaps you haven't heard. They arrested that guy for fraud.' He tosses a sports newspaper down in front of me. There on page three is the name of Reiji Gosaka.

'I'll Turn You Into a Famous Singer' – 50-Million Yen Fraud

'What?'

Songwriter Reiji Gosaka (real name: Gensaburo Nomura; age 47) has been arrested on charges of fraud. Police allege that Gosaka persuaded a large number of unknown singers to pay him a total of some 50 million yen by cleverly duping them into believing that he would arrange their recording débuts on major labels. Gosaka is closely associated with Kenjiro Yoshii, the Japanese enka singer currently riding a wave of popularity in Taiwan. Widely rumoured to be the Svengali behind Yoshii's rise to stardom, Gosaka has been under the spotlight as the composer and lyricist of Yoshii's hit single, 'Man of Japan'.

'I was a bit worried, since it said he was in the habit of conning singers on the cabaret circuit, so I rang up Kaho on her mobile. She said it was all true. By the way, that girl has really changed for the worse . . .'

Gosaka admitted the charges, saying that he had used the money he obtained from the singers to finance production of the promotional video for Yoshii's second single, 'Rambling Gambler'. Gosaka commented, 'He's a really promising talent, but the agency and record company were reluctant to commit themselves to a second release – so there was nothing for it but to make the advance investment myself.'

My hand trembles as it clutches the newspaper. But, at the same time, I feel swathed in a mysterious feeling of relief.

'You don't need to make any more tapes', I say, throwing the newspaper aside and reaching out to switch off the tape deck from which my own voice is wafting, 'because I'll sing for you any time – live.'

Thank you very much indeed, Mr Mysteron, for taking me back to Daiki – the biggest Christmas present I've ever had.

'Well, Rinka, all I can say is that it's great to have you back at Tsurukame Productions.'

'Thinking about it coolly, there's no way something like that was really going to happen to someone like me, right?'

'Perhaps you're right. But at least we can be grateful that he didn't fool *you* out of your life's savings. I'm just glad to have you back. Work's going to be fun again.'

We clinked our glasses together. Funny to think that it was just the other day I was clinking glasses with that old fraudster, Reiji Gosaka. Makes you wonder, doesn't it?

'Well, it's nearly the end of the year, Rinka, and it's been quite a topsy-turvy sort of year for you, eh?'

'People say that to me every year, Mr Hirata.'

'I must say, Rinka, for a young 'un you've had your fair share of life's ups and downs. You've done well, you know, keeping your head above the water and smiling through it all. Don't know how you do it.' Hm, yes, I suppose you could indeed say I've had my up and downs. Mr Hirata paused to blow his nose loudly in an excess of emotion, and I took the opportunity to make a slightly theatrical statement myself.

'Quite a lot of stuff's happened to me, it's true. But whatever happened to me, I always accepted it as part of my destiny. After all, I've only got one life. No original songs, perhaps, but an original life.'

'Goodness, Rinka, you really are smart for a young 'un.'

Yes, he's right. I *am* smart – for a young 'un. I sat there for a moment, staring at the counter of the cheap sushi restaurant with the plastic dishes chugging around on their little conveyor belt, intoxicated with myself. I drained my beer with a mighty gulp and felt a sharp pain shoot through the cerebral cortex, just where it links to the spinal column. Maybe I hadn't quite got rid of that cold, after all? No, I rather thought the pain was a little corrective punishment from God, for getting a little too smug about my turbulent life. 'Don't forget, you're the one who caused all the turbulence in the first place' – that's what He's saying to me.

'Yes, Rinka, you really are fantastic. And so you know what? I'm going to give you a little present today – a little prize for being so fantastic.' He spoke with such emphasis that I was quite intrigued. 'Right, remind me how old you are now?'

'You mean my real age?'

'No no, dear, your stage age.'

'Well, I used to be twenty-six, then I became twenty-four and these days I'm twenty-two.'

'OK, Rinka, I've got good news for you. Starting from today, you are twenty years old precisely. I look forward to helping you celebrate your Coming of Age. Ha-ha-ha-ha!'

The following day Daiki and one of his workers got my things out of the flat and dumped them back in his place. I hadn't got properly sorted out yet, but I already had a gig at a health spa lined up for the day after that.

'Honestly, your belongings consist almost entirely of clothes.' Mr Wild sighed deeply as he briskly bundled my stage boxes into a large closet. He looked as if he were about to cry.

'How about a little break?' I suggested tactfully. 'The beer's had time to cool. I'll call the workman in, too.' I looked down from the window. Daiki's workman was standing next to the truck, talking to a young man. When he heard me calling he waved back with tremendous enthusiasm.

'Miss Rinka. We've got a celebrity here. I just got his autograph.'

I took a closer look, and realized that the youthful 'celebrity' was none other than Kenjiro. He was dressed all in black: black hat and sunglasses, black-leather bomber-jacket, black trousers. This rather showy kind of anonymity is favoured by celebs when they're at the airport *en route* for Hawaii, the traditional New Year getaway for Japanese stars. I gave a good-humoured little snort. Kenjiro looked up and waved to me, flashing his familiar tombstone teeth.

'It's your friendly neighbourhood celebrity. Mind if I come up? Is that scary boyfriend of yours up there?'

Kenjiro came up to the apartment, bearing a gift from Taiwan of durian, that delicious but remarkably smelly fruit. Daiki didn't mind too much. Despite their unpleasant previous encounter he'd been rather impressed by Kenjiro's performance on television.

'That wasn't bad, I'll admit. C'mon then, you'd better have a beer.' Daiki cracked open a can of lager and handed it to Kenjiro. Grinning in exaggerated embarrassment, Kenjiro accepted the peace offering and drank it down in one. As if taking this as a sign that things were going to be OK, Daiki's workman immediately became very animated. He watched a lot of television, apparently, and knew all about Kenjiro and his budding career. He knew Kenjiro had been nominated in the Best Newcomer section of the Radio Entertainment Awards; he knew that 'Man of Japan' had made it into the Japanese pop charts, currently riding high at Number 48, and he even knew that Kenjiro had plans to expand his sphere of activity to New York shortly. Kenjiro gave an embarrassed laugh and broached the one topic the workman had tactfully omitted.

'Yep, things are going great for me, really great – except for old Gosaka getting arrested. He wasn't really a bad guy, he just put a lot of money into making songs, like a gambler. Always looking for the one big hit that would get him out of trouble. Oh, it's been a very tiring few days.' I had been hoping that particular topic wouldn't come up, and I tried to start talking about something else, but now Daiki had a gleam in his eye.

'Actually, I was meaning to ask you about that. The guy who introduced Rinka to that composer-cum-con-man – that was *you*, wasn't it?' The lively drinking party suddenly went very quiet. This could turn ugly. But Kenjiro didn't turn a hair.

'Yes, as a matter of fact. What of it?' Kenjiro's composure somewhat took the wind out of Daiki's sails, but he none the less added, almost as an afterthought, 'And did you know he would try and con her?'

'Did I *what*?' Kenjiro stuck out his jaw defiantly and defended his position. 'What makes you think he'd try and con Rinka? There's no way she'd be taken in. The ones that get conned are cleverer than her. They're proper singers. They're the only kind that you can set up for that kind of con. Now listen to me, pal. I don't know how many years you've been knocking about with our Rinka, but I bet I know her a damn sight better than you do. She ain't got no plans or secrets. She ain't got nothing. She's naked as the day she was born. You just can't con her type. When a bad guy sees a woman like that, he wants to befriend her, make her one of the family. So all's well – end of story.'

Eyes wide with tension, I waited for the words to pass. How was I to stop Daiki's iron fist from swinging into action? That was the only thought in my head. But, quite contrary to expectations, Daiki threw back his head and gave a delighted roar of laughter.

'Of course, of course, that's exactly how she's come to be living with me right now. Why, when I first met her she seemed like an easy lay, and I thought I'd just fuck her a few times and then give her the old heave-ho. But somehow everything went weird and now look at me. Ha-ha-ha-ha!'

Kenjiro started laughing, too. Somehow the laughter even spread to the workman, who really didn't have anything to do with it all. Now all three men were laughing themselves silly, slapping each other on the shoulders with tears running down their cheeks.

'Ah-ha-ha-ha-ha – and now just look how I've ended up. On the rare occasions when I go home my kids don't recognize me, my wife's gone and joined some creepy religious cult – my whole damn life's a complete fucking mess. Hey, Kenjiro, why don't you come over and join us on New Year's Eve? I haven't got the heart to go home for it. You're not going to be on the New Year's Eve TV variety show, I don't suppose, so I expect you'll have time on your hands. So why not come over here?'

Kenjiro bashfully assented. 'OK, why not? My boss has to go back to her husband for New Year, so I'll be on my own. She did invite me to their place, but under the circumstances I don't really want to meet her husband face to face. I'll come round here instead, and we'll have ourselves a sexy little threesome, eh?'

'Ah-ha-ha-ha-ha!'

'Ha-ha-ha-ha-ha!'

Daiki and I went down to the street with Kenjiro to see him off. As we were about to part, for no apparent reason, he said, 'I don't know how long I'm gonna carry on in this line of business, actually.'

Daiki's eyes flashed with fury. 'Leave it out – I don't want to hear that kind of talk.' Kenjiro seemed to shrink away before him in fear, as Daiki seized a muddy shovel that was standing by the roadside and raised it high above his head. Towering over Kenjiro he loudly berated him. 'Anyone'd want to live a flashy life like yours. Why, there are millions of people right here in Tokyo who'd give their eye teeth to be in your fancy shoes, chum. Don't you forget that. If you're gonna come this far and then give up, you're just a waste of space. You'd do a lot better to get off the fucking road in the first place and make way for some of the others. Got that?'

His arms, his head, his body, all were bathed blood red by the setting sun. The bloody tide shone right through him; he blazed brilliantly.

It's 29 December. I'm sitting on a plane – All Nippon Airways, Flight 65, a little domestic shuttle from Hokkaido back down to Tokyo. We left Chitose airport at 2 p.m. and the flight takes slightly more than an hour. I've just finished my last job of the year, a three-night engagement at a health spa in Sapporo. Outside the window, the tasty-looking fluffy clouds form a kingdom of their own.

Three o'clock. I wonder where we are.

We'll be touching down in Tokyo very soon. Thinking back to my shows in Sapporo, the face of one particular old man comes floating into my mind. He was there for my final show, just last night.

'Oh, but, you know, for an old man like me this is paradise. Steaming hot baths and a chance to hear some songs. That really was a great experience for me. So, will you be back to sing for us again tomorrow, my dear? Or will we not be seeing you any more?'

Truth to tell, I don't suppose the two of us will ever meet again. But I laughed, and said, 'Sure we'll meet again tomorrow night – but I'll be a different singer tomorrow.'

The old man's eyes sparkled. 'I see. So, we will be able to hear some songs tomorrow, then.'

I'm a travelling singer. People remember my name just on the day they see my show, because it's written in big letters on the drop curtain. They soon forget it, but that's all right, because an angel like me only really exists as long as she's singing.

'The current temperature in Tokyo is 15 degrees centigrade. Cloud cover is giving way to blue skies, and it's so warm it feels like spring.'

The soul always wants to conceive something. It'll give you a tantalizing peek at life rooted in solid ground. But I can always float up into the air. That's because I have wings growing out of my soul. This pain, this sadness – truly, I am all mixed up with the songs now. It can often be tough when I throw myself into it – but I'm going to carry on flying.

In each individual's personal paradise.

And in my own space.